Meet Me
under the Ceiba

Meet Me under the Ceiba

Silvio Sirias

Arte Público Press
Houston, Texas

Meet Me Under the Ceiba is made possible in part from grants from the city of Houston through the Houston Arts Alliance, the University of California at Irvine Chicano/Latino Literary Prize, and by the Exemplar Program, a program of Americans for the Arts in Collaboration with the LarsonAllen Public Services Group, funded by the Ford Foundation.

Recovering the past, creating the future

Arte Público Press
University of Houston
452 Cullen Performance Hall
Houston, Texas 77204-2004

Cover illustration by Esperanza Gama
Cover design by Mora Des!gn

Sirias, Silvio
    Meet Me Under the Ceiba / by Silvio Sirias.
    p.   cm.
    ISBN 1-55885-592-2 (pbk. : alk. paper)
    1. Murder—Investigation—Fiction. 2. Nicaragua—Social
life and customs—Fiction. I. Title.
PS3619.I75M44 2009
813'.6—dc22   2009036688
                                                        CIP

9 0 1 2 3 4 5 6 7 8   10 9 8 7 6 5 4 3 2 1

For Rhonda, who kept me honest,
Nina, who kept me precise,
and Magee, who kept me creative

and, of course,
for María Auxiliadora Pavón,
who is at the heart of this story

This work of fiction was inspired by a true story described in the author's postscript.

In memoriam

Aura Rosa Pavón
and
Carla Vanesa Muñoz

*... ninguno de nosotros podía seguir viviendo sin saber
con exactitud cuál era el sitio y la misión que le había
asignado la fatalidad.*

(... none of us could continue living without an
exact knowledge of the place and mission
assigned to us by fate.)

—Gabriel García Márquez
Crónica de una muerte anunciada

CONTENTS

PART I: CHRISTMAS MORNING

One	*The Last Farewell*	1
Two	*A Descendant of Pirates*	14
Three	*Incense and Mirrors*	25
Four	*The Former Lover*	33

PART II: THE FERRIS WHEEL

Five	*The Mastermind*	43
Six	*Splitting Melons*	53
Seven	*The Ferris Wheel*	61
Eight	*The Object of Desire*	72
Nine	*The Old Man*	85

PART III: DECLARATIONS AND CONFESSIONS

Ten	*The Messenger*	101
Eleven	*The Threat*	111
Twelve	*The Arrangement*	118
Thirteen	*No Harm in Killing a Freak*	128
Fourteen	*The Marriage*	137

PART IV: DISCOVERIES, TRIALS, AND FUNERALS

Fifteen	*The Discovery*	151
Sixteen	*The Foundation*	160
Seventeen	*Smokescreens*	173
Eighteen	*The Trial*	180
Nineteen	*Death Without a Statement*	189

PART V: EVERYTHING UNDER THE CEIBA

Twenty   *What Fate Has Assigned*   199
Twenty-One   *Entryway to Heaven*   209
Twenty-Two   *A Fatal Delay*   215
Twenty-Three   *Her Last Moments*   227

                Postscript   239

PART I
Christmas Morning

ONE

The Last Farewell

On that *Navidad*, the Christmas Day Adela Rugama was murdered, the sudden blast of fireworks and the explosive first notes of the brass band's off-key music—each trombone, trumpet, tuba, saxophone, clarinet, and drum competing to see who could play the loudest—startled her awake shortly before the break of dawn. But Adela didn't really mind. In fact, she was grateful for the commotion. Just earlier that week, the battery in her alarm clock had died, and the night before, she had gone to bed afraid that she might miss the Procession for the Infant Jesus.

Two thoughts crossed Adela's mind the instant she opened her eyes that morning, her last morning alive. The first one was that that evening, after six long months apart, she was going to be reunited, and this time forever, with Ixelia Cruz, the love of her life. Her second thought was that later that morning she would get to see the excitement on the faces of her nieces and nephews as they opened the gifts she had bought them for Christmas.

I didn't see Adela that day. It was her sister, Mariela, who, three-and-a-half years after the tragic incident, shared with me how Adela had felt that Christmas, shortly before dawn. As I sat in Mariela's living room, listening to her story on an unusually cool June morning, she paused occasionally to soak up her tears with my handkerchief. She remembered that the first thing Adela did upon arriving at her house was to pour herself a cup of *café con leche*, her second of the day. She then sat down and told Mariela about the dream she'd had the night before.

In that dream, Adela was working on a coffee plantation, picking the ripening beans as fast as her sprightly fingers allowed.

At quitting time, right before the dimness of the evening engulfed the tall trees that shaded the coffee shrubs, she found herself alone and completely disoriented. There wasn't a single landmark Adela recognized. She began to walk as straight a line as possible through the curving rows of stout, green bushes, searching for a trail that would lead her out of the plantation and on her way back home. But always, after wandering aimlessly for what seemed like hours, she'd return to what in her mind had become the center of a labyrinth—a dark, foreboding house . . . a house she knew all too well and whose shadow filled her heart with gloom. After finding herself at the same spot a fourth time, Adela began to sob and shudder uncontrollably. Her knees buckled, and she fell to the moist ground, surrendering to despair. Just then, the warmth of a brilliant light made Adela lift her gaze. To the right of the house, resplendent under the magnificent ceiba tree and poised before her like a bold knight was San Jorge. At once, Adela's grief turned to amazement and relief. She was convinced that her patron saint had come to save her. But the look on his face quickly transformed her joy to concern. After staring sadly at her for a moment, San Jorge spoke: "I cannot hold back the dragons any longer, Adela." And just as suddenly as he had appeared, he vanished. Everything around her, without the light of the saint's sword, went pitch black. At that instant, the thunder of the fireworks and the ragtag band's loud, cheesy music awakened her, and for the time being the dream was lost.

"San Jorge tried to warn her," Mariela said to me with a sigh so deep that it made her tremble. "That statue over there belonged to my sister," she added, pointing toward the table where two large religious figures made out of plaster stood: a sixteen-inch Virgin of the Immaculate Conception, with three lit votive candles at her feet, and a foot-tall statue of San Jorge, dressed in a metal breastplate and clutching a sword in his right hand. At the feet of the saint laid a slain dragon. His right foot rested on the beast's neck, and his hand firmly grasped the handle of the blade that he had plunged deep into the creature's heart.

That morning, the morning of Adela's murder, the dream came back to her in a forceful, disturbing wave as she relived every detail the instant she took the first sip of her second cup of coffee. In a rush of words, she told Mariela about her encounter with her patron saint. Immediately after Adela finished telling her tale, the excited chatter of her nieces and nephews filled the small house as they hurriedly dressed, thrilled about opening their presents. The excitement of Christmas and her anticipation over being reunited with Ixelia, helped Adela shake off any impending sense of doom.

On the fingers of her left hand Mariela recounted the gifts her sister had bought for the children. For Gema, eighteen years old at the time and Mariela's oldest, Adela had chosen a pair of Wild Things blue jeans. For Nubia, sixteen, pregnant, and looking forward to getting married the following month, Adela had purchased pirated compact discs of Shakira *Unplugged* and Maná—*Grandes Exitos.* For Tulio, fifteen years old, Adela had bought a pair of baseball cleats, made in Taiwan, of the finest imitation leather. And for Javier, the youngest at fourteen, Adela had got a Jonsport backpack: a surprisingly good reproduction of a Jansport with a reinforced leather bottom.

Although Adela's nieces and nephews were thrilled with their aunt's gifts, the biggest stir that Christmas morning was caused by the used Rali mountain bike that Mariela had bought for Tulio. It cost five hundred *córdobas*: a small fortune for her. But in return, since Tulio was not doing well at school, she expected the eldest of her two sons to start looking for work in the nearby communities of Niquinohomo, Nandasmo, Pío XII, Las Crucitas, or Masatepe, as well as in the small town in which they lived: La Curva. Mariela's children quickly gathered around the bicycle, each of them begging Tulio to allow them to take the Rali for a spin.

Three-and-a-half years later, Mariela still recalled that moment perfectly. "Adela took me aside and whispered, 'You can't give Tulio a bike in that condition; especially if it's a Christmas gift. It needs a lot of work. Look at it! The gears need adjusting, several spokes are shot, the brake pads need replacing, the tire rims are bent, and the frame is beginning to rust in places. I'll tell you what . . . if you invite me to dinner, I'll take the bicycle home, and by the end of the day I'll have it looking like new.'" Mariela smiled longingly as she evoked her sister's most remarkable talent. "That Adela, she could fix anything."

Bicycle in tow, the aunt, accompanied by Tulio, walked the three blocks that separated the sisters' houses. Before beginning the repair work, Adela headed for her bedroom to change out of her carefully selected Christmas outfit. As Tulio's aunt entered the bedroom, he saw her remove the key chain that always dangled from the second right-hand belt loop of her pants and take out an unopened pack of Belmont cigarettes from her shirt pocket.

When Adela came out of her bedroom, dressed in old clothing and ready for the grimy work ahead, she stopped abruptly to glance down at her chest. Tulio noticed that his aunt's gaze lingered on the medallion of San Jorge that she always wore on a silver chain around her neck. Adela studied the relic, holding it between her thumb and index finger. After a few moments, during which she appeared to be praying, she kissed the medallion and placed the saint inside the well-worn T-shirt a former lover had brought her years earlier from Costa Rica. Across the chest, in large orange letters, it read: *PURA VIDA*.

"San Jorge is my patron saint. He's the protector of good husbands, which means that he watches over me." Tulio chuckled as he recalled Adela's irreverent sense of humor, but remembering her statement also made him awfully sad.

Tulio and his aunt spent the entire day, until shortly before dinner, working on the bicycle. Adela performed the most difficult repair work, and it was Tulio's job to run to Bicitaller El Gordo, knock on the door—because, this being Christmas, the bicycle shop was closed—and buy whatever part she needed. But Tulio also helped tighten the new spokes and painting the frame. In the late afternoon, they both stepped back and nodded approvingly at their handiwork. To them, the Rali mountain bike looked as if it had just come out of the factory.

Tulio's aunt Adela was quite the worker. Eight years before the murder, she built her own house, almost single-handedly. She only asked for her brothers' help with the electrical wiring and the plumbing. Her dwelling had three rooms: a living room, a bedroom, and a spare room that she used for storage. The kitchen, which was outdoors in the backyard, consisted of a wood-burning stove, an oven made out of clay and stones, and a sink she used for washing both the dishes and the laundry. Close to the stove she kept an unpainted wood table, on which she prepared the food and ate afterward. As with the other houses in the neighborhood, the outhouse was in the backyard, in the corner farthest away from the stove and the house.

Adela started her apprenticeship in construction when she was only ten years old. That's when she offered to help her uncle Casimiro build his home. She assisted, observing carefully everything he did: the leveling of the plot of land, the cutting of wood to construct the framework, the mixing of mud and grass to just the right consistency to make long-lasting adobe, and the mounting of the beams that would support the zinc roof. By the age of fourteen, Adela had helped all four of her brothers build their houses. After that, she was ready to construct her own.

"Adela always wanted to have me nearby," Mariela said. "For years my sister begged me to leave Las Crucitas and join her in La Curva. I finally did when she offered to build a house for me. Of course, I helped," the surviving sister said proudly. "We added a cement finish to the walls so it looks like they're really made of concrete. It fools everyone." I nodded, feigning agreement, as I glanced around Mariela's humble home, its layout identical to Adela's.

Suddenly, Mariela's expression turned melancholic. "You're sitting in the exact same chair and in the exact same spot as Adela during her last visit," she said. By the end of the statement, her voice trailed off, dropping to barely above a whisper. Her large dark eyes still bore the pain of her sister's murder. Mariela sighed deeply and then continued. "That evening Adela was so nervous. Her right knee kept bouncing up and down, up and down. I don't think the poor thing could have stopped doing that if she tried.

And about every two minutes, she would glance up and look from clock to clock." I scanned the room and saw that there were indeed four clocks: three hanging on different walls and one on the table, to the left of the statue of the Immaculate Conception.

"If only I had trusted my instincts. If only I had listened to that voice inside trying to tell me that something was terribly wrong. If I had, Adela would still be alive," Mariela said, sighing yet again. "The signs were everywhere, but I just chose to ignore them."

Mariela rested on a hammock strung across her living room. Its ends were tied to the wooden beams that supported the zinc roof. She had also been in that exact same spot during Adela's last visit.

"Adela was more than just my sister, you know. Because of our age difference, she was more like a daughter to me. I helped raise her. After our mother's death, I had no choice but to fill that role. That never bothered Adela, though. Even as an adult, whenever she left La Curva, she'd let me know where she was going. But, much more than being without my little sister, I miss Adela terribly because she was my best friend as well."

Mariela took a sip from a cup of hot lemongrass tea. A drop of a baby boy's first morning urine had been added. For the last three years her neighbors had assured her that the potion would relieve her of her gurgling stomach. Without respite, her stomach had been bothering her since the day she was asked to identify Adela's body.

Seeing Mariela once again after my last prolonged stay in Nicaragua, nearly four years ago, helped to sharpen the image I had of Adela—an image that had become hazy, indistinct, but that I intended to rescue from the recesses of my memory. As I now remembered, the sisters looked very much alike, in spite of Mariela being eleven years older. Short in stature, they drew people's attention because of their compact, muscular bodies. Their strong torsos made it appear as if they lifted weights, which neither of them did. In fact, as I observed Mariela resting on the hammock, wearing a yellow blouse held up by dangerously thin spaghetti straps, I couldn't help but admire the rigidity of her biceps. They had a tautness many a man would envy.

In spite of their rather masculine physiques, the sisters had pretty, delicate faces: nicely rounded jaws, large dark eyes, appealing smiles, and full lips. Mariela wore her hair long; it serpentined down her back until it reached the middle, ending in flurries of small, upside-down question marks. Adela, on the other hand, always wore hers very short.

Where the sisters differed greatly was in their demeanor. Although Mariela had a brawny physique, she was unquestionably feminine. Adela, though, was just the opposite. As most folks who met her commented afterward, she acted just like a man.

Of both parents, Adela most resembled her father, Nemesio Rugama. From him she had inherited an astounding capacity for work. A simple *campesino*, his skin prematurely leathered and cracked from a lifetime of hard labor in the tropical sun, Nemesio had been sought out by the wealthiest landowners in the region for his diligence, as well as his honesty.

That is, until one exceedingly hot, humid day, when Adela was seven years old. Nemesio, while harvesting *pitahayas* in the full sun, suffered a stroke. He was only forty-two years old. The tragedy prompted Adela to abandon school, which she hated anyway, to help pay the medical bills.

"How can *you* go to work?" Pastora, her mother, argued with the child back then. "Who's going to pay you to do anything? You're just a little girl. Stay in school. You're the smartest of my children, Adelita. Besides, someone in this family has to learn to read."

"Don't worry about me, mamá. I can work as hard as any grown man," answered the child. "I can take care of myself, and I want to help take care of papá and you."

She was determined to prove that she could bring money home, so with the help of her brothers Adela built a handcart. Early each morning, she walked through the haciendas near her home gathering dry, fallen branches that she sold as firewood to her neighbors. By the time she reached adolescence, when her robust body could meet more demanding tasks, she began to haul water from the nearby creek, pulling the heavy cargo up a steep hill. She sold it by the bucketful and was soon earning more money than anyone else in the family. Shortly after Adela turned fourteen, the wealthier *hacendados* competed for her services, especially on the coffee plantations where her quick, nimble fingers were perfect for harvesting beans. They sought her out just the way they had once sought out her father, who was never able to work another day, but whose formidable strength allowed him to cling to life nine more years after the stroke.

At a young age, then, Adela learned everything she needed to know to earn a living, except how to read and write.

Adela's capacity for work is what I most remembered about her. Over the three days that she worked for me, I found her endurance stunning. Adela was able to work on a steaming zinc roof for nine hours straight with only a few short breaks to rest. The seriousness with which she approached the project I had hired her for also impressed me.

At the time, I was living in Managua, spending a year there on a Fulbright scholarship while conducting research for a book on an obscure Nicaraguan poet. This poet wrote his earliest verses in English, lived and published his work in New York, and had been one of Edna St. Vincent Millay's first lovers.

During the first torrential downpour of the rainy season, water flowed freely through the seemingly infinite leaks in the roof of my rental house, flooding the entire building, and almost ruining my computer. Between Mariela, who was my housekeeper, and me, it took three hours to push out the invading rainwater with the help of brooms.

"Do you know anyone who can fix the roof?" I asked Mariela once we had reclaimed the floor. She would serve me faithfully and flawlessly that entire year.

"My sister, Adela, can do it. She's honest, hardworking, and will only charge you half as much as someone who lives in Managua."

I confess that, initially, I had severe doubts about giving Adela a job that, in Nicaragua, is entrusted only to men. But over the few months Mariela had been with me, I had come to trust her judgment. So I asked her to go ahead and contact her sister.

At the head of a crew composed of Adela and her two brothers, she led and supervised the repair work. It was a challenging project. The entire roof needed to be replaced, and quickly, before the next deluge of the rainy season forced me to move about the house in a canoe. Adela handled the job professionally. After three days of working in the relentless, muggy heat—although the persistent rain clouds protected her and her brothers from toiling directly under the blazing sun—the task was completed.

Our time together was brief, but I became well acquainted with Adela, and I liked her. Each day, worried about the heat, I urged this small group to take frequent breaks, which, since they were in a hurry to finish the job, they did reluctantly. During those moments of rest, we all sat in the backyard porch with tall glasses of ice water in hand, and I listened to the brothers and sisters as they recounted their family's story. Through this, I came to understand and appreciate Mariela much more.

In the end, as Adela and I shook hands in farewell, right after I had handed her the payment, I was happy with my decision to hire her for the job. I promised that if I ever had a similar project I would call her. (As it was, during the remainder of that year I didn't encounter another such crisis in the house.) But not once did I suspect that only a few months after my return to the States, Adela, so strong, so vigorous, would be dead.

Here I was, three-and-a-half years after the murder, back in Nicaragua to spend the summer vacation. A local university had invited me to teach a graduate seminar. My students were excited about what they had heard was an exciting and rapidly growing field: U.S. Latino and Latina literature.

The day after my arrival, I visited some former neighbors of that Fulbright year, and they informed me of Adela's tragic fate. The next morning I went to La Curva to find Mariela.

When she finished telling me the story of her sister's death with tears in her eyes, she said, "The saddest part, for me at least, is to imagine how terrifying it must have been for her to face death all alone like that. Since the people who killed her have always denied having anything to do with it, I'll never know what she went through. It may seem strange, but even though the truth may be horrible, I believe that if I knew the last things she said and did, I'd find some consolation in that, and my sleepless nights would finally end."

For several years, I had been toying with the idea of writing a novel, my biggest fantasy, but as hard as I invoked the muses, inspiration never came. On the morning of my visit with Mariela, they started to sing to me in clear, distinct voices.

Under their battering assault, I shoved caution aside, and, thoroughly surprising myself, I blurted out, "Mariela, I'll find all of that out for you."

Mariela turned to look at me, astonished, and, after recovering from the initial shock, she asked, "How are you going to do that?"

"I'll write a book about Adela's murder. I'll talk to everyone who was involved in the case, and I won't let up until I discover the truth."

"You'd do that?" Mariela exclaimed. "It would be so good to know what really went on that Christmas. Maybe then Adela and I will be able to rest in peace."

That was the first of many trips to La Curva and to the surrounding pueblos. While in Nicaragua I stayed with my uncle Guillermo, who lives in the city of Granada. He generously offered me the use of Si Dios Quiere—his ancient, thirty-year-old Subaru.

"Why do you call it that?" I asked.

"¿Si Dios Quiere? Use your imagination, *muchacho*. Just look at this car: the door handles are missing and they've been replaced with wire; you need two hands to raise or lower the windows; on occasion, the brakes will go out on you, although I think the mechanic finally took care of that problem; the floor on the driver's side has been replaced with sheet metal; the head-lights work when they want to; the turn signals, forget it; if it's windy when it rains, the wipers flop all over the place; so, if in spite of all this you still make it to your destination, it's because it was God's will. ¿*Comprendes*? But the engine works fine, usu-ally, although it often backfires; and you'll have to turn the key several times before it starts. But Si Dios Quiere will get you where you're going . . . most of the time."

To save money on car rentals, as well as to avoid Nicaragua's dreadful public transportation, I accepted my uncle Guillermo's offer. With the help of Si Dios Quiere, I traveled throughout the province of Masaya where Adela lived and the crime was com-mitted. And throughout the nine weeks of my investigation, with the thirty-year-old Subaru usually within sight, I conducted countless interviews, talking to anyone who knew anything about the murder in the hope of uncovering the truth about Adela's last moments.

On the Christmas that Adela was killed, after helping to repair the Rali, Tulio returned to his mother's house an hour before dinner. The young man sped into his backyard on the mountain bike and fishtailed to a halt, lifting a thick cloud of dust. His huge grin caught the immediate attention of the entire family. The bicycle gleamed, thanks to a new coat of quick-drying paint, the rims of the wheels had been straightened, the spokes, which had all been replaced, now sparkled, and the gears shifted noiselessly, with an ease that would meet the approval of most racers.

Before going back to Mariela's house, Adela showered and changed back into her Christmas outfit: a pair of blue denim pants, held up by a brown leather belt with hand-engraved drag-onflies; a blue and white checkered long-sleeved shirt; an almost new pair of Caterpillar work boots, purchased only the previous week; and a new pair of white socks with light green trim around the top, a gift from Mariela. The bulge from the still unwrapped pack of Belmonts showed in her breast pocket, and, as usual, her key chain dangled from the second loop of her pants. The medal-lion of San Jorge hung outside her shirt once again.

"I kept my part of the deal, Mariela. And my work today ended up saving you about two hundred *córdobas*. Now, where's my dinner?"

Upon seeing that their aunt had arrived, the nieces, Gema and Nubia, took the turkey out of the stone and clay oven. The young women had spent eight months raising the bird, and, shortly after dawn, they had gotten it drunk on *kuzusa*—the local version of moonshine. Once the bird passed out, with a stone-sharpened machete, Gema chopped off its head. Before dinner, as the family sat under the rickety shelter that protects the rustic wood table, Mariela made the sign of the cross and led the family in saying grace, ending the blessing with the Lord's Prayer.

During dinner, the chatter of Mariela's children, still excited over their Christmas gifts, did not allow the sisters to converse. As soon as everyone finished eating, Tulio and Javier rose from the table.

"We'll be right back," Tulio said for Mariela's benefit. Although at the time she didn't think much of it, as the boys excused themselves, they were looking directly at their aunt Adela. Mariela told them to leave the Rali, afraid that the boys, unaccustomed to the bicycle, would have an accident in the encroaching darkness of the evening. At first they protested, but, well versed in their mother's resoluteness, they soon gave up and left.

While the younger women cleaned up, the mother and aunt sat in the living room, chatting. "My sister was concealing something from me. She was awfully nervous that evening, her knee bouncing up and down so rapidly that I thought she was going to leave a big hole in the floor. We talked, but all the time I had the impression that Adela wasn't paying attention to anything I said. Although she looked right at me, her gaze was distracted. Then, just as I was telling her about the names we were considering for Nubia's baby, my sister worriedly glanced from clock to clock. I should have stopped her from going out that day," Mariela said to me as she quickly brushed away tears with the back of her hand.

"Several times I asked her what was wrong, but Adela didn't give me a straight answer. Suddenly, glancing around and seeming very concerned about something, she asked, 'Where are the boys? They're supposed to go with me on an errand.'"

Mariela asked Adela where they were going, but her sister's answers, as before, were vague. She kept on insisting that the errand was nothing important.

Adela, with her knee bouncing ever more furiously, checked each clock in the living room one last time. "I'm late, Mariela. I can't wait for the boys any longer. Can I borrow Tulio's bicycle? I'll only be about an hour."

"Of course, I let her take the bike," Mariela recalled. "How could I not? After all, she had spent the entire day fixing the damn thing. Plus, Adela was a stubborn person, just like me. It would have been useless to try to stop her. Deep in my heart, I knew that something was wrong, and I suspected that it had to do with Ixelia. But when I suggested this, Adela laughed and said that I was just being silly. Before she got up to leave, I asked her to wait a few more minutes for the boys. I said that if she ran into any problems, they would be there to help her. But Adela merely repeated that she was already late and that she had to go."

Ignoring Mariela's concerns, Adela stepped out of the house, mounted the refurbished Rali, smiled at her older sister, told her not to worry, waved farewell, and took off down the dirt road leading toward the town of Pío XII.

That was the last time Mariela saw her little sister alive.

TWO

A Descendant of Pirates

That Christmas, before the violet hues of dawn outlined the grove of mango trees east of La Curva, Lizbeth Hodgson was up and sweeping the sidewalk in front of the small neighborhood store she ran out of her home. She hummed along to the music of the brass band. Lizbeth had hung Christmas decorations from the eaves of her house the first Sunday in Advent. The twinkling lights cast a soft, comforting glow, enough to work by. In the dimness, Lizbeth froze for an instant when she heard the sound of a door opening. She squinted to see who was across the street. Soon she recognized Adela Rugama, her favorite neighbor, stepping out of her house and turning to lock the door.

As Adela approached, greeting Lizbeth with her customary parrot trill—a high-pitched sound she had picked up through her fondness for birds and also because she had never learned to whistle—Lizbeth took note of the outfit her neighbor had chosen to wear that Christmas: a blue and white checkered long-sleeved shirt; blue denim pants held up by a dragonfly-engraved leather belt; and a mustard-colored pair of Caterpillar work boots. As usual, a long key chain dangled from one of the loops of her neighbor's pants.

The women had known each other for almost seven years. Lizbeth had met Adela the same day she moved to La Curva from her native Pearl Lagoon, a fishing village on Nicaragua's Caribbean coast. The storeowner had come to the town after marrying Roberto Pereira, who had made the arduous journey expressly to find a wife. He had traveled first by land, then down the Río Escondido to Bluefields, and from there up the coast on a fishing boat. Lizbeth's husband was a small, frail man, and when the couple first arrived in La Curva, they drew plenty of stares, as the stunning *mulata* bride towered over the groom. Lizbeth now

14

believed the disparity had been merely another bead in a long rosary of omens that she freely recited the afternoon of my visit. "My father, an Anglican minister, cautioned me against marrying Roberto. I should have listened to him. 'Lizbeth,' he said, 'the man you've chosen to be your husband is a weak, useless human being. He also looks queer. Don't marry him, daughter.'"

The afternoon I interviewed her, Lizbeth spoke to me in English occasionally sprinkled with Spanish and in an accent that was drenched in that magical Caribbean lilt. "The problem," she continued, "was that Roberto dazzled me. Somehow, he hypnotized me. Besides, that asshole completely seduced me when he spoke about his wealth. He especially took my breath away when he said that he owned a sprawling hacienda full of coffee plants. I just couldn't see straight at the time. It was as if someone had put blinders on me. The evening Roberto proposed to me, as he got down on one knee in front of all of my family, I felt powerless; I could only give him one answer: 'Sí.'" Although their marriage was doomed from the start, the couple tried to make the relationship work. They remained together for three years, producing two daughters.

But there was another important reason that Lizbeth married Roberto, one she had shared with everyone shortly after arriving in the town. The tall, broad-shouldered woman made it no secret that all her life she had desperately wanted to escape the mosquito-infested marshes of Pearl Lagoon. Marrying the delicate stranger allowed Lizbeth to trade the stifling, insect-riddled heat of the Caribbean coast for the damp coolness of the coffee-growing highlands. Because of her move and later because of her two daughters, the woman from the coast believed that accepting Roberto's marriage proposal had not entirely been a mistake.

The afternoon of my visit we sat in a room to the side of her store, chatting. Lizbeth chose a spot where she could see the customers that entered. Our conversation was occasionally interrupted by seemingly insignificant purchases: an aspirin, a box of matches, a Rojita soft drink, a pair of shoelaces, two packs of Belmont cigarettes, a liter of milk. However small these transactions appeared, they helped the woman from Pearl Lagoon sustain herself and her daughters.

While we spoke, in between clients, Lizbeth waged war on a persistent swarm of flies with a wire-handled swatter. "It's almost impossible to find these in western Nicaragua," she said, brandishing the mortal instrument. "On the east coast you can get them anywhere. Let me tell you something, though, it's worth the trouble shopping all over for them because they're deadly. The swatters with plastic handles just don't move as swiftly. By the time I begin to move my wrist, the flies have already flown away. But with this type, I can kill three times the number of these little bastards. I know. I've counted."

Lizbeth then continued her story. Almost immediately after arriving in La Curva, she was relieved to discover that the man she had wed did, indeed, own a large hacienda. But for several years Roberto had left the land unattended, and she was alarmed to see that it was mostly covered with brambles. Still, he survived fairly well on the money he had inherited from his parents, both Brazilian immigrants who found good fortune in Nicaragua's coffee boom and what little his hacienda produced. Roberto also owned a comfortable two-bedroom house in La Curva. Behind the building were thirty coffee shrubs, which yielded just enough each year for their morning coffee that and a few citrus trees.

The problem with their marriage, then, had little to do with money. The reason resided elsewhere. Only two months after Lizbeth arrived from Pearl Lagoon, the magnificent *mulata*, the descendant of a fiery eighteenth-century affair between an English buccaneer and a freed African slave, concluded that her scrawny husband would never be able to satisfy her amorous needs, no matter how hard he tried.

Since La Curva is a town where secrets do not exist, the thought of people openly questioning his manhood terrified Roberto. To help conceal his inadequacy, he started to hang out with the toughest, meanest men in town, drinking cheap rum, and playing cards most nights of the week. But when he returned home, early in the morning, broke, stumbling drunk, and nearly incoherent, Lizbeth would put on a performance that thrilled the neighbors, all of whom loved to see a wealthy man humiliated in public. Belt in hand, she would greet her husband at the door. As the woman from Pearl Lagoon lashed Roberto across his backside, she'd shout out his shortcomings as a husband and a lover for everyone to hear. On these occasions, Adela would be the only neighbor moved to compassion, and she'd cross the street to plead for mercy.

"I know he's useless, Lizbeth, but that doesn't mean that you can kill him," she'd say while staying the woman's hand.

One terrifying, stormy evening, thick veins of lightning descended furiously from the heavens upon La Curva and the neighboring pueblos. A fierce bolt struck the beautiful *guayacán* tree that had stood proudly for decades in the middle of the small park in front of the church. The lightning left the noble tree charred and Don Virgilio Gómez, the sacristan, deaf for life. Another bolt struck the television antennae on top of Roberto's house. In spite of Lizbeth's warnings to unplug the set, her husband foolishly insisted on watching his favorite program, *Sábado Gigante*, with Don Francisco, who he considered a comic genius. The lightning's fury coursed its way through the wires, and the television exploded like a grenade. The force of the blast sent Roberto tumbling back, rocker and all. A shard of glass from the screen lodged itself in his neck, just millimeters from the jugular. Dazed, but grateful that God had spared him, Roberto stumbled out into the middle of the street as the winds and floodwaters threatened to sweep other parts of the town away. Despondent over his failures, he decided at that instant to change his life. Roberto fell to his knees in a bubbling pool of mud and repented of his many sins, screaming each one out loud, arms outstretched as he faced the storm, begging the Lord for forgiveness.

After the danger had passed, sparing the town of greater tragedies, Roberto stopped drinking. Instead, he started to spend his days in church, crying and beating his chest before the altar. He also sought solace by praying the rosary every afternoon in the company of La Curva's most devout women. As rumor spread about Roberto's conversion, a group of prosperous and pious Catholic men from the city of Masaya inducted him into a secret society that to this day no one in La Curva knows anything about. Upon formally accepting Lizbeth's repentant husband into their order, they made him repeat their sacred vow—to support one another in their quest for sainthood. They also made Roberto pledge to give his life, if necessary, to prevent the return of a socialist government. The members of his new fraternity unquestioningly believed that God favored the rich, rewarding them with wealth so they could lead the floundering nation back toward the narrow, moral, and traditional path of orthodox Catholicism. The Lord's trust, then, placed them under a sacred obligation to protect their material possessions from Marxist radicals and religious liberals. But more relevant for Roberto, these saintly men urged one another to be the undisputed leaders of their households. They firmly maintained that a husband's place, that is, above his wife, was also God's will.

"I've never been a person to put up with such bullshit, and I wasn't about to start with Roberto," Lizbeth stated. The low rumble in her voice echoed her resoluteness, and her resentment toward her husband resurfaced in the sternness that darkened her luminous, emerald-green eyes as she retrieved that memory. Throughout Roberto's conversion, the woman from Pearl Lagoon suspected that his newfound righteousness was nothing more than a poorly veiled attempt to conceal the insecurities that resided deep within the fissures of his tormented soul. "I had no use for Roberto's phony piety," Lizbeth said as in one swift movement she killed three flies with a single stroke of the wire-handled swatter. Still, intrigued by what was going on in the minds of her husband and his new friends, she joined them for a few family prayer meetings.

At first, the fervor of these gatherings impressed Lizbeth, who started to believe that there might be a possibility that Roberto would become more of a man, like her father, the Anglican minister. She attended once a week, on the days that wives and children were invited, and for a time her husband seemed to be gaining confidence in himself. "I actually began to think that the marriage could be saved." But that hope ended the day Roberto returned from a meeting demanding that she leave her heathen Anglican sect and convert to Catholicism. With this, the minister's daughter reached the borders of her scant patience. Ignoring the desperate cries of her young daughters, Lizbeth threw her husband out of the house, his house, for good. Then, to further disgrace "that Catholic hypocrite," she seduced Padre Uriel, La Curva's parish priest, with whom she had been flirting since shortly after her arrival in the town. And, to aggravate the insult, she tortured Roberto by letting him know that that man of God was much better at satisfying a woman than he could ever hope to be.

Although the affair was born out of spite, Lizbeth quickly settled into a comfortable relationship with Padre Uriel. The woman from the Caribbean coast found it liberating that the parish priest wasn't in a position to demand anything of her and that, at last, she could enjoy the independence she had been seeking her entire life. All Padre Uriel asked from her was discretion and that she visit him in the church's rectory twice a week: on Mondays and Thursdays. She readily agreed to both conditions. On the Christmas Adela was murdered, Lizbeth and Padre Uriel's pact was entering its fourth year.

"¡*Feliz Navidad*, Lizbeth!" Adela called out from across the street as her neighbor busily swept the storefront sidewalk.

"It was strange," Lizbeth said to me as she struggled to light an inexpensive cigar, "but for an instant, when I first saw Adela that morning, in the glow of the Christmas lights and with the sun yet to rise, I thought I was seeing a ghost."

As her neighbor crossed the street, coming into full view, the huge grin on her face surprised Lizbeth. "Adela, I didn't realize that Christmas made you so happy."

"Yes, woman. Today I'm happy, but it's not because of Christmas. This evening my life's going to become complete."

"Adela's eyes shone so brightly that I immediately knew what she was talking about. She had been depressed the last few months, and there was only one thing that could suddenly lift her spirits like that," Lizbeth said. As she started puffing again on the cheap cigar, a thick cloud of dull gray smoke floated straight toward me. The stench of the low-grade tobacco made it difficult to remain in the same room with her, but I was bolted to the rocker, wanting to learn more about the role the woman from Pearl Lagoon played on that fateful day.

"Are you and Ixelia getting back together?" Lizbeth asked Adela, half jokingly.

Her neighbor responded by smiling even more. "When I saw that she intended to join up again with Ixelia, I became alarmed. I knew nothing good could come out of that relationship. I told Adela that it would be better for her to forget that woman. I reminded her of all the grief that girl had already caused. I recited a long list of offenses that would have stopped anyone from going back. But Adela was too far gone, too much in love. You know how that goes," Lizbeth said. She stopped rocking, removed the cigar from her mouth, and stared wordlessly toward the house where her neighbor had lived.

Lizbeth Hodgson didn't mind that Adela preferred women to men. Early in their relationship, though, that preference nearly ruined their chances of becoming friends. "In the beginning, Adela kept coming on to me, and she was too aggressive about it. Once she set her sights on a woman, she wouldn't take no for an answer. When I first moved to La Curva, she stalked me . . . literally. At first, shortly after I arrived, Adela would stand for hours at her doorway, looking intently in the direction of my house. Then, whenever Roberto stepped out, she'd come by, pretending it was all part of a casual visit. We'd chat while I worked around the house. The entire time she'd follow me until I would find myself cornered. I always had to struggle to get out of those tight situations because, if nothing else, Adela was persistent.

"'Lizbeth,' she at last declared one day, 'I've known your husband for years, so I know that he can't possibly satisfy someone as magnificent as you. Give me a chance. I can teach you the meaning of pleasure, I swear. Besides, I've never been with a *mulata*, and I'm dying of curiosity.'"

Lizbeth firmly rejected Adela's proposal. She let her neighbor know that she was a man's woman all the way and that there was no chance of a lesbian seducing her. But Adela persisted . . . that is, until the day she went too far.

"One morning," Lizbeth said, her rainforest eyes widening at the recollection, "when she had me cornered, that song by Juan Luis Guerra, *Burbujas de amor*, came on the radio. Before I could react, Adela had taken me in her arms and we were dancing. She led perfectly, even though she was shorter than me. Let me tell you, that woman knew what she was doing on a dance floor." Lizbeth looked at me and smiled. "I didn't really think much of it. I mean, I used to dance with my girlfriends back in Pearl Lagoon. Plus, that song is so beautiful that I immediately became lost in the words and the music. I was fully enjoying myself when Adela's voice brought me out of the trance.

"'Woman,' she whispered, aiming her voice up toward my ear, 'I'm tired of just being your friend. I want to be your lover as well. I can make you happy, I know it. Not only that, I'll make you come endlessly.'

"With that, Adela slowly reached around me and started to caress my behind. The heat of her hand stunned me. I thought that only the hearts of men were capable of such lust. Then Adela started to kiss my shoulder, her mouth slowly moving toward my neck.

"Well that did it!" Lizbeth leaned forward, adamant that I listen closely to this passage of the story. "Firmly, I pushed Adela back. 'Listen,' I said to her, 'if you can't be happy as just friends, then I will have to ask you to stay away from me. I mean that, Adela. I like you, very much. But as a friend only, never more than that.' I tried to let her down as gently as I could, but at the same time I also wanted her to stop that nonsense. Let me tell you something, she must have known that I meant business because she never bothered me again."

Over time, the neighbor from across the street earned Lizbeth's respect, yet she never came to trust Adela completely. Having experienced her aggressive pursuit, the woman from Pearl

Lagoon repeatedly warned her daughters to be careful whenever they found themselves alone with her.

"Adela's taste for women kept getting her into trouble. But, honestly, I never dreamed that being a *cochona* would get her killed."

We rocked for quite a while in our chairs amid a dense cloud of cigar smoke, neither of us speaking. When Lizbeth at last broke the silence, she credited Adela with teaching her an important lesson, one for which she would be eternally grateful: that a woman could survive, and even prosper, without the help of a man.

"It was her idea that I open this store to support myself and my two girls. And it was a great idea. Thanks to Adela, I've managed just fine without Roberto. I've even been able to save some money, you know. I'm going to buy a small farmhouse, one that I've had my eye on since I arrived in La Curva. I don't mind telling you that at the beginning the thought of making it on my own was frightening, but once I made the decision to open the store, Adela was there to help me every day. She was very good to me during that difficult time. She went with me to Nandasmo, helped me buy the wood, and then built the shelves, the display cabinets, and the counter. I just assisted, handing her the boards and the nails."

The information Lizbeth didn't share with me that afternoon was that Adela often minded the store while the descendant of an English pirate visited the church sacristy. It was Mariela who mentioned this prior to my meeting with Lizbeth. In the town everyone knows what takes place whenever she walks toward the parish rectory every Monday and Thursday morning after Mass, her formidable hips wrapped in tight skirts. No one in La Curva, however, seems scandalized. People in Nicaraguan pueblos tend to overlook the indiscretions of their priests when they involve a woman. "It's better than their molesting children," Mariela stated emphatically once. The folks of La Curva accept without question that Padre Uriel is a man as well. Even the older *ciudadanos*, who sit on the stone ledge behind the church, dunking *rosquillas* in their morning coffee, see the priest waving goodbye to Lizbeth at the rectory door, pretending she had been there for confession.

On the morning of that fateful Christmas, a Thursday morning, the woman from Pearl Lagoon would not visit the chamber at the rear of the church until well after Mass. She had to wait for the Procession for the Infant Jesus to complete a second journey up and down the streets of La Curva. That morning, after Adela returned Lizbeth's greeting, the sound of the musicians—their trumpets, trombones, clarinets, saxophones, and tubas blaring against the reckless beating of drums—interrupted their chat.

The neighbors turned their heads toward the town's main street, half a block south. They caught sight of the first procession of the day as it appeared at the corner. The statue of the Infant Jesus was destined to go west, down the main street of La Curva, to the small baseball stadium, to circle the field, and then return to the church to celebrate Christmas mass. As the faithful advanced, their faces illuminated by the candles they held in their hands, Lizbeth and Adela spotted Padre Uriel; he was walking directly ahead of four men who carried on their shoulders the wooden platform with the statue on their shoulders. The priest walked meditatively, his hands serenely clasped across his chest in front of the Holy Infant. But as Padre Uriel reached the middle of the intersection, he glanced in the direction of Lizbeth's house. When he recognized her voluptuous figure, distinct in spite of the murkiness of dawn, he waved at her discretely, barely releasing one hand from the other. Lizbeth smiled and returned the greeting with an almost imperceptible wave of her left hand at the height of her hip.

"Adela laughed when she saw that," Lizbeth recalled as she leaned back in the rocking chair. She relit the cigar, which had gone out, and quickly blew on the match before it burned her fingers. "After the procession had passed, Adela said to me, 'You know, Lizbeth, in reality, we both like the same thing . . . almost. You like men who aren't really men, and I like women.'"

Chuckling at her own joke, Adela said farewell to her neighbor, stating that she was going to check out the procession because she was curious to see who was there. "I then warned Adela once more about trying to get back together with Ixelia. I told her to be careful. I reminded her that, in my opinion, that girl was nothing but trouble and that she was better off without her. Adela laughed and answered, 'Don't worry about me, woman, I know how to take care of myself.' Sadly, that was the last thing we ever talked about."

That afternoon, as Lizbeth and I finished our conversation, I knew that those final moments with Adela had been etched in her memory, as if in granite: a heartbreaking gash, a lingering sore that would never heal completely.

Adela smiled, waved farewell, and then left in the direction of the procession. "At that moment I never suspected, even for an instant, that it would be the last time I would see her alive."

THREE

Incense and Mirrors

A s Adela Rugama said farewell to Lizbeth Hodgson to join
the Procession for the Infant Jesus, the golden luster of
the rising sun began to glance off the tile rooftops of La
Curva, making the town look as if it were covered in the embers
of a dying fire. Gema, Mariela's oldest daughter and Adela's
favorite niece, sighed that morning when she saw the Christmas
lights sparkling against that smoldering, amber background of
dawn.

"It was so beautiful! A gorgeous daybreak. For an instant I
thought that I was strolling through the streets of La Curva in a
dream. I had to pinch myself to make sure that it was real," she
said, handing me a cup of lemongrass tea. I had stopped by to
visit Mariela yet again, thankful that Si Dios Quiere made it all the
way without incident, to talk about that fateful day.

That Christmas, Gema had gotten up early to join in the procession. As soon as Adela saw her niece, she trilled like a parrot in
greeting and then wove her way through the crowd to walk
alongside her.

"Believe it or not, my aunt attended religious ceremonies out
of faith," Gema assured me. "She loved the Catholic Church, in
spite of the way Padre Uriel sometimes treated her." Gema had
graduated from high school thanks to her tía Adela who paid her
tuition. As a result, she had more education than anyone else
from the Rugama family. Because of this, I could discuss issues
with her that, at times, most other family members had difficulty
grasping.

"When I would remind my aunt that Padre Uriel had once
said that he would not welcome her into the church unless she
stopped being a lesbian, she would laugh and reply, 'I don't care
what that robed man says. I bet you that half the nuns and half
the women saints are repressed lesbians. And the other half . . .

25

well . . . they're not so repressed. Do you really think they spend the entire day in prayer?' My aunt Adela was so comfortable with who she was. Nothing scandalized her. She believed that everyone was entitled to enjoy their bodies, even the nuns. Her open-mindedness was one of the things I admired most about her."

Adela also attended church events because she enjoyed the pageantry. According to Gema, the grandeur of Catholic rituals always moved her aunt. Adela wasn't bothered in the least by the condemning glares of the pious, who, prompted by their deep-rooted religious prejudices, would turn their heads unreflectively to glare at the lesbian the moment she stepped into their sanctuary. In fact, she loved to return their hostile stares. Sometimes she'd scandalize the faithful even further by giving them the *guatuza*—flipping them off Nicaraguan-style—with her thumb crammed deep into the gap between the index and the middle finger.

"Also," Gema said, "my aunt Adela believed that church events were a great place to scout for horny women. 'What they're really looking for is that breathtaking experience of ecstasy, and, as a couple of them had already discovered, I can give them that . . . easily,' she would say."

That Christmas morning, according to Gema, when Padre Uriel saw Adela join the Procession for the Infant Jesus, he began to scowl. Everyone in La Curva knew that their parish priest strongly disapproved of lesbians. On several occasions Padre Uriel had preached homophobic homilies from the pulpit. Once, during an impassioned Sunday sermon, he called all *cochones* and *cochonas* an abomination. In that memorable lecture, the priest reminded his parishioners that for two millennia the church had condemned homosexuality as the worst of sins. Pointing toward heaven with his right index finger, Padre Uriel said that going to bed with a person of the same sex was *contra-natura*, absolutely, because it didn't lead to procreation and because it didn't create devoted adherents to the Holy Roman Catholic faith. But Gema suspected that, in reality, Padre Uriel was jealous of Adela because he feared that in spite of Lizbeth's denials, the *mulata* was strongly attracted to her scandalous neighbor.

"*Cochones* and *cochonas* have their places reserved for them in hell," Padre Uriel shouted that Sunday—in a single stroke condemning all faggots and dykes to eternal damnation. As the priest said this, he glared directly at Adela. Instead of being offended, she chuckled, leaned toward Gema, and whispered in her ear, "I guess that adulterer and I will be seeing each other in hell. I'll then have the rest of eternity to convince the man that, in reality, he's one big queer himself."

The Christmas of Adela's murder, during the Procession for the Infant Jesus, Gema was pleased to see her aunt in a good mood. For six months the woman had been brooding, ever since Ixelia Cruz broke up with her. But that morning, during the short breaks the musicians took to rest their instruments, sore lips, taxed lungs, and tired arms, Adela joked and chatted away as she and Gema strolled amid the faithful, about twenty yards ahead of the statue of the Infant Jesus.

Suddenly, about a block before the procession reached the baseball field, Gema saw her aunt become anxious. She stopped talking, hunched down, and tried to become invisible by crouching low and slinking along with the crowd. Gema glanced around and saw nothing alarming. She then stood on her tiptoes to try to get a better view. To the right of the procession, she spotted the reason for her aunt's nervousness: looming above everyone's heads was Don Roque Ramírez, mounted on his palomino. Later that Christmas, a little past seven-thirty in the evening, he would murder Adela Rugama.

From atop his golden-haired steed, with its immaculately trimmed, light brown mane, Don Roque scanned the crowd. "I instantly knew that he was looking for my aunt Adela. But that day I thought he only wanted to intimidate her," Gema said, sadly shaking her head at the recollection.

Everyone in La Curva knew that the wealthy *hacendado* wanted Adela dead. He had said so himself, several times, in front of witnesses, threatening to kill the lesbian with two bullets from his .22 caliber rifle. But Adela assured her family and friends that Don Roque would never carry out his threat. "I'm not afraid of that old man," she had once boasted to her niece. But in that instance, Gema heard her aunt's voice falter, if only slightly. "She was trying to be brave, but I could tell that she was really scared of Don Roque."

That Christmas morning, the last thing Adela sought was a confrontation with the wealthy *hacendado*, so she hurriedly kissed Gema on the cheek and told her that she would see her later, at Mariela's house. Still crouching among the faithful, the aunt discreetly weaved her way through the crowd to the side opposite to where Don Roque sat astride his horse. When the Procession for the Infant Jesus passed before Don Erasmo Alemán's house, she swiftly dodged inside, startling the old man who was standing at his doorway enjoying the religious spectacle.

Once in the living room, Adela rushed to hide behind one of the front doors. Through the crack at the hinges she spied on the procession until she was certain that the danger had passed. Feeling safe, she stepped toward the center of the room and glanced around. For a moment Adela felt faint, when she saw her image repeated to infinity, and she was forced to hold herself steady by clutching the backrest of one of Don Erasmo's rocking chairs.

To this day, virtually every square inch of the walls in the old man's living room is covered with mirrors, and not a single one of these matches another. People in La Curva believe that all of them are stolen. Whenever Don Erasmo drops by for a visit, his hosts watch him closely. And usually, in spite of their vigilance, after he leaves, when they take inventory, a mirror has inexplicably vanished. No one knows how Don Erasmo manages the feat. Many an owner of a missing mirror has stopped by the old man's house a few days later, feigning a casual visit. They then search, as inconspicuously as possible, for their mirror among the countless reflections hanging on his walls. But not once has a lost mirror been found or reclaimed. If what the people of La Curva believe about him is true, even the most ornate, the most unique mirror loses its identity the instant it passes through his doorway.

Before Adela broke the spell her other selves had cast on the moment, prior to saying anything to Don Erasmo, she lingered, studying her likeness before a full-length mirror. The glass was cracked straight across the middle. (When the mirror first broke, Don Erasmo, an expert on these matters, threw handfuls of salt on it to ward off bad luck.) That morning, what startled Adela about her reflection was that she saw herself cut perfectly in half—at the waist.

"She just stood there, off to the side, staring in that mirror for the longest time," Don Erasmo told me the evening of my visit. "I then saw the poor thing shudder, as if a gust of cold wind had passed through the living room, chilling her. For an instant, Adela seemed to be on the verge of crying. At last, she took a deep breath, turned to me, and said, 'Don Erasmo, looking into this mirror makes me feel like a ghost.' At the time I thought that was a strange thing to say, but I never imagined that the Lord had blessed her with a clearly prophetic moment."

Turning away from the vision to face a bewildered Don Erasmo, Adela decided to visit with the old man for a while to repay him for providing a safe harbor. She chose the largest rocking chair in his living room and sat down. Don Erasmo, still stunned over Adela's abrupt entry, left the doorway and took a seat across from her. Before long the man of the mirrors had placed her sudden appearance out of his mind and was telling her the story of his life.

"I talked about my childhood, about growing up in Granada. It's such a beautiful city—the most beautiful in the world, I'd say. I still ask myself why I ever left to move to La Curva. Anyway, I told Adela stories of when I was a boy, about all the trouble I used to get into with a friend of mine, Nicolás Salazar. As I was wondering aloud about what had happened to him, I looked at her and saw that she was distracted, not listening to a word I was saying.

"'Adela, are you all right?' I asked.

"'I'm sorry, Don Erasmo. I'm fine, thank you. But I've got to hurry to my sister's house. She's expecting me, and I'm already late.'

"What happened to Adela later that day is terrible," Don Erasmo said the evening of the interview. "She was a good person, a hard worker as well. I have to admit that it bothered me a bit that she was a *cochona*. I mean, it doesn't seem natural for women to go to bed together. But Adela had a good heart, and, in spite of her preferring women over men, I liked her as a person. Some of my neighbors would get upset whenever I defended Adela, but I had learned to respect her," added the man of the mirrors, smiling sadly. "Getting back to the story, that morning Adela rose from her chair and asked me if she could leave the house through the backyard. 'Of course,' I answered. She then kissed me on the cheek and left through the kitchen door. Right before she reached the banana trees, she turned, waved farewell, and then disappeared among them. I never saw her again."

Don Erasmo paused, remaining quiet while he gazed into the mirrors, as if he were trying to recapture a lost image. After a few moments of reflection, he went on with his story. Shortly after Adela's departure, Don Roque, mounted on his palomino, pulled up in front of the house.

"He jerked his head a couple of times, you know, signaling for me to step out. The old man's eyes were bloodshot, as if he had been drinking all night.

"'Don Erasmo,' he said in his low, gravelly voice, 'where's the *cochona*? I saw her come in, so don't deny it.'

"'Yes, Don Roque. She was here, but she has already left.' I had no choice but to be honest."

"'What did you two discuss?'"

"'Nothing really,' I answered.

"'You shouldn't get mixed up with dykes, Don Erasmo. It doesn't look good. People are going to talk.'

"I wanted to say 'Go to hell, you old son of a whore!'" The flash of anger in Don Erasmo's eyes, as he reached back into that memory, startled me, and his outrage beamed back in a thousand different ways through the mirrors. "But it's not that easy to cuss at a wealthy *hacendado*, even though he may be the worst person on earth. Besides, I knew I had to be careful. That man is capable of anything. So, in spite of being pissed-off, I bit my tongue.

"'Be careful, Don Erasmo,' Don Roque continued, 'that *cochona* can get you into a lot of trouble. Someday, someone will take care of her once and for all, and if I were you, I wouldn't want to be caught up in that mess.'"

"'Sir,' I answered, 'the funny thing is that I was just telling Adela that I've been in trouble all of my life.' Don Roque stared at me for a long time. Then, slowly, he turned his palomino and went off to rejoin the procession."

I nodded in appreciation of Don Erasmo's moment of rebellion, but seeing my gesture repeated over and over again made me dizzy. Like most people who visit Don Erasmo, I became disoriented as I glanced around his living room. Seeing my image reflected without end made me feel as if I had lived through that interview many times before. I rose from the rocking chair, thanked him for his time, said farewell, and left. But for days afterwards I was haunted by the eerie sensation that I had left several replicas of myself behind.

Through Gema I learned that Don Roque, after talking to Don Erasmo, returned to the procession. "That old man was obsessed with Ixelia's young pussy, and he hated my aunt Adela for taking her away from him," she said, referring to the source of Don Roque's animosity. Gema watched the *hacendado* closely, and was relieved when she saw that her aunt had eluded him. Don Roque rode alongside the Procession for the Infant Jesus; he scanned the faces from up on his steed until he was satisfied that Adela wasn't back among the pious. He then turned and dashed off in the direction of Las Dos Balas, his hacienda.

Adela, in the meantime, made her way through the labyrinth of banana trees that grow wild behind Don Erasmo's house. Because the man of the mirrors never thinned them out, they had taken over his backyard, sprouting up everywhere, without order. When Adela at last discovered a way out of the maze, she found herself standing at the edge of the alleyway that runs behind Don Erasmo's property. She turned right, heading east. The United Fruit Company, during its glory years, had cut the wide path between the region's towns to lay down railroad tracks. The train used to carry wagons full of coffee and bananas to the port of Corinto, and from there the products were shipped to the United States. Today, like the vestiges of an ancient civilization, all that is left is a trackless alleyway that leads west to Jinotepe and east to Niquinohomo. In the early 1990s, Doña Violeta's government removed the rails to sell them on the international market as scrap iron. The final destination of the proceeds is anyone's guess.

Heading east, the former railway passes directly in front of Mariela's house, which faces what used to be La Curva's train station. Although dilapidated, the wooden structure—a small, one-room building—is still standing. The station's elevated cement foundation has withstood earthquakes, hurricanes, revolutions, and a civil war without a single crack. The withered testament to the banana boom of the 1920s is now home to two families of squatters, who divide their quarters with a bed sheet that hangs from a wire across the middle of the room.

On her way to her sister's, Adela stopped to buy a pack of Belmont cigarettes at Doña Matilde Chacón's store. Nearly two months later, when her corpse was discovered, the pack would be found in her right breast pocket, still unopened.

"*Feliz Navidad*, Adela," Doña Matilde greeted her cheerfully. "How much money did you spend on your nieces and nephews this year? I remember that last Christmas you invested a small fortune in them."

"I couldn't afford to spend much this time, Doña Matilde."

"Adela then looked around the store," Doña Matilde said when I stopped by her store to chat. "After that she poked her head outside, glancing up and down the street to see if anyone else was nearby, eavesdropping nearby. That morning Adela was acting as if she had something to hide. But at the same time I could tell that she was eager to share a secret with me."

"No, Doña Matilde," Adela continued once she was sure they were alone. "I barely spent any money on gifts this year. I've been saving most of it because, beginning tomorrow, I'll be starting a new life."

FOUR

The Former Lover

On her way to Mariela's house after leaving Doña Matilde's store, Adela paid Gloria Obando a quick visit. She wanted to wish her former lover a Merry Christmas. She also wanted to view the nativity scene that La Curva's midwife dutifully laid out every Christmas. In spite of having seen the display for seven consecutive years, four of them while living with Gloria, its delicate intricacy always left Adela feeling as if she had witnessed a miracle. The menagerie of toys occupied more than half of the midwife's living room. Seemingly endless strings of small blinking lights surrounded the miniature community, there to pay homage to the Lord's birth. Little plastic toy soldiers, firemen, cows, elephants, giraffes, gorillas, glass ballerinas, clowns carved from wood, cast metal airplanes, helicopters, U.S. military ships, and land vehicles of every type were spread out before the Infant Jesus' feet. The exhibit was placed upon layers of blue, green, and gold felt cloth.

On the morning of Adela's final visit, the morning of her last Christmas, the Infant had awakened to his first day of life in his crib. The night before, at the tolling of the church bells calling the faithful of La Curva to midnight Mass, Gloria placed him there with reverence, cradling the plaster Jesus in her arms as if he were a real child. She then sat on a rocking chair to enjoy her creation. Without knowing when, she fell asleep. A few hours later the midwife awoke, turned off the lights, and went to bed. The next morning she got up early because she expected her former lover, as was her custom every Christmas, to drop by for a visit.

Gloria invited Adela to join her for their traditional breakfast: a *nacatamal*, toast with guava jelly, and *café con leche*. On Adela's last day of life, she only had time for the cup of coffee.

"You should at least have some toast," Gloria had said.

33

"I can't. I'm in a hurry. I want to get to Mariela's house before the kids wake up. I'm dying to see the expressions on their faces when they open their presents," Adela had answered.

"She was the love of my life," Gloria sighed the morning of my visit; her gaze became distant as my questions sent her rummaging through the attic of her recollections. The two women had lived together for four years, very happily, or so the midwife thought, until Ixelia Cruz came between them. "I couldn't stand the notion of carving up Adela's affections. At first she begged me to think about the three of us living together, but I knew that with that girl under the same roof, it wouldn't be long before I became a bother. I always thought of my relationship with Adela as a marriage, and I simply couldn't accept the idea of sharing her on a permanent basis with another woman. To be honest, I wanted Adela all to myself."

On that fateful Christmas, the former lovers, in spite of three years having elapsed since their breakup, approached one another with caution. Their meetings often ended in arguments and bitter recriminations. To remain on neutral ground, they talked about the weather. "The day was rather chilly; a cool breeze blew steadily from the north. That's why Adela was wearing her long-sleeved checkered shirt."

On Adela's last Christmas morning, the women avoided, as they had learned was wise, the subject of Ixelia. Whenever that topic came up, the discussion would inevitably culminate in a swift current of angry reproaches. "I knew that little whore would bring Adela nothing but trouble," Gloria said to me. Although more than three years had passed since her former lover's death, and more than six years since their sentimental parting, I could detect a swell of resentment in her voice. Adela's betrayal had left a gaping wound in the midwife's soul, which I suspected would never be completely healed. "How could that girl not be trouble, considering the way her mother raised her! They were both nothing more than common whores and, believe me, the daughter liked what she did—she enjoyed selling herself. What's worse, her mother acted as her pimp, placing her in anyone's bed for whatever she could get in return."

Gloria rose from the dining room table, walked to the refrigerator, took out a Rojita, and offered me a bottle of the strawberry soda as well. I declined, not being too fond of the medicinal taste of Nicaragua's favorite soft drink. Using an opener that, years before, Adela had screwed to a wooden column that helped hold up the eave out in back, Gloria took the top off the bottle. She then returned to her seat to continue talking about her role on the day of her former lover's death.

Throughout the interview, Gloria's mood wavered between melancholy and bitterness. "All the years we lived together, Adela and I were happy. We understood one another perfectly. I was the wife, which is what she wanted out of a partner, and she was the husband. We took care of each other's needs . . . every single one of them. What's more, I put up with Adela's previous friendships without complaining."

When Gloria noticed my puzzled expression, she explained further. "Everyone in this country pretends that lesbians don't exist. Men especially. They're so damn *macho*; their little brains can't imagine that a woman can find pleasure outside of their pitiful dicks. But let me tell you something, there are more *cochonas* and bisexual women here than anyone would ever care to admit, in spite of those stupid laws against loving someone of the same sex. What's more, we come in all shapes, sizes, colors, and social classes. Believe me. In fact, several women, wealthy ones at that, used to drive all the way to La Curva to spend time with Adela."

Gloria smiled when she saw that because of her candor I was caught somewhere between a grin and a blush. She took a long sip from the bottle of Rojita, licked the moisture off of her lips with the tip of her tongue, and went on with her explanation. "Adela had been meeting with these women for several years before she and I got together. It all started when she met a widow who lives in Managua and owns a coffee plantation near Masatepe. The woman, recently freed from having to put up with a man in her life, fell hard for Adela. She was the aggressor, even though she didn't need to be because Adela seldom turned down an opportunity to get to know a woman in the flesh. They became lovers. All this time, back in Managua, the widow sang

Adela's praises to her closest friends. Before long, a handful of these women started driving all the way up here just to spend a few hours with Adela. They'd arrive disguised in scarves and dark glasses. Although on the surface that scene was funny, it also made me want to cry. Now, since these women were married to rich, powerful men, they were generous with Adela, giving her nice gifts that sometimes included money, because they wanted to make sure that Adela wouldn't talk. If their secrets ever leaked out, their comfortable lives would be ruined. But Adela would never have said anything, even if they hadn't given her a cent. She wasn't like that. In fact, Adela felt sorry for them. These rich women were risking everything, their families, their reputations, and their wealth, just by coming to La Curva to see her. But they didn't drive all the way out here only because she was a great lover: they liked coming to La Curva because very few people in Managua have ever heard of this miserable little town. Two women still visited her, on and off. In this way, their indiscretions were sure to remain private—up until the time Adela was murdered.

"During these visits, I'd sometimes sit quietly in the living room, knitting. At first I could hear Adela and her guest in the bedroom, talking normally and giggling. But little by little their conversations became whispers; then the sighs would come; and, finally, Adela would have the woman gasping for breath, lost in ecstasy. Do you know what made her such a great lover? Three things, I'd say. First, she lived to give other women pleasure. She considered that the main reason God had placed her on this earth. Second, she had a talent for quickly discovering what made a woman lose control. Let me tell you, Adela was incredibly skilled as a lover. Plus, she was tireless. And, last, and perhaps most important, Adela was a wonderful listener. These women would dump their frustrations on her, and she'd always be completely understanding."

I expressed my surprise that Adela's friends didn't make Gloria jealous. "Who said they didn't make me jealous!" she replied loudly, without hesitation or shame, while slapping the surface of the rustic dining room table. "But, shit, we needed their gifts! Do you know how hard it is to earn a living in this damn country?"

Biting her lower lip, Gloria waited until she was calm again. At the height of the outburst, her gaze startled me: Gloria's eyes had blazed with the intensity of hot, burning coals. But once she had regained her composure, the fire dampened, and her once-blistering stare turned warm, compassionate.

"Really, I feel sorry for these women," she went on at last. "As hard as it is to make a living in Nicaragua, it's harder still to be a woman who likes other women. Adela's most faithful visitor, for example, was very lonely. She was the one who spent the most time here, lingering around afterward, just pouring her heart out. This woman is married to a well-known man who at one time headed a government ministry. I still see the couple on television, to this day. Everyone knows them as devout Catholics. Most Sundays, after the cardinal's mass, they're standing at his side as he shakes people's hands after the service. Every day of her life that poor woman has to put up a front, pretending that she is happily married and free from sin. But we got to know her as she really was. After making love with Adela, as they sat at this table and drank coffee, her face was radiant. But always, toward the end of her visit, she'd become sad because she was faced with returning to a self-righteous man and a loveless marriage. About a month after Adela's funeral, she came by to see me. She had read about the murder in the paper and decided to wait for the commotion to die down before risking a visit to La Curva. She sat right there, in the chair you're sitting in now, sobbing. We talked for several hours. Over and over she kept telling me how important her relationship with Adela had been to her. Since that visit, she hasn't returned."

The recollection brought tears to Gloria's eyes. I reached into the back pocket of my pants, pulled out my handkerchief, and handed it to her. She dabbed her eyes for a few moments and then looked at me, smiling in thanks. After taking a sip of Rojita, she continued. "But Adela's relationship with that little whore was another matter altogether. She placed poor Adela under a spell. I really believe that. That's why I'll never let her name cross my lips. Several people swear that they saw her consulting a sorcerer in Diriomo. Who knows what curse that little bitch had that evil man conjure up to keep Adela so needy, so dependent on her? She probably gave her some panty water to drink as well. Adela was a strong-willed person, but when it came to that girl she could never say no.

"The worst part was that Adela's pathetic obsession with that whore put her straight on a collision course with Don Roque and Doña Erlinda, the girl's mother. That old man, just like Adela, was crazy over the girl. Not long after the little bitch left Don Roque's house to go live with Adela, Doña Erlinda started her plot. She desperately wanted her daughter to return to Don Roque. She figured that the old man wouldn't be around much longer, and she hoped that when he died he would leave everything he owned to her daughter. So, both Don Roque and Doña Erlinda saw Adela as a problem, like an old *guachipilín* tree that has fallen across a road after a heavy rain and needs to be chopped into sections to be removed.

"Plus, there was another thing, beyond losing Ixelia that drove Don Roque insane: he knew that men were snickering behind his back, questioning his honor. He was sure that they were saying that he was too old to satisfy someone as horny as that little whore, and that's why she left him for a woman! Don Roque's a very proud man. He simply couldn't handle the idea of his sweet young thing leaving him for a woman. Can you imagine what all the *machos* around here were saying? 'Don Roque's prick is so old and withered that his girl has to find a woman to feel satisfied.'

"That final Christmas morning," the midwife went on, "the last thing I wanted to talk about was that little whore. I didn't want to get into an argument. Besides, I could see that Adela was very nervous. The entire time she sat here, at this table, drinking her *café con leche*, her knee kept bouncing up and down so fast it reminded me of a jackhammer. I knew Adela well enough to realize that she was terribly worried about something.

"'What's the matter? Why are you so tense?' I asked her. Adela didn't answer. She simply stared at the floor. That was enough for me to guess what was going on.

"'Are you going to be seeing her today?' I asked. Again, Adela said nothing.

"'Are you crazy? Do you have a death wish?' I scolded her, angry that she would even consider getting back together with that whore. 'You know that both Don Roque and Doña Erlinda have threatened to kill you if you go anywhere near her again!'

"Adela laughed and began to cough. That cough was from the cigarettes. I was always ranting that smoking wasn't good for her. But I have to admit that toward the end of her life, she had been trying very hard to quit. Anyway, when Adela finally recovered, she said, 'Don't worry, woman. I can take care of myself. Just try not to worry.'"

Gloria became silent. In her gaze I could clearly see that she was reliving those last moments with Adela. At last, from the core of her being, a deep sigh sprung forth. She then looked at me directly, her eyes brimming with tears, and said, "I should never have let Adela go. But how could I stop her? Once she made up her mind about something, it was impossible to get her to even consider changing course."

That Christmas, after Adela finished her cup of coffee, she rose from her seat, stepped toward Gloria, and gave her a long, tight hug.

"I thought that was strange," Gloria said. "It was as if she knew that she was saying goodbye forever." Once again, Adela wished her former lover a Merry Christmas. Before leaving the house, she stood before the manger scene, admiring the toys and the lights.

"What I wouldn't give to be a child again," she said out loud, smiling sadly.

Adela then walked to the door, turned, waved farewell, and left for Mariela's house. That was Gloria's last living memory of the love of her life.

Nearly two months passed before the midwife saw Adela again. On that morning, Mariela sent her oldest daughter, Gema, to call Gloria because she needed her to help identify Adela's body.

PART II

The Ferris Wheel

FIVE

The Mastermind

Doña Erlinda Cruz, the mastermind behind Adela Rugama's death, spent Christmas Eve in the city of Masatepe, dancing away in the company of several relatives and acquaintances. She assumed that by being in a community hall full of witnesses at the precise hour of the murder she would have an airtight alibi. In spite of this, the jury felt there was enough circumstantial evidence against Doña Erlinda to sentence her to thirty-five years in prison.

I could rightly grasp Don Roque's reasons for killing Adela. His obsession with Ixelia, plus his humiliation over losing her to a woman, resulted in an implacable desire for revenge that refused to yield to the healing powers of time and ultimately led the _hacendado_ to commit a reckless crime of passion. Most of us know that nothing is more difficult than being madly in love and having to accept that the object of our desire does not feel the same. We also know that at its darkest, the human heart is capable of mangling simple realities, unleashing legions of pent-up demons that can plunge a person into such depths of despair that even the meek can sometimes commit infernal acts, including murder.

But comprehending what led Doña Erlinda to plan the execution of her daughter's female lover was far beyond my reach. Nevertheless, as chronicler of this tragic event, I was obliged to penetrate her motivations, as well as to try to understand how she had managed to persuade two others that Adela Rugama's death would be in their best interest. Thus, armed with a brand-new notepad, a concealed tape recorder, and great trepidation, I went to Nandasmo, Si Dios Quiere sputtering as it fought its way up the hill between Masaya and Catarina, to interview Ixelia's mother.

43

When I visited Doña Erlinda for the first and only time, her appearance surprised me. Because of the hateful character of the murder she had planned and because of the things people had said about her, I was expecting a woman who outwardly revealed the heartless, dark, and sinister soul that dwelled within. What I found, instead, was a thirty-nine-year-old mother of four who could still make a man's heart beat faster. Doña Erlinda's expression upon greeting me at the door of her house was so open, so innocent, that for an instant I asked myself whether I had found the right person.

The woman standing before me that morning certainly didn't appear capable of planning the brutal crime of which she had been convicted. Doña Erlinda's beauty was, and I believe I use these terms without exaggeration—seraphic, otherworldly. If she had truly played such a prominent role in Adela's murder, then her mesmerizing presence attested to the possibility that those beings expelled from heaven alongside Lucifer could, indeed, once have been angels. In spite of her age, Doña Erlinda's allure was so disquieting, so disturbing, that I could easily imagine how, at its peak, as several persons had affirmed, she had driven several men to the brink of madness. At present, the only detail that detracted from her loveliness was the reddish-brown tone of her hair, the result of a cheap dye job that had also left a somber halo of dark roots along the surface of her scalp. People who had known Doña Erlinda as a teenager stated that she had gained a couple of pounds from the days when her own mother had, with dogged determination, sought a wealthy husband for her. But she could still command attention. As we stood at the doorway chatting, I witnessed how the men who passed before her house stared hungrily at the roundness of her hips and at her firm, upright breasts.

What I found most unsettling about Doña Erlinda were her eyes. Her irises were like two pools of honey into which pinpricks of bright mustard had been dropped and smeared. When she looked straight at me, the harshness of the yellow flecks reminded me of the spine-chilling stare of cinematic vampires, who with a single gaze can detect a soul's deepest fears.

That morning, excruciatingly awkward gaps of silence turned our conversation into a marshy pit where, without a thing to latch onto, I was sinking helplessly. Doña Erlinda replied to my questions in as few words as possible, and when I pushed her to elaborate on terse answers, she exhibited the astonishing gift of stringing together sentences that seemed coherent and fluid, yet ultimately were hollow of meaning. Still, at the time of the interview, I had the impression that I was gathering a respectable amount of information, perhaps because of the hypnotic effects of her honey-mustard stare. But later, when I listened to her replies on my tape recorder, I realized that Doña Erlinda had told me nothing.

A couple of weeks after my visit as I reviewed the court transcript of her testimony, I discovered that she is, in fact, a master in the art of disguising her thoughts and deeds with discreet, resonant words that at first impress, but that later, upon further scrutiny, end up being pointless. For instance, when the judge, Leticia Solórzano, frustrated at Doña Erlinda's evasiveness on the witness stand, pointedly asked her if she had planned the murder. The woman replied, playing with the multiple meanings of the somewhat archaic word *merced*, in Spanish: "Your Grace, the grace that people grace me with is impossible. For not only do I not possess the grace they think I have, but thanks to my gracelessness I am innocent."

In my quest to understand the paths Doña Erlinda's life had taken that would one day lead her to plan Adela Rugama's death, most of what I learned arose during conversations with people who knew her well. In Nandasmo, her hometown, where she had spent all her years, her neighbors actually felt sorry for her. They tended to exonerate Doña Erlinda from responsibility in Adela's murder because of the miserable circumstances of her upbringing. But in La Curva, sentiments ran quite to the contrary: the majority of the people I spoke to in that town thought that the woman was nothing but pure, unadulterated evil.

In retracing Doña Erlinda's life, I discovered that her mother, Doña Rebeca Cruz, had never sent her to school. She didn't believe that learning to read and write was necessary to succeed in life. It was more important, Doña Rebeca told neighbors, for the child to know how to make money. Ultimately, the mother reasoned, what mattered most to others was how much money a person had. With this in mind, every day, including Sunday mornings, she took Erlinda to the small produce stand she owned in Managua's Mercado Oriental. By the time the little girl could talk, she was already an experienced merchant, aggressively peddling plantains, yuca, mangos, and *pitahayas* to the shoppers who bravely ventured into the capital's most pulsating and dangerous marketplace.

At the Mercado Oriental, a sprawling city itself, Erlinda witnessed every conceivable dark act in human existence. She was raised among people whose lives were caught in webs of deceit, theft, assault, alcoholism, drug addiction, prostitution, and murder. Years later, as an adult, Doña Erlinda admitted to her neighbors that her experiences in El Oriental, as most Nicaraguans refer to the open-air market, had taught her to admire people who went to any length to get whatever they wanted.

Shortly after Erlinda's thirteenth birthday, Doña Rebeca took notice of how her daughter's budding sexuality began to attract the lewd comments of grown men. So promising was the adolescent's appeal that news of her remarkable potential reached a *coronel* in the Guardia Nacional, the owner of a brothel in the heart of old, pre-earthquake Managua. Through an intermediary, the officer offered the mother three thousand *córdobas*, a small fortune at that time, to have Erlinda join his stable of young apprentices. The emissary promised Doña Rebeca that the child would be treated royally. What's more, he assured her that the country's military elite would help introduce her with honors into the profession.

"What do you think I am, you son of a bitch! Who would do that to their child?" Doña Rebeca answered. Her angry shouts could be heard throughout the marketplace. Instead of being offended, the emissary, a wily sergeant dressed in civilian clothing, walked away, chuckling at what he knew was a barren display of outrage.

The surrounding merchants, on the other hand, applauded the mother's moral integrity and her courage in snubbing the representative of a high-ranking officer in Somoza's army. Doña Rebeca bowed deeply in acknowledgment.

That afternoon, as the passengers dozed on the bus ride back to Nandasmo, exhausted after a hard day's work, Erlinda's mother leaned toward the girl and whispered in her ear. "Men are starting to pay close attention to you, *hijita*. You won't be this pretty for long. We need to take advantage of that, and quickly. But don't worry, I've got a plan."

Two months later, on a cloudless Sunday afternoon, Doña Rebeca dressed her daughter in a bright, flimsy dress that flaunted the adolescent's incipient voluptuousness. They climbed aboard a bus headed to Masatepe, a relatively wealthy community only a short distance from Nandasmo where several coffee plantation owners lived. As soon as they arrived, they walked from the Central Park to El Chilamate, the town's best restaurant, named after the dense tree that shaded the courtyard. Once there, the mother sat the beautiful young girl at a table, alone. Erlinda distractedly sipped through a straw from a bottle of strawberry soda—a stunning portrait of innocence. From another table in the corner of the yard, Doña Rebeca watched as young *masatepeños* stopped by to chat with the dazzling teenage girl. If the mother learned that the unsuspecting young man came from a family of scant means, the mother would shake her head, and Erlinda, as instructed, would neither speak nor look at the boy. Soon, the rejected suitor would depart, accepting that this particular round of seduction was not one he was going to win. But if a young man was a good candidate for marriage, Doña Rebeca would nod affirmatively, and Erlinda would then, like a cat, alternate between disarmingly affectionate purrs and the occasionally painful clawing.

By the fourth week, the adolescent's table had become Masatepe's most popular gathering place for young men from well-to-do families. Every Sunday afternoon, the finest marriage prospects in the town sat at Erlinda's table. Shortly after her arrival, a cologne-soaked cluster of fifteen- and sixteen-year-old boys, all still too young to shave regularly, would surround the lovely adolescent. Like Romantic poets, they competed fiercely for the girl's affection, each of them vying to deposit the seed of his raging hormones into her pretty, shapely vessel. They each hoped to become her boyfriend—at least for a while—and were so intent on this goal that not once did they take notice of the woman who sat in a corner, sternly examining them.

From the beginning of her quest, Doña Rebeca paid the town's most lucid drunk one *córdoba* to sit at her table and tell her about the background of each of the boys. She wanted to know which ones came from the wealthiest families. With that information, she discarded Erlinda's favorite suitor: a tall, thin youth who looked like he never got enough to eat and who told the girl that one day he would be a respected writer.

"I don't know, but they've told me that in Nicaragua all poets starve to death," Doña Rebeca stated emphatically on the bus ride back to Nandasmo as she ordered Erlinda to forget that loser. (Nevertheless, this young man did go on to become an internationally renowned novelist and politician.)

After six months, the commotion surrounding Erlinda's table resembled a pack of pubescent dogs in heat. To put an end to the turmoil the gatherings were beginning to cause, the mother finally made her choice. The boy who won the right to possess Erlinda Cruz was Raúl Dávila: the handsome son of Don Ramiro Dávila, owner of Masatepe's largest hardware store. What secured the victory for Raúl was Doña Rebeca's discovery that his family also owned El Carmen, a placid coffee plantation nestled in a quiet valley south of the city.

With the mother's encouragement, the teenagers swore to get married as soon as the groom could get his parents' permission. To distance Erlinda and Raúl from the unruly and burgeoning pack of horny male adolescents, Doña Rebeca had the teenagers begin to meet in the park. There, they would spend the entire afternoon sitting on a bench under a canopy of mango trees, holding hands and playfully kissing. Over time, and under the mother's intentionally neglectful performance as chaperone, these innocent forays of affection turned into passionate groping as the young couple took full advantage of the protective veils of the encroaching evening.

At first, Raúl's family accepted the boy's obsession with the daughter of a simple merchant from El Oriental. They thought of his crush as something quaint, a mere phase of his passage into manhood. The parents reasoned that the boy did, after all, need to become experienced in lovemaking before marrying an appropriate candidate—a young woman from a wealthy and well-respected family.

But that all changed the day Raúl returned home after a particularly inspiring groping session that had left him breathless and dizzy. As soon as he walked into the family's living room where his parents were entertaining three of Masatepe's most prominent couples, he announced, "Mamá, Papá, . . . I want to marry Erlinda as soon as possible."

The thought of their son marrying the daughter of a common merchant from El Mercado Oriental terrified the Dávilas. At once, and in the presence of their company, they exerted the full measure of their parental authority.

"Do you really think we're going to allow you to marry the daughter of a common merchant? The girl's nothing but a tramp! We'd rather see you dead first!" the teenager's father shouted before the embarrassed guests.

In response to the Dávilas' reaction, Doña Rebeca gave the young couple enough money so they could run off to San Juan del Sur, a tranquil port town on an expansive, quarter-moon bay of the Pacific. There, they holed up in a cheap hotel for an entire week, only coming out of their room when their bodies absolutely needed sustenance beyond what they could provide each other.

When Erlinda and Rául returned to Masatepe, she had just turned fourteen and, although no one knew it at the time, she was pregnant. Doña Rebeca tried to persuade Raúl's family to do the proper thing and have their son marry Erlinda, thus restoring the girl's honor. Instead, through their lawyer, the Dávilas denied that the boy had any responsibility in the occurrence. Raúl was quickly shipped off to San Pedro Sula, in Honduras, where he was locked up in a Catholic boarding school. His parents were willing to wait as long as necessary for the teenager's loins to cool off and for his brain to once again assume control over his thoughts. The Dávilas' lawyer then met with Erlinda's mother, and through him, they bought her silence. She signed a document in which she agreed that neither she nor her daughter would ever try to contact Raúl. In return, Doña Rebeca received what she believed to be a small fortune. But with the passage of time, the mother realized that she had sold Erlinda's purity for far too little.

Before long, and as the parents had hoped, Raúl outgrew his obsession with the daughter of the merchant from El Oriental. After two years in San Pedro Sula, the young man returned, having by then completed high school. He went on to study at the Jesuit university in Managua, became a lawyer, and married an artistic young woman from the respected Cárdenas family, who specialized in painting scenes of the Virgin's Ascension into Heaven. At the time of Adela Rugama's murder, Raúl Dávila was a member of Nicaragua's Supreme Court, as well as a staunch member of Opus Dei. And not once did he make an effort to meet Ixelia Cruz, his daughter.

In spite of the failure of her initial strategy, Doña Rebeca stubbornly clung to her plan. "You're still pretty, *muchacha*. Don't worry, even though you now have a child, we'll find a husband for you with plenty of money. He may not be as rich as Raúl, but he'll have enough to take good care of us." But their attempts on the affections of unsuspecting young men didn't fulfill the mother's goals: Erlinda never married. Instead, she gave birth to four different children from four different men, each man of less means than the one before.

When Erlinda was twenty-five years old, she had her last child: a boy, her second son. One can argue that this is where the tragedy of Adela's death really begins. The father was Bayardo Ramírez, the eldest of Don Roque Ramírez's numerous bastards and the only one the *hacendado* ever legally recognized. Bayardo, however, never acknowledged the child he had with Erlinda. Prior to the boy's birth, during a loud argument that all of the neighbors overheard, Bayardo adamantly refused to assume responsibility for the kid.

"You're joking, right? Any man from around here could have been the father. Everyone knows what a slut you are. You've got to be kidding if you think I'll give your child my last name!"

In spite of this, one Sunday afternoon a few days after Don Roque learned that he had a grandson, he mounted his palomino and rode the five kilometers from his hacienda, Las Dos Balas, near the town of Pío XII, to pay the mother his respects. At first, Erlinda's glacial beauty startled the *hacendado*. He was particularly disturbed by her eyes: their stern color reminded him of lemon zest. But all that was forgotten, and the grandfather's life was forever altered the instant Erlinda's eldest daughter, then only ten years old, entered the room.

"And who is this precious child?" Don Roque asked, giving the little girl his most endearing smile.

"This is Ixelia, the oldest of my children."

"Well, then, that almost makes her my granddaughter. Isn't that so?" Ixelia smiled at the old man's joke, enjoying the thought of at last having a real grandfather.

One drunken night, according to the men who played cards every evening with Don Roque, the *hacendado* confessed that the moment he first set eyes on Ixelia, the little girl's splendor left him gasping for breath. The air in his universe became thin in her presence, sucked in by the vacuum of his desires. Ixelia was, he thought, as perfect as an angel. Her light brown hair, just a shade darker than blonde, fell in soft, captivating curls all the way down to her waist. The girl reminded him of a high-spirited filly as she skipped across the room, playing with her siblings. Her honey-colored eyes made the old man want to break out in sobs; although she had inherited her beauty from Doña Erlinda, Don Roque breathed a sigh of relief when he discovered that genetics had withheld the golden harshness of her mother's eyes.

But what kept the *hacendado* spellbound, what made his usually dry mouth salivate, were the little girl's legs. He couldn't take his eyes off their tender, graceful curves. Don Roque felt his heart strain to continue its labor when he saw, thanks to the short skirts that Doña Erlinda always made Ixelia wear, the glory of the child's firm limbs, already shapely in spite of her young age. And in his mind, the *hacendado* became absolutely sure that one day the taut flesh of her celestial thighs would spread far apart, like the doors of Paradise, to let him in.

SIX

Splitting Melons

"To be honest," Mariela said while she stared vacantly at the old train station, her gaze fixed sorrowfully on the dilapidated building, "the color of Doña Erlinda's eyes make me think of the devil." For a moment, I imagined her wishing that the extinct United Fruit Company train would return to take her away from the painful memories of Adela's death.

I had spent the morning questioning Adela Rugama's sister, trying once more to breathe life into her recollections. Toward the end of my visit, Nubia, the youngest of Mariela's two daughters and the single mother of a three-year-old boy, stopped sweeping the floor, stepped out into the kitchen, and returned with a cup of lemongrass tea. I accepted the drink with a smile and took the tiniest sip, hoping that it didn't contain a drop of the neighbor's remedy for anxiety.

"That woman," Mariela continued through teeth clenched so tight her statement came out as a hiss, "is the most manipulative person on this earth."

When Ixelia left Don Roque to start living with Adela, Doña Erlinda did not seem upset in the least. In fact, she often boasted to her neighbors, in the guise of a joke, that her daughter's amorous talents were so unique that they annihilated the borders between the sexes.

"It was clear to everyone that Doña Erlinda didn't care one bit if her daughter was in a lesbian relationship. And you know why she didn't care? Because when they first came together, Adela worked her ass off for that woman . . . and for free," Mariela told me.

Her daughter's relationship with the future murder victim turned out to be a highly profitable arrangement for Doña Erlinda. Several times during the first three months Adela lived with Ixelia, she'd rent a pickup truck and a driver, travel to

53

Chontales, a good six-hour drive from La Curva, and buy as many piglets as the vehicle could hold. Adela would bring the animals back and sell them at a considerable markup to *campesinos* of the coffee region; they, in turn, would raise the pig to slaughter on a special occasion, such as Christmas or a wedding. She'd then hand over half of the profits to Ixelia's mother. What's more, in between runs for piglets, Adela picked fruit and plantains from several haciendas near La Curva, keeping a portion as pay, which Doña Erlinda would then sell at her stall in El Oriental. Everyone who knew the woman with pale yellow eyes agreed that, thanks to Adela, she was raking in more money than ever.

"At this rate," she once crowed to her neighbors, "within a couple of years I will have made more money on my own than Ixelia could have made from inheriting everything Don Roque owns."

Whenever people asked Erlinda if it didn't bother her that her daughter was living with a *cochona*, she would laughingly reply, "Everyone wants to possess Ixelia. There's nothing I can do about that. But let me tell you something, there's always been plenty of that girl to go around."

For several months, the three women seemed happy with their unspoken arrangement. Through their alliance, each of them gained something they had always wanted: Adela, to save a beautiful damsel in distress; Ixelia, to be in an honest relationship; and Doña Erlinda, to begin her long-desired journey toward wealth.

But before long, Adela became restless. Having fought her entire life to be independent, she soon grew tired of being exploited for the right to love. Although Adela sought Doña Erlinda's approval, she didn't want to become a slave to the woman's obsession with wealth. Still, she was well aware that her submission to Doña Erlinda's greed was the price she needed to pay if she wanted to live in peace with Ixelia. However, in the end, Adela followed the dictates of her conscience. She informed Ixelia's mother that she wouldn't continue handing over the hard-earned rewards of her labor because, from that point on, she intended to save money to buy some property. But Adela assured Doña Erlinda that her daughter would be well taken care of, never wanting for anything.

"When my little sister told Doña Erlinda that she'd had enough, that she now needed to work for herself, that woman became venemous. All the poison stored inside of her started to ooze out in everything she did," Mariela said, shaking her head. "I don't know why Doña Erlinda expected Adela to work for her forever. Did that woman really think that my sister was willing to pay any price, including giving up her own freedom, for a relationship with Ixelia?"

Doña Erlinda, distraught over losing Adela's income, turned her eyes again toward Don Roque. During those months his fortune had moved far from her grasp, a barely visible speck on the horizon. But knowing that the old man was still madly in love with her daughter, she sent Don Roque a message with Arquímedes Guadamuz, asking the *hacendado* to drop by her house for a meeting.

According to the court testimony of Doña Verónica Bustamente, one of Doña Erlinda's neighbors, the old man responded to the summons late one Thursday afternoon, mounted on his palomino. The witness overheard their conversation because Don Roque's visit caught her while she was using the outhouse. Sitting on the commode, Doña Verónica eavesdropped on their conversation, observing the conspirators through a crack between the boards.

"Don Roque," Ixelia's mother said, "I've been feeling terrible ever since my daughter left you. That girl made a mistake. I've asked her over and over, why did you do something so stupid?"

"That's not what I hear, Doña Erlinda," the old man answered, a stinging bitterness evident in his growl. "People tell me that you were dancing with joy because of the money the *cochona* was giving you."

"People lie, Don Roque. How can you even think that I would be happy knowing that Ixelia was involved with a lesbian? The whole thing is unnatural."

Don Roque just stared at Ixelia's mother for a long time without making a sound. In court, Doña Verónica stated that the *hacendado* seemed to be measuring the veracity of her words. Nevertheless, the witness added, the excitement evident in his eyes revealed his fervent hope that Doña Erlinda was telling the truth. She, in turn, offered the old man her most innocent, blank expression.

"Now, the reason I called you, Don Roque," she continued at last, breaking the wordless duel, "is to ask if you'd like to have my daughter back."

Don Roque didn't answer; he simply kept staring at Doña Erlinda. But Doña Verónica testified in court that upon bringing up the possibility of Ixelia's return, the *hacendado* leaned forward slightly, and appeared to start shaking.

"Don Roque, if you'd like my daughter to return to you, I think I can help. I'll do whatever I have to for Ixelia to come to her senses, for her to realize that being with you is what's best. But you need to promise one thing: you will forget that she ever left you for that woman. That *cochona* has to disappear from our lives, forever. You can't hold anything that has happened against my little girl. If Ixelia goes back with you, we all have to leave what the *cochona* did to us in the past. Do you think you can do that, Don Roque?"

Through the gap, Doña Verónica observed closely as the coarse knot of the *hacendado*'s Adam's apple slid up and down the dry, sagging wrinkles of his throat. At last, in a barely audible rasp, Don Roque answered, "You know I want Ixelia back, Doña Erlinda. My life is worthless since she left. You know that."

"Well then, Don Roque, leave the whole thing up to me," Erlinda said, smiling. She reached out, took his large hand, stained with age in hers, and patted it gently on the back. "Soon Ixelia will be back. I promise."

From that conversation on, Doña Erlinda devoted all of her energies to hatching schemes that would force her daughter to return to the wealthy landowner.

"The first thing that woman did was to lock poor Ixelia up. Imagine that, trying to keep her own daughter a prisoner," Mariela said to me, her voice rising in disbelief.

According to Mariela and to several *nandasmeños*, with the help of her two sons, Doña Erlinda kidnapped Ixelia several times. Twice a month, the young woman would ride Adela's bike to Nandasmo to visit her mother. The day Doña Erlinda set into motion her plan to persuade Ixelia to return to Don Roque, as soon as her daughter arrived, she and her boys forced the girl into a windowless storeroom, closed the door, and then secured it with a strong padlock.

"I'm not letting you out, you little whore—not until you come to your senses and promise to go back to live with Don Roque! You're acting like a common slut! No, you're worse than a whore because you're making a fool of yourself over a lesbian. Did you hear me? I know you can hear me, Ixelia! I won't let you out until you promise that you're going to leave the *cochona* and return to Don Roque! From now on, stay away from that dyke!" Doña Erlinda shouted, to the delight of her neighbors who came out of their houses to witness the spectacle. They were thrilled to have enough grain to feed the gossip mill for weeks.

The first time Doña Erlinda kidnapped Ixelia, she kept the young woman locked in the stifling storeroom for two days. The morning of the second day Adela came looking for her, but the brothers greeted the distressed lover with a hailstorm of rocks, forcing her to return home where, with great anxiety, she had little choice but to await the outcome of her lover's imprisonment. On the third day, at dawn, Ixelia finally surrendered. She told her mother that she had come to realize what a terrible mistake she had made, and she promised to return to Don Roque. Doña Erlinda, relishing the victory, unlocked the door and let her daughter out. She proclaimed her triumph over the lesbian lover in a passionate speech that several neighbors overheard.

"I knew that you'd come to see things my way. We can't afford to let Don Roque's fortune slip away. Now, if you're patient and do what I tell you, with time we'll become very rich." But late that afternoon, the first instant Ixelia was left unguard-

ed, she escaped, mounting the bicycle and racing all the way back
to La Curva and to Adela.

This scene was repeated several times, in spite of the outcome
being so predictable. Whenever Ixelia went to visit her mother,
like Rapunzel, she'd be locked up. And each time she'd find a different way to escape.

"Poor Ixelia," Mariela said, sighing heavily before taking
another sip of her lemongrass tea. "That girl couldn't get away
from her mother. Ixelia was drawn to her the way an iguana is
drawn to the sun. She was easy prey for such a ruthless hunter.
But it was strange because Ixelia could not seem to survive without her mother's abuse. Doña Erlinda had exploited her for so
long that it seemed that she couldn't handle the freedom Adela
gave her. Ixelia always talked about how she wanted to be independent, but in spite of what she said, in the end she still needed
her mother's approval. More than anything, she wanted Doña
Erlinda to agree with the choices she had made in her life and to
share in her new dreams."

"When her first plan failed, Doña Erlinda started to show up at
my aunt's house to try to scare her into giving Ixelia up," said
Nubia. She had stopped cleaning the house to sit with us and
recount yet another fragment of the sad tale. "Whenever Doña
Erlinda came by, she threatened to have my aunt Adela thrown in
prison for being a pervert. My aunt would then, very calmly, try
to explain that it was Ixelia's decision to live with her. She'd also
tell Doña Erlinda that for once in her life the girl was happy. But
that woman didn't care about her daughter's happiness. All she
could think about was Don Roque's money. What Ixelia thought
or felt didn't matter to her mother one bit. Every time Doña
Erlinda came to threaten my aunt Adela, she'd leave in a fury, rav-
ing like a lunatic because she couldn't scare her into sending
Ixelia back to live with Don Roque."

The last time the mastermind of the murder came to see
Adela, Ixelia was out, but Nubia was there. That Sunday, right
after lunch, Adela and her niece sat in the living room, the front
door wide open to let the breeze in, listening to music on a

Korean sound system that had cost the coffee-picker a fortune, but was also her most treasured possession. Then, Doña Erlinda appeared in front of the house, standing in the middle of the street while glaring at them. Under the blazing midday sun, she spread her legs apart like the cowboy gunslingers Nubia had seen on television. Doña Erlinda scowled so menacingly that the younger of Mariela's two daughters was instantly overcome by a tidal wave of terror. In her left hand, Ixelia's mother held a machete and, in the other, a large melon. Doña Erlinda waited outside, wordlessly, for what seemed to Nubia like an hour. She merely stood there, staring at Adela, who continued rocking in her chair as if nothing unusual was happening beyond her doorway. At last, Doña Erlinda took a deep breath, and, with the explosive rage of a long dormant volcano, she roared, "Hey, *cochona*, come out of the house this instant, and give me back my daughter!"

"I nearly jumped out of my seat when I heard Doña Erlinda shout that. Never in my life have I been so scared. I started shaking, and, no matter how hard I tried, I couldn't stop," Nubia said. As she relived the moment, I could see the cinders of that frightening incident still glowing in the young woman's eyes. "But my aunt Adela just sat there, rocking in her chair. Then, she smiled sadly, glanced at me, and shook her head. At last, she brought her rocking to a halt, rose slowly from her seat, and walked to the door."

"I've told you many times, Doña Erlinda, I'm not keeping Ixelia here by force. She's living with me because this is where she wants to be."

"In that case, if you're not going to return my daughter, I must warn you that you're headed for big trouble, *cochona*!" the woman said. Doña Erlinda then stepped slowly toward the house. When she reached the curb, with much drama, she carefully placed the melon on the sidewalk, making sure the fruit was perfectly balanced.

"I'm telling you now, dyke," she said in a deep snarl, "if you don't send Ixelia back to Don Roque, you'll end up either in prison . . . or in the cemetery."

With that, Doña Erlinda took a small step back, raised the machete high above her head, and brought its glinting edge down on the melon. A chilling metallic crash rang out as the sharp edge of the blade met the concrete, and the melon fell open in two perfect halves, its entrails falling in one squishy lump onto the steaming sidewalk.

SEVEN

The Ferris Wheel

As I sat in Gloria Obando's living room sipping on a bottle of Rojita in between questions, I could clearly see how painful it was for La Curva's midwife to recall how Adela and Ixelia had come together. Although these memories made Gloria sad, I really had no choice but to prick the soothing wrapping of time, let the recollections seep out, and hope that on that afternoon she could summon the murder victim's spirit. She, the woman in Adela's life prior to Ixelia, was the only person who knew how the couple's love story began. The murder victim, in the forthrightness that characterized her in life, had shared every detail with her former lover.

"My aunt used to tell me everything," Gema had said to me a few days before. "But she never told me how she had broken up with Gloria. 'I want to keep that private. . . . I owe Gloria that much . . . ' she said to me."

Although six years had passed since their breakup, the memories of how their relationship ended still brought large, glistening tears to the midwife's eyes. "It was November, toward the end of the rainy season, just around the time of year when you notice the days getting shorter," Gloria began. "That's when the coffee beans begin to ripen and there's a rush to gather them before they turn completely red."

As harvesttime approaches each year, plantation owners hire as many men, women, and children as possible to pick the coffee beans. Adela, renowned for being the best picker in the region, was particularly sought after for hire. Several months before, aware of her harvesting prowess, Don Carlos Somarriba, Don Roque's foreman, had offered her a bonus if she would sign on early to work among the rows of coffee shrubs at Las Dos Balas.

"Adela? Adela Rugama?" Don Carlos said to me as he let out a long whistle of admiration. He then lifted the tip of his

61

Pittsburgh Pirates baseball cap and pushed it back on his head to reveal more of his rough yet handsome face. "Let me tell you something, I've seen coffee pickers come and go. Working on plantations is what I've done all of my life. But even the best pickers couldn't come close to Adela. She was one of a kind. That woman had these agile, nimble fingers that could reach between the twisted branches of the coffee bush and pick beans at a speed you wouldn't believe. Plus, Adela was a workhorse. She never seemed to get tired. She alone could almost do the job of two good pickers."

Don Carlos then patiently explained how a very good worker can pick three sacks of beans a day, for a total of seventy-five pounds. An outstanding one could harvest up to four sacks.

"But Adela is the only picker I've ever seen who completely filled five sacks in one day. And I saw her do it three times. You could always count on Adela to harvest more than a hundred pounds of coffee beans before the sun set," Don Carlos said, smiling at the memory. "It's a shame what happened to her. But that's all I'm going to say about that," he added quickly, holding up the palm of his right hand.

Adela's work was so astounding that during dinner one evening, at the beginning of the harvest season, Don Roque Ramírez told his live-in lover—sixteen-year-old Ixelia Cruz—about the coffee picker's peculiar genius. The story of a woman who could outwork any man intrigued the beautiful teenager so much that the next day she sought Adela out, wanting to see the talented harvester for herself.

As Ixelia stood at a discrete distance, trying to observe Adela without being noticed, the legendary coffee picker felt a pair of eyes piercing the moist, sweaty skin of her back, like the pinpricks of a small insect bite. She turned her head several times, trying to find the source of her discomfort. At last she spotted Ixelia. Instantly, as if an invisible fist had struck her in the middle of her chest, Adela felt breathless and faint. The beans she was cradling in her hands began to slip between her fingers as Ixelia's stare held her transfixed. Adela then got down on her knees to recover the fruit from the damp, shaded earth. Having seen enough, Ixelia decided to return home.

"I don't see what's so special about her," she told Don Carlos, strolling past him on her way back to the house. "If you ask me, the woman's downright clumsy. Half the beans she picks end up on the ground."

Adela stood there, unable to move. Her heart pounded as she watched Ixelia leave. She knew that a man would become aroused by the way in which the young woman's well-rounded hips swayed invitingly as she walked. She knew that the short skirt that Ixelia wore, revealing her splendid thighs, would be a provocation too tempting for any man to turn down. And she also knew that the girl's tight pink blouse, insinuating a perfect pair of breasts underneath, could drive a man to madness. But what really struck Adela about the visitor was the melancholic expression on her face. Although stunning, Ixelia seemed like a sad, desperate young woman in need of help.

At that very instant, Adela started to forget who she was, as well as everything she had ever been. She started to forget her commitment to Gloria. She started to forget that she had sworn to remain at the midwife's side for the rest of her life. At that very instant, Adela began another existence, this one expressly devoted to making Ixelia's life blissful. And at that precise instant, she began to plan their coming together.

Never known for being timid in her amorous pursuits, that same day, after the blossoming shadows of the evening made picking impossible, Adela rushed home on her mountain bike, got undressed, showered, splashed on Mennen aftershave lotion, put on her best clothes, and once again climbed aboard her bike to visit Ixelia. At work she had questioned Don Carlos briefly and learned that every evening Don Roque rode his palomino to Nandasmo to play cards with a group of old-timers he had known most of his life and who always let the *hacendado* win a few *córdobas* to keep the peace. And the wealthy landowner, seduced by the illusion of his invincibility, never missed the opportunity to flaunt his skills.

Adela pedaled her bicycle as fast as she could, driven by a compulsion she didn't even attempt to resist. Her only desire in life now was to see Ixelia, to meet her, to talk to her, to worship her, to convince her that their destinies were irrevocably intertwined and that somewhere in this vast universe, at the dawn of creation, God had mapped out the everlastingness of their union on a stone tablet.

When Adela reached the turnoff to Las Dos Balas, her heart was beating so feverishly that she took a few deep breaths and imagined she was getting ready to go to sleep. Her mother had taught her this trick when she was a child. The practice helped calm the anxiety attacks Adela had experienced shortly after her father had suffered his stroke. When she turned off the main road, she pedaled harder, lifting a small cloud of dust on the dirt path leading to the house. As Adela approached the building and while the bicycle was still in motion, she stood on the left pedal, rode on it for a short distance, and then hopped off to a trotting dismount. Before coming to a complete stop, she propped the bicycle against the clay and stone oven that was on the northern side of the house. As Adela walked toward the main entrance, she took a moment to admire the majestic ceiba, a gigantic tree of the tropics that stood a hundred yards to the south and was the tallest of the region, looming above the rest. Taking one last deep breath she stepped onto the long, concrete front porch, dried the palms of her hands on her blue denim pants, walked up to the door, and knocked.

When Ixelia opened the door, her amber eyes, at first wide and curious, became a dark, harsh squint as she struggled to recognize her visitor. After a few seconds of scanning the faces and names stored in her memory, she gave up and said, "Don Roque isn't here right now."

"I'm here to see you, Ixelia. You were watching me pick coffee this morning."

"Oh, of course! Now I remember you."

"I just came by to say hello. I mean, you seemed so interested in what I was doing that I decided to come by to see if you had any questions. Or, if you don't, then maybe we can just talk."

Ixelia stared at the coffee picker, studying her intently, saying nothing. Adela felt her blood thicken, straining to flow through her veins as she gazed into the young woman's honey-colored eyes. At last Ixelia smiled, opened the door to the house, and said, "Very well, come on in."

From that evening on, during the remainder of the harvest season, Adela worked as if possessed by demons so she could get off earlier. Evoking Ixelia's eyes fueled the astonishing pace with which she picked the beans off of the bushes. In spite of leaving thirty minutes earlier each day, Adela always picked well over four sacks—to Don Carlos Somarriba's delight. More than once, Don Roque's foreman proclaimed out loud to the other coffee pickers that he did the right thing in giving her a signing bonus. After work, Adela would race home on her mountain bike, get undressed, shower, splash on Mennen aftershave lotion, put on clean clothes, and, without bothering to eat dinner, begin the six-and-a-half kilometer ride back to Don Roque's hacienda so that she could spend the evening with the object of her growing obsession.

One Tuesday night, after Adela's visits had been going on for two weeks, the women were sitting on the front porch of the hacienda house, drinking Victorias from a six-pack the coffee picker had brought along. Without Adela asking, Ixelia, pausing frequently to bite her lower lip, told her the entire story of her unhappy life. That night Adela learned how Doña Erlinda had been exploiting her daughter from the time she was eleven. She also learned that it was her mother who urged Ixelia to wear provocative clothing: a trademark she was well-known for.

"So that men will go crazy with desire and pay well for you," Doña Erlinda would say, promising her daughter that eventually some fool with money would fall madly in love with her and take care of the entire family.

"I hate doing this, Adela. I hate depending on men. I hate to use them and to be used. But my mother has never taught me anything else. She never sent me to school because she said that she would teach me everything I needed to know. I can't read or write, Adela," Ixelia said, shaking her head. She kept her teary gaze on the coarse cement floor of Don Roque's house, unable to sustain the longing stare of her newfound friend.

But that evening the revelation that most startled Adela was that the girl absolutely hated living with Don Roque. "The only reason I'm here is because my mother thinks he's going to leave me everything he owns when he dies. And she believes that since he's old, he's going to die soon. But what I try to tell her is that that old buzzard has plenty of years left, a lot more than me. He's still going strong. Why, every night, Adela . . . every night . . . he fucks me. He returns home from playing cards, reeking of alcohol and cigarettes, and he forces me to do whatever he feels like in bed. And I can't fight him. My mother has made me his property, his slave. And you know what's the worst part, Adela? You know what I hate the most? Don Roque has the breath of an old man. I hate it when he kisses me, especially in the morning. His mouth always smells stale, rancid."

As Ixelia brushed away her tears with the back of her hand, Adela placed an arm around her shoulders and made a silent vow to take care of the young woman, to take her away from that misery, to keep her safe from Doña Erlinda and Don Roque. By now, the coffee picker was passionately in love with the girl, far beyond redemption. At this point, Adela's only recourse was to keep moving forward: Ixelia's fate, whatever it may be, was now her own. As they said farewell, Adela held the young woman in a brief, loving embrace. She did, though, withhold her feelings; she didn't think it was the proper time—yet.

But the following night, overcome by the torment of her love, Adela opened her heart to the young woman. Like water rushing down a mountain stream, all of her feelings flowed out, without reservations. Adela confessed to Ixelia that she thought about her every second of the day; that she wanted to take her away from the cesspool her mother had thrown her into; that she wanted to slay all the dragons that threatened her; that she wanted to wake up every morning entangled in her sandalwood hair; that she wanted to teach her to think of herself as the most perfect woman in God's creation.

Throughout Adela's declaration of love, Ixelia remained quiet, listening intently, her eyes wide open, revealing nothing. She didn't reject Adela, nor did she seem shocked that a woman could desire her. Ixelia merely sat there, paying close attention to the reasons Adela gave for their loving one another until the list was exhausted. Ixelia then escorted her visitor to the front door, where Adela quietly refused to leave as she fervently prayed that God would allow them to share a loving first kiss. Instead, after the object of her desire excused herself, saying that it was getting late and that she'd better go in before Don Roque returned, the gifted coffee-picker experienced an overwhelming sense of frustration because she had no clue as to how Ixelia felt about anything she had said.

Several days later, during the cooler days of early December, the feast of the Immaculate Conception converted the town of Pío XII into a carnival. Among the attractions that invaded the village, altering its usual peace and drawing visitors from the entire area, were a small circus, with no animals—only two dwarf clowns, one clumsy magician, two quivering acrobats, and three inept jugglers; several gambling booths; a ride of flying chairs; a merry-go-round; a Ferris wheel; large open-sided tents under which people danced and drank; and several freak shows that included a young man whose hair and skin had become translucent, making it possible for everyone to see the shadows of his internal organs, after he had narrowly escaped the mortal grasp of La Llorona, the weeping woman whom most believed was not merely a legend.

One of those nights, as Adela tossed in bed formulating and then discarding plans for persuading Ixelia to become her mate, inspiration struck. Early the next morning, before dawn, she rushed to her sister's house and pulled Gema out of bed, drowsy and complaining the entire time, out of bed. Disoriented and rubbing both eyes with her fists, she heard her aunt saying, "I want you to write a note to a girl named Ixelia. She lives at Don Roque's house. Tell her to meet me in Pío XII tonight at eight o'clock by the largest roulette wheel. Later this morning, send Javier to deliver the message. Can you do that?"

Gema nodded, stumbled back to her bed, climbed in once again, and immediately went back to sleep. She woke up unsure of whether her aunt's request had been a dream or not, but the details were still so vivid, especially the notion of a girl with the strange name of Ixelia, that she decided to write the note anyway, just in case her aunt's message had been part of reality. After Gema finished, she asked her youngest brother to take the note to Don Roque's hacienda.

"Since Ixelia couldn't read," Javier told me during my investigation, "she asked me to read the message to her."

"Tell Adela that I'll be there," Ixelia answered after he had finished.

That evening, at exactly eight o'clock, Adela waited anxiously near the largest roulette wheel. At eight-twenty, she started to think that Ixelia was not coming. Adela nervously scanned the swarms of faces that moved about the plaza of Pío XII. By eight-thirty, her temples were throbbing because of the music that blared from two massive speakers in the beer booth next to the roulette wheel. Adela then tried to distract herself by watching people lose their money as they played roulette.

"Thirteen red," she suddenly heard a saintly voice say inside her head. She immediately believed the voice belonged to San Jorge, her patron saint. His tone was charged with such certainty that Adela almost pushed aside those standing around the table to place a bet. But before she could do so, the operator called out the end of betting, and she was relieved she missed the chance because the pin stopped on seven black. There was one winner, a middle-aged woman, who smiled delightedly as the roulette operator handed her two crisp twenty *córdoba* bills.

For an instant, Adela forgot about Ixelia, her thoughts drawn to the woman's good fortune. It was precisely at that moment when she felt someone tap her on the shoulder. She turned around, and there was Ixelia, dressed in a short, pink satin dress that clung snuggly to the arresting outline of her body. This was the first time that Adela had ever seen Ixelia in full makeup. The vision took her breath away, and when the love of her life smiled, looking absolutely happy, Adela had to fight back the tears.

"I was beginning to think you had stood me up," she said.

"I'm sorry," Ixelia replied. "At the last minute the old man decided to come to the fair with me instead of going to Nandasmo to play cards with his buddies. He said that there would be too many young wolves around here tonight and that it would be best if he were around to protect me." For an instant Adela saw a flicker of apprehension in Ixelia's eyes. The young woman glanced over her shoulder to see if Don Roque was anywhere behind her. Once Ixelia was sure that the *hacendado* had not followed her, she smiled and continued talking. "But first he insisted that I go dancing. The strange thing, Adela, is that he never dances with me. He just likes to watch as I dance with other men." Ixelia glanced around to see if anyone was listening; she then leaned so close that Adela could smell beer on her breath. Placing her mouth next to Adela's ear, so her secret could be heard above the music, Ixelia said, "The old man likes to pick my dancing partners himself. Watching me on the dance floor with a handsome young man that he picked to be my partner always gives him a hard-on."

Both women giggled, their heads slightly bumping against one another. After they had finished chuckling, Adela said, "Would you like to try your luck at roulette? After that we can get a beer."

"I'd love to," Ixelia answered. But she then frowned and said, "The problem is that I don't have any money."

Adela reached into the pocket of her jeans, and pulled out a handful of one *córdoba* coins. "Here you go."

Ixelia smiled and stepped up to the roulette table. She studied its layout for a moment and then began to place two coins on nine black. But before Ixelia let go of the money, Adela reached out, put her hand on top of the young woman's, and whispered, her lips gently brushing her ear, "No. Thirteen red." Her hand then guided Ixelia's to the correct spot. They watched as the wheel spun, never seeming to come to an end. At last, when the dealer called out that no more bets could be placed, Ixelia reached out and took hold of Adela's left hand. They laced their fingers together and clasped them tightly. Both women held their breath as the wheel began to slow down, their number looming on the curved horizon as a possible winner. As the roulette finally approached its halt, the pin bent forward as far as it could, and when at last it stopped, the winner was indeed thirteen red. Adela and Ixelia jumped up and down, squealing in delight. They hugged one another as the operator handed Adela a fifty-, a twenty-, and a ten-*córdoba* bill.

"Now we can celebrate by having four beers each," Adela said with a beaming grin. The women searched for a beer stand without loud music so they could talk. When they found one, they scrambled to occupy a table that had just been vacated. In the time it took to finish three Victorias each, the women had discussed every topic imaginable, with the exception of how they felt about one another. When they were close to finishing their fourth beer, Adela suggested, "Let's go on the Ferris wheel."

Ixelia agreed with a nod. In quick gulps, they finished what was left in their bottles, rose from their seats, and walked toward the ride.

"That's what did it," Gloria Obando said to me, sighing as she approached what for her was the most painful part of the story. "If they had never gotten on the Ferris wheel, perhaps Adela would be alive, and we would still be together."

Gloria's former lover stepped up to the booth and bought two tickets—five *córdobas* each. Adela and Ixelia then got in a short line of customers and waited for the wheel to end its current voyage. When the ride finally came to a halt and its passengers got off, the women followed the operator's hand signals and stepped into their carriage. They sat close together as he lowered the safety bar, locking them in place.

They were the last passengers to climb on board, so the Ferris wheel immediately began its journey. The first time that Adela and Ixelia reached the apex of the circle, each of them let out a loud sigh as, high above the world, they gazed out at the view. From the highest point, they saw the lights of Pío XII and of other nearby communities. On the second turn, Adela pointed out the scarce lights of La Curva, six kilometers to the east. On the third turn, they marveled at the silhouette of the colossal ceiba that stood out impressively next to Don Roque's house—the tree reminded Adela of a noble, venerable grandfather, there to protect everything under its generous canopy—against the background of the lights of Niquinohomo. By the fourth turn of the Ferris wheel, Adela and Ixelia were no longer gazing out at the rest of the world. The women had their eyes closed as they shared their first deep, passionate kiss.

EIGHT

The Object of Desire

The press in Nicaragua feasted on Adela Rugama's death. The story had all the markings that guarantee high ratings: lust, greed, jealousy, prejudice, murder, and the right amount of kinkiness. Mariela told me that while the trial lasted, reporters constantly assailed her, wanting to record her opinion on every word uttered in the courtroom.

"The experience was terrible," the surviving sister said, leaning back in her hammock. "I just wanted the judge to punish the people who killed my little sister. I never imagined that asking for justice would mean having microphones shoved in my face and questions shouted at me everywhere I went. It was scandalous. The whole thing made me feel like a carnival freak."

Since I didn't learn about her death until three-and-a-half years later because I was living in the United States, I missed what television and radio had to say about the tragedy. But I visited the online archives of Nicaragua's leading newspapers, where I downloaded every article that dealt with the crime. Viewing the coverage through the dispassionate lenses of distance and time, I was startled to discover that one of the reporters assigned to the story had become emotionally involved in the case. I can't pinpoint exactly what led me to this assumption, but after carefully reviewing each one of the printouts, there was something about his treatment of the subject, something about the tone of his prose, something about the way his words became sultry whenever he referred to the young woman who had been at the axis of the murder that convinced me that Esteban Padilla had, like others before him, fallen under the spell of Ixelia Cruz.

What I liked about Padilla's writing was that his articles were more detailed than those of his colleagues who worked for the rival papers. I found Padilla's approach to the tragedy far more thorough, interesting, and humane than anyone else's. But also,

72

after reading his work, I got the impression that Padilla was trying to write his way out of an obsession. On several occasions, the
reporter's thoughts seemed to be more focused on what Ixelia wore
to the courtroom than on the proceedings. He had gone as far as to
create an endearing moniker for the young woman, referring to her
at least once in every article as "the alluring *nandasmeña*." In my
eyes, it was obvious that the beautiful young woman from
Nandasmo, with her seemingly lethal charms, had taken possession of Esteban Padilla's heart.

Wanting to know exactly why the reporter had set his objec-
tivity aside, highlighting Ixelia's attractiveness in terms that
teetered dangerously on the precipice of terrible clichés, I called
him on the telephone to request his help. After I told Padilla that
my intention was to write an account of Adela Rugama's murder,
he agreed to meet me for lunch at a Mexican restaurant in
Masaya, the city where he lived.

Three days later we stood at the entrance of El Charro, shaking hands. A man in his early thirties, Padilla could have stepped
out of one of the many photographs from the Mexican
Revolution that adorned the restaurant walls. The only things
missing were the wide-brimmed sombrero dangling down his
back and the trite image of the crisscrossed leather bandoliers,
loaded with ammunition. His dark mustache, thick and bushy,
gave him a fierce expression. But his small, obsidian eyes gleamed
with mischievous intelligence, letting one know that the reporter
would always have a quick, witty reply, even in the most stressful
situations. What really stood out about Esteban Padilla, though,
was his size: he was over six feet tall and weighed close to two
hundred and fifty pounds. But a lot of this corpulence was mus-
cle: most college football coaches in the United States would
have unquestionably recruited Padilla if he had grown up there.
And, if the reporter had ridden alongside Pancho Villa, he would
certainly have needed a sturdy horse.

I requested a table on the second-floor balcony of the restaurant where we could enjoy a superb view of the city's colonial
architecture and its red tile rooftops while we chatted. Once we
were seated, our waiter brought us our menus. As Padilla's eyes

scanned down the list, I noticed his expression becoming increasingly perplexed. I concluded that he, like most Nicaraguans, knew virtually nothing about Mexican cuisine. He accepted my offer to help, and I described several items for him. In the end, the reporter left the decision up to me, so I ordered what I knew was always a safe choice with his compatriots: a beef and bean burrito—in his case extra large. As for myself, I chose my favorite: chicken *mole*. When I explained to Padilla what I had picked, he grimaced. For some reason beyond my understanding, Nicaraguans, to a large extent also descendants of the Aztecs, who gave the world the cacao bean, cannot conceive of the notion of eating chicken smothered in a dark, chocolate-based sauce.

Over beers, while we waited for our orders, we became involved in a lively discussion about our favorite writers. Before long we were talking freely, like two good friends who had not seen each other for quite a while. I was pleased to find that Padilla was, indeed, outgoing and witty. After lunch, as we basked in the pleasant radiance of our fourth beers—he ordered Victorias, while I ordered Toñas—I decided that it was time to be forthright.

"Esteban," I said, taking a deep breath and hoping that after I placed my cards on the table he would not flee, "after reading your articles about Adela Rugama's murder, in particular those you wrote during the trial, I came away with the distinct impression that you had developed . . . well . . . some strong feelings for Ixelia. I mean, based on your reports . . . well . . . you seemed to have fallen for her."

Padilla, who was just about to take another sip of his Victoria, stopped abruptly, the tip of the bottle only millimeters from his lips. His expression darkened, reminding me of college students caught cheating on an exam. Without taking the drink, the reporter put the bottle of Victoria back on the table and gazed mournfully out over the rooftops in the direction of the bell tower of the church of San Jerónimo. I didn't want to lose the trust we had so readily built that afternoon, so I continued speaking, trying to restore the ease with which we had been chatting.

"Look, Esteban," I said, "I'm not here to judge you. I'm only trying to understand what happened to Adela, especially Ixelia's role in her murder. In reading your articles, I saw that you had interviewed her, which is something no other reporter took the time to do. Please, Esteban, I'd be greatly indebted to you if you'd share your impressions of Ixelia with me . . . please."

Padilla didn't answer immediately. I started to worry and was about to apologize for having jumped to the wrong conclusion when the reporter nodded, leaned back in his chair—making it creak ominously under the strain—cast his gaze out on the sea of red roof tiles, and began to tell me everything he knew about the alluring *nandasmeña*, from the beginning.

The day Mariela visited the newspaper, asking the publisher to help locate her sister, Padilla's editor, acting on a hunch that a murder had been committed, assigned him to the case. His first article, in fact, simply stated that a woman named Adela Rugama had been missing for a month. The reporter urged anyone with information regarding her whereabouts to contact the newspaper. Alongside the piece was a picture of Adela, straddling her mountain bike. A month passed without further news, and then her body was found. After that discovery, Padilla wrote a series of articles about the murder, the earlier ones based on interviews he conducted with Mariela and with the Niquinohomo chief of police, Commissioner Gilberto Wong.

"From the beginning, everything about this case seemed fascinating, novelesque. You know what I'm saying, don't you?" Padilla said, turning to look directly at me. He was relaxed once again and had set caution aside, having determined that I was worthy of his trust. "Of course you do. Otherwise, why would we be here? Anyway, the more I learned about the case, the more I wanted to talk to the young woman who had apparently driven these people to commit murder." But at the time, because of his other writing assignments and because it didn't seem pertinent to his initial reports, Padilla didn't seek Ixelia out. It wasn't until the murder trial, four months later, that the reporter first set eyes on the alluring *nandasmeña*.

"She was so beautiful." Padilla sighed as he looked out at an indefinite point in the midst of Masaya's rooftops. "She took my breath away the instant she walked into the courtroom. My chest tightened, and I had to gulp for air in short, painful bursts. I remember being terrified because I honestly thought that I was having a heart attack."

According to the reporter, the way Ixelia entered the building, her square shoulders drawn back on her exquisite and surprisingly boyish frame, gave her the appearance of being much taller than she actually was. Her stride, fluid and sensuous, reminded Padilla of the movements of a jaguar—a cat he had often seen in the jungles of northern Nicaragua where, as a teenager, he served his country in the war against the Contras, a soldier in the Sandinista army. As Ixelia walked to the front of the courtroom, the reporter couldn't stop staring at her long, firm legs, proudly displayed by a splendidly short skirt that he thought inappropriate for such formal proceedings. Directing his gaze upward, Padilla paused to admire Ixelia's bare arms, soft and enticing. Then the young woman's shimmering, light-brown hair, just a shade darker than blond, caught the reporter's full attention. Ixelia's thick mane descended to the middle of her back in generous, lively curls.

"Man, I was hypnotized. She was so magnificent, so seductive, that my pulse ran wild whenever she roamed about the courtroom. Let me tell you something: that girl was nothing but pure, condensed sexuality."

After Ixelia took a seat, she turned and glanced around at the gathering. For a brief moment, her eyes met Padilla's straight on. His heart strained again as he stared into one of the most beautiful faces he had ever seen. The young woman smiled at him, and the reporter was startled to discover that although she was looking directly at him, he felt invisible, disembodied, as if her luminous amber eyes had the power to see right through him.

"To be honest," Padilla said, turning his eyes away from Masaya's rooftops to look at me, "the first time I saw Ixelia, the only thing I could think about was how glorious it would be to get under that skirt. She was so sexy, so extraordinarily sexy that for the remainder of the trial I had trouble concentrating on my work. My eyes kept wandering toward her as if I had lost control of them. But I couldn't help myself, you know? I wasn't the only one, though: Ixelia commanded the attention of every man in that courthouse. I spent hours looking at the way she played with her hair, twirling the ends around one finger. I also watched the way she pushed back her cuticles with her fingernails whenever she became nervous, and I carefully studied the way she ran her hands up and down her thighs to dry her sweaty palms. I have to admit that I somewhat neglected my duties as a reporter, barely paying attention to what was going on. But when the trial was over, I understood completely the motivations of those who had been convicted; I could easily see how they would commit murder to possess Ixelia."

Once the jury reached its verdict, and Doña Erlinda, Don Roque, and the messenger had each been sentenced to thirty-five years in prison, the reporter, obsessed with the idea of taking Ixelia to bed, devised a plan to seduce her.

"I confess that I was dying to get into her pants," Padilla said, his voice trailing off at the end of the statement. "I also have to admit that during parts of the trial testimony I'd get really turned on by the thought of Ixelia doing it with another woman. What man doesn't get excited by the thought of screwing a lesbian? Admit it, I know the idea excites you." Padilla smiled after saying this, but I found his expression sad, sterile.

A couple of days after the sentencing, under the pretext that he was still covering the story, the reporter drove out to Doña Erlinda's house, where Ixelia had returned to live after her mother's arrest, and invited the gorgeous *nandasmeña* out for a drink. Padilla was surprised when, without hesitation and with a smile that made him feel faint, she accepted. They headed for the area's most elegant restaurant, on the outskirts of Niquinohomo. On the way there, he nearly got into two accidents because, instead of paying attention to the road, he kept glancing down at Ixelia's bare thighs.

They were fortunate, the reporter told me, to have arrived safely at their destination. Once seated, Padilla ordered a quarter

liter of Flor de Caña rum and a bottle of soda water. But he soon
realized that he didn't need the alcohol to loosen Ixelia's tongue,
as was called for in his plan. Ixelia was eager to talk, and she
answered all of his questions in a steady stream, not even pausing
for an instant to think about her replies. For the rest of the afternoon and part of the early evening, Padilla became her prisoner,
as the dazzling creature gave him little choice but to listen to her
story.

"Her life was so sad, so tragic," the reporter said as he tilted
the empty bottle of beer toward him with one finger and then
made it turn in circles. "You know, I might as well tell you the
whole truth. When I walked into the restaurant that day, I had a
tremendous erection. The sight of those incredible legs aroused
me beyond anything I'd ever experienced. I remember feeling
terribly self-conscious because, although I was seated, I thought
everyone in the place could see my hard-on. In all honesty, my
plans were completely dishonorable: to get Ixelia drunk and then
take her to a nearby motel. I just wanted to squirm in pleasure,
my hands gripping that gorgeous ass of hers, while she rode me
as if I were a thoroughbred. Well, let me tell you something, I
could've fulfilled my fantasy. Easily. The poor girl's self-esteem
was completely wrapped up in her talent for pleasing men. That
afternoon I learned that the only time that Ixelia felt worthy of
being loved was when she was in bed with another man. Knowing
that changed everything for me. After she told me her story, I
couldn't go through with it. She had already been exploited
enough, and I would have felt like shit if I had added my name
to that list. After what I heard that day, I couldn't carry out my
plan. I could never be that much of a bastard."

During Padilla's afternoon outing with Ixelia, he learned that
Doña Erlinda had raised her daughter to become a slave and that
the young woman could neither read nor write because her mother had never sent her to school. "Just look at the court records;
look at the declarations she made to the police," he said to me,
vehemently tapping the tip of his right index finger on the table-
top. "That poor thing could barely sign her name. Every time she
did, she spelled it differently: 'Ixelia,' 'Yselia,' 'Icelia,' and so on.

And her handwriting was worse than that of a five-year-old. For people like you and me, who know how important it is to have a good education, that, if anything, is reason enough for her mother to have been sent away to prison for the rest of her life."

The reporter also recalled, between sips of Victoria, how Doña Erlinda, even before Ixelia could speak clearly, had put her daughter to work selling fruits and vegetables in El Oriental. And Esteban Padilla became grim when he told me that shortly before Ixelia's eleventh birthday, her mother began to lavish praise upon her because grown men started to show a lurid interest in the child.

"I'm convinced that from the moment Ixelia was born, that woman had been waiting for the day when she could place the child's virginity up for sale. Can you believe that?" The empty bottle of Victoria shook as Padilla slapped the table with the open palm of his right hand. He then leaned back in his chair and gazed out silently over the rooftops. All the while, with the thumb and forefinger of his left hand, he pulled on his mustache, waiting for his anger to subside.

Once the reporter had calmed down, he continued with the story, telling me that for several months Doña Erlinda took bids to see who would be the first man to have the honor of deflowering her daughter. "She did a great job running up the price," Padilla said, shaking his head in disbelief. In the end, the winner came from the capital. The man signed over the deed to a parcel of land he owned just outside Nandasmo—half an acre's worth. Doña Erlinda would later sell the property for three thousand dollars. In reality, the amount wasn't all that much, but to her it seemed like a fortune. So it came to be that when Ixelia was eleven years, one hundred and twenty-seven days old, she lost her virginity in a scorpion-infested beach house that the victor, a fifty-three-year-old insurance executive, owned in Casares, a hamlet on the shores of the Pacific Ocean.

"You want to know the saddest part about the whole thing?" the reporter asked. I leaned forward, eager to hear the answer. "The entire time that man was with Ixelia, in spite of the awkwardness, pain, and discomfort, the little girl was happy, ecstatic.

She thought it meant that she was getting married. That idea thrilled her because she honestly believed that she would be leaving her mother and starting a family of her own. While the man lay on top of her, humping away, Ixelia, in her naïve understanding of what was taking place, silently vowed to treat her children right."

Although Ixelia had already lost her highly flaunted virginity, Doña Erlinda knew that she could still exploit the girl's youth, as well as her extraordinary beauty. Throughout the bidding war, the merchant from El Oriental had compiled a list of twenty-nine men, all of them eager to follow in the insurance executive's wake. The mother had ranked each man according to his offer, and every one of them had his turn, taking his pleasure with Ixelia, but for much less than the winning bid. The child, not really understanding what was going on, grew terrified of the seedy drive-in motels where she was forced to submit to the ravenous impulses of perfect strangers.

Once Doña Erlinda reached the end of the list, she began another commercial practice: as soon as a man set eyes on Ixelia, she would become her daughter's pimp, negotiating a price for the privilege of sleeping with her "precious little girl." And the mother would accept not only cash, but she would barter for her daughter's body as well. In return for being allowed to take Ixelia to bed, a man could pay in the form of a truckload of *pitahayas*, a couple of pigs, sheets of corrugated zinc for the roof, bags of cement, rocking chairs, and anything else that Doña Erlinda believed that she could sell or that would make her life more comfortable.

"I almost started to cry when Ixelia, with tears streaming down her face, told me that the only time her mother showed concern for her was when she thought that she had a customer for her body," Padilla sadly recalled. "I'm not kidding. She felt completely abandoned by the world. Her only confidants were her brothers and her sister, who were too young and fearful of their mother to do anything about the situation."

After nearly two years of pimping, when the price for sleeping with the beautiful little girl began to wane, Doña Erlinda thought of a new plan, one that would take advantage of Don Roque's obsession with Ixelia.

The mother, her sights now set on the sixty-three-year-old man's fortune, set in motion her scheme to bring the *hacendado* and her thirteen-year-old daughter together, permanently. Doña Erlinda estimated that the old man had, perhaps, ten more years of life, and she reasoned that if Ixelia became his sole heir, she and her daughter could still end up being well-to-do women. She found these thoughts comforting, but she was careful to curb her enthusiasm so as to not scare Don Roque away. The next time the *hacendado* begged Doña Erlinda to allow the child to become his woman, promising that he would look after her, she, as usual, refused. Yet on this occasion she wasn't as adamant; instead, she subtly displayed a willingness to begin to consider his petition.

According to Esteban, Ixelia told him that during Don Roque's visits (at this stage he had started dropping by the house almost every evening), the mother would observe how the old man's Adam's apple, in a reflex that looked painful, slid slowly up and down his long, wrinkled neck whenever Ixelia ran by—her short skirt springing up in the air as she played with her brothers and sister, chasing them through the building and out into the backyard. The *hacendado*'s eyes would then glaze over, becoming two misty clouds moist with longing, at the tender sight of his fantasy.

"When Doña Erlinda estimated that the old man's passion for the girl had reached its boiling point," Padilla said while shaking his head as if he found what he was about to say incredible, "she made her pitch, one she had been rehearsing for weeks.

"Don Roque, you know I just can't give my daughter to you. I'm a woman raising four children—the youngest one your grandson, by the way—all by myself. Since Ixelia is the oldest, she helps out a lot. She takes care of them when I have to go out, does the laundry, cooks, and helps clean the house. As you can see, to replace her I would need to hire some help, and you know that takes money. Besides, there are plenty of men, rich men at that, who say they want to marry Ixelia once she turns fifteen. They tell me that that's a good age to take her as a wife without it seeming so scandalous. Living with you would ruin that for her. So, you see, and pardon me for asking this so bluntly, Don Roque, but . . . what would I gain by allowing my daughter to become your woman?"

Don Roque promised Doña Erlinda all the plantains she could cut down and transport to El Oriental. He also promised that while oranges were in season, she could have a pickup full each week. When the *hacendado* saw that Doña Erlinda greeted his offer in silence, he continued adding more produce to the list: avocados, mangos, *pitahayas*, yuca, and coffee. Although the growing inventory delighted Ixelia's mother, she feigned disinterest. When Don Roque had run out of crops to offer, Doña Erlinda remained quiet. She knew this would make the landowner nervous, as he would assume that she was disposed toward rejecting his proposal. At last, she said, "I like what you're offering, Don Roque. But, really, to be honest, and, again, I don't mean to offend you, but . . . I'm also worried about your age. I mean, what will become of Ixelia if something should happen to you. How will my little girl take care of herself?"

Without hesitation and with his mouth so dry that the words stuck like *mantequilla de maní* to the roof of his mouth, Don Roque replied, "Ixelia will inherit everything I own. You have my word."

"That very evening," Padilla assured me, "Doña Erlinda ordered her daughter to pack her things because the next morning she was going to move in with Don Roque."

"But, mamá, he already has a woman living with him . . . and they have children!" Ixelia protested.

"He's telling them to leave at this very moment," Doña Erlinda replied.

"Mami, he's an old man. Please, don't make me do this. I don't want to be with him. I hate him. He makes my skin crawl. I hate his breath as well—it reminds me of death. Let me stay here, with you. Please, don't make me go live with that man. *Por favor*, mami." And at once Ixelia burst into tears.

"Stupid girl, you said it yourself; the old man is close to dying. Don't be an idiot. Be patient. Don Roque has promised me that you will inherit everything he owns. Just put up with him for a few years. He's going to die soon, you'll see. You'd be foolish to let an opportunity like this get away. In the end, we'll both be so rich that you'll thank me for what I'm making you do today."

In spite of her mother's arguments, Ixelia kept rejecting the notion of living with Don Roque. But Doña Erlinda insisted that Ixelia pack her things at once and move to Las Dos Balas, her new home. The daughter, though, remained steadfast, refusing to obey. Losing her scant patience, the mother went to the shed and brought out a whip—a sun-dried bull penis that she used to keep the pigs she raised from coming into the house. She lashed away at Ixelia until the girl surrendered, dashing tearfully to her room to begin packing, angry welts on her forearms, legs, and across her back.

The afternoon the stunning *nandasmeña* met with Ernesto Padilla, she told him that from the moment she had finished taking her scant belongings into the old man's house, she knew that the whole thing would end tragically. But Doña Erlinda never shared her daughter's fear; all she saw was the inheritance.

"For three years," Padilla said, "the poor thing lived with an old man who was convinced that one day she would leave him." At first, Don Roque was so preoccupied with the thought of Ixelia running away that he'd leave her tied to a chair, naked, whenever he went out at night to play cards. "Worse yet, the poor girl never imagined that a man in his sixties could have so much energy and could get it up every night. And, although she didn't say a word to me about it, I'm sure that he beat her whenever he felt she was getting out of line."

"Mamá, he's never going to die!" Ixelia cried hysterically one morning when her mother dropped by Las Dos Balas to harvest tangerines. "That old man is stronger than you and me put together. He's going to outlive me. I'm going to die first!"

Not long after that outbreak, nearly two years after Ixelia had moved in with Don Roque, Adela stepped into her life. By then the young woman had lost hope of ever being happy, and thoughts of suicide constantly assaulted her. Adela, madly in love with Ixelia, was the only person who listened to her, the only one who understood how desperate her life had become, and the only one who cared enough to try to change the young woman's sorrowful situation.

It was my turn now to gaze out in silence at Masaya's rooftops. I was struck by how quickly time had passed. The sun had begun to set with a vivid red glow that seeped into the roof tiles, making them seem as if they were covered in blood. I had become so absorbed in the story that I didn't even notice when we switched to drinking coffee instead of beer. But I did know that the sadness of Ixelia's story had a sobering effect on both of us.

"She told me that the happiest days of her life were those she spent with Adela," Padilla said toward the end of our meeting. "Adela made her feel worthy of being loved, of being treated with dignity. Even though people ridiculed Ixelia because of her relationship with another woman, telling her that it was a perversion, she told me that Adela made her feel complete. In Adela, Ixelia found everything she ever wanted out of life."

Padilla watched in silence as I pulled a debit card out of my wallet to pay the bill. After the waiter left, the reporter continued. "You know what I still find interesting? By the end of my meeting with Ixelia, I no longer wanted to screw her. And I could have taken her straight to bed. All I had to do was ask. She was immensely grateful that someone, anyone, especially a man, had taken the time to listen to her story. But, tell me, how could I fuck her and add my selfish pleasure to an already long list of miserable memories? Poor thing. That girl had already suffered enough. Besides, it was getting late and I knew that my wife and kids were getting worried, wondering what was keeping me. So we just hopped into my car, and I took Ixelia straight home."

NINE

The Old Man

S hortly after dawn I arrived at Las Dos Balas—notepad in hand, a tape recorder hidden in my pants pocket, and a rosary around my neck. Maresa, a cousin of mine who lives in Masatepe, had hung the string of beads there for my protection.

"You're insane if you insist on talking to that murderer, little cousin. I'm giving you this rosary, and I expect you to wear it. It was blessed by His Eminence himself. Now, thanks to the cardinal's intercession, the Lord will be looking after you. You should be safe." Knowing that Maresa was well acquainted with Don Roque's history (she had served on the jury that found him and the two other defendants guilty) increased my already significant apprehensions about the interview.

Si Dios Quiere complained loudly during the last stretch of the journey: the chassis groaned in pain as the old Subaru wobbled along the rain-gutted dirt road leading to the hacienda. The sun had yet to ascend fully above the vibrant tropical landscape. Tall, thick, seemingly prehistoric weeds with gigantic leaves grew wildly along both sides of the road, defying all attempts to tame them.

In spite of the early hour, I missed Don Roque: he had already departed on his morning rounds of the hacienda. Luckily, Don Carlos Somarriba, foreman of Las Dos Balas, who'd become one of my most valuable informants, was still at the house, replacing a termite-infested porch railing. Graciously, he invited me to take a seat and wait for his boss.

The foreman then excused himself to return to his work, and I moved a chair to the south side of the porch, where I could gaze at the ceiba that stands a stone's throw from Don Roque's house. From there, one-hundred-and-thirty feet tall, the tree majestically governed the region's skyline. Its sprawling, massive boughs, all at the very top of the trunk, covered almost an eighth of an acre, shading everything underneath from the harsh tropical sun. Much like the way that Atlas supports the globe, the ceiba's root system reaches up from the earth's throbbing depths and extends itself toward the heavens, bracing the tree's broad, columnar trunk. From ten feet out, the veins rise gradually in slowly winding arms that become as thick as a muscular human thigh when they approach the core. There, they form imposing buttresses whose walls reach ten feet in height. Each of the crevices between the roots is large enough to be a resting place for the gods and small enough to be a perfect hiding place for mortals.

As I sat there, quietly trying to unravel the ceiba's secrets, I imagined a compelling spiritual force emanating from the tree, reaching out to every living thing under the shadows of its canopy. In my mind, that pulse, like the waning ripples of a pebble tossed into a pond, traveled from the core of the ceiba, through its outer, elephant-skin layers, and straight to our hearts, reminding us that all life is sacred. Struck by that flash of grace, I realized that if I could communicate with the kingly tree, then Adela's last moments would cease to be veiled in darkness, becoming clear, even luminous. I sat as still as possible and started to breathe slowly, trying to discard every worry in the hope of drawing out the ceiba's knowledge, of penetrating its thoughts and sentiments. Slightly more than an hour later, the hollow clanking of hooves disrupted my meditations as Don Roque, mounted on his palomino, returned from his inspection of Las Dos Balas.

In the eyes of the people who live in the vicinity, most of them simple *campesinos*, Don Roque's resources are boundless. He is the sole owner of Las Dos Balas—fifty-three hectares of lush, fertile land. The property is dotted with shade trees, above which the ceiba reigns supreme, planted generations before to protect the coffee shrubs. Don Roque's father, Don Manrique Ramírez, named the property after two bullets he wore on a chain around his neck: a keepsake from a bar room shootout in which, as a young man, he had been wounded twice in the chest, slightly above the heart, and he nearly lost his life.

Standing a quarter of a kilometer east of the main entrance to Las Dos Balas is the hacienda house. The building, a large, foreboding structure that gives the impression of being haunted, has four spacious rooms: a living room and three bedrooms. Because Don Roque seldom invested in maintenance since inheriting the property, nearly forty years ago, the outside walls are worn, cracked, and covered in a thick, charcoal-grey layer of mold.

When Don Roque Ramírez returned home that morning, he glanced at me and, without offering the slightest greeting, walked straight to the other end of the porch to speak to Don Carlos. The *hacendado* stared at me as his foreman informed him that I was there in the hope of being granted an interview. Don Roque then walked toward me and curtly nodded his head, a welcome so cold that in spite of being in the tropics I almost shuddered. I did, however, understand his apprehension: in the *hacendado*'s mind I was an intruder who had dared to enter his lair without an invitation.

I rose from the chair and held out my hand, doing my best to disguise my trembling. With great reluctance, he returned the greeting.

"Don Roque, I'd like to ask you a few questions about Adela Rugama's death. I'd like to hear your side of the story." His expression froze into a harsh, menacing scowl. I quickly went on to assure Don Roque that I was neither a lawyer nor working with the police. "I'm just gathering information to write a book about the tragedy."

The landowner turned away to face the ceiba. I had been warned that, even under the best of circumstances, he was a taciturn man and that to coax him into open conversation would be next to impossible. Don Roque, as if to confirm this, stood there, silently stroking the gray stubble on his chin.

At last, mumbling to himself throughout, Don Roque wearily pulled up one of the chairs and sat down. I thought that meant that he was ready to talk, but instead he remained quiet while gazing broodingly at the ceiba. Confronted with this stony reception, I wondered how such a reticent man could have convinced five different women to bear the nine children he had scattered throughout the region. After the interview, I became convinced that their attraction to the *hacendado* had little to do with his vivaciousness; either the women had been drawn to his wealth, or they had submitted to his amorous demands out of fear. Based on the stories I heard about him, plus what I had learned on my own, of one thing I was absolutely certain: Don Roque Ramírez was capable of anything.

When I announced to my friends in Nicaragua that I intended to write an account of Adela's murder, they tried to persuade me to abandon the idea of interviewing the landowner because his violent past terrified them, and, in this nation's tragic history those who resort to violence usually end up being forgiven with alarming speed.

"Take a gun along when you go to visit that animal," my cousin Maresa had urged me at first, before she finally settled on the rosary. "Or at least take someone with you, little cousin. Don't go alone, please. That man is evil."

A few friends in the United States, aware of the project I was working on, became concerned about my safety. "Are you sure you want to go visit that man?" one of my colleagues in the States wrote in an email. "He sounds downright treacherous to me."

Even his foreman, Don Carlos, once whispered in my ear a warning about his employer: "Be careful. He's dangerous. He's not like other people."

Throughout the interview, Don Roque clung stubbornly to terse responses, without showing a trace of remorse. In spite of the brevity of his answers, they confirmed that, indeed, he was far more educated than the other actors in this tragedy. Informants knowledgeable about Don Roque's history told me that he had attended the Colegio Don Bosco, in Masaya, up to the sixth grade. His father, Don Manrique, had enrolled him and his younger brother, Julio, in the all-male Salesian school as boarders.

Not expecting any success, I called the Colegio. I was startled to learn that Don Roque's former principal, Padre Gino

Benedetti, was still alive and residing in Nicaragua. The priest was now in his nineties, in remarkably good health, and could be found at the Colegio Salesiano in the city of Granada. I called the school and made an appointment to chat with him. Two days later we met amid the lush vegetation of the school's courtyard, which was closed off to students, and we spoke while sitting on a concrete bench next to a whitewashed statue of the Virgin of Cuapa.

Padre Gino was from Turin, Italy, and had arrived in this country in his mid-twenties, not knowing the language. But the priest would spend the remainder of his life here and, as a result, he spoke Spanish like a Nicaraguan. His astonishing memory justified my search. Padre Gino remembered the Ramírez brothers, vividly.

"It's funny, you know, old age. I can't remember whether or not I celebrated Mass this morning, but I can remember every single detail about things that happened several lifetimes ago, especially if the experiences were sad."

"Was this story sad, Padre? The story of the Ramírez boys?"

"Yes, I'd definitely say that their story is sad," the priest said with a sigh. "Their father, Manrique, was incapable of showing the boys any affection. All he cared about was to spread his seed around and then only with young girls. Those two boys had many illegitimate brothers and sisters. Sadly, their mother, the only woman Manrique ever married, died when Julio was still an infant. Even though those of us in the Salesian order live in relative isolation, spending most of our time behind the walls of our schools, the rumors involving our students and their families still reach us. Those two boys had a desolate childhood. At the Colegio we tried our best to become their family, but in this case we would have needed a miracle to fill the void."

"Padre Gino, what was Don Roque like as a boy?"

"When he first came to us, he was pleasant enough. But as the years went by, he increasingly became a loner, and then his quick temper started getting him into lots of fights. As he became older, I noticed that most of his schoolmates were afraid of him. I never found out what he would do to them, but I do know that very few students ever dared to be alone with him. Roque was capable of being quite cruel, you know? In all honesty, I'm not surprised that he ended up in so much trouble."

"How do you know that he was capable of cruelty?"

"Because I had to expel him for his malice, that's how. When he started the sixth grade, his last year with us, we began to find mutilated carcasses of small animals in the school: birds, lizards, cats. At first we had no idea who was responsible. Then, one of the priests, it was Padre Eusebio, I believe, caught Roque in the act. The boy had climbed the church bell tower and caught a pigeon. He then tied the bird to a stick and was roasting it alive, in the chapel, over the candles that were lit before the statue of the Blessed Mother. Can you believe that? That's blasphemous: torturing a poor, innocent creature at the feet of the Virgin! I sent Roque home immediately. The sad part of the story is that the father decided to withdraw Julio from the school as well. Now that one was a good child, pious even. We had our eye on Julio because several of us thought that he would have made a good priest, you know? Because of his older brother's sins, Julio's education remained incomplete. There's the real tragedy. But as for Roque, we had no choice but to send him home . . . permanently."

My conversation with Padre Gino confirmed what others had told me about Don Roque: that he could be brutal in the extreme. The card players in the town of Pío XII, who, prior to the murder, had entertained the *hacendado* by losing to him almost every evening, later shed more light on the family's history. They told me that, as a young man, Don Manrique Ramírez had failed miserably at several businesses (including smuggling American cigarettes and batteries from Costa Rica, and opening a house of prostitution—an offense for which he spent several months in prison because he refused to give a percentage to the local *comandante* of the Guardia Nacional). But his dismal fortunes all changed one night when, during a glorious streak of astonishing luck while playing cards, he won a neglected coffee plantation, which he soon renamed Las Dos Balas.

"Don Manrique turned out to be fairly good at running a plantation, much better than either of his sons," one of the card players said. "But he had a cold heart. He didn't seem to care at all for his boys." The other men nodded and then added that the Ramírez family was not particularly close. When Don Manrique passed away, his sons shed no tears. What's more, some people suspect that Don Roque may have contributed to his father's death.

"Don Roque slowly poisoned his father so he could get to the inheritance sooner," Don Erasmo told me. We had stopped to chat in front of Lizbeth Hodgson's store where he had gone to buy glass cleaner for his mirrors. "One day Don Manrique told me that the doctors said he had diabetes. But he was optimistic because they also told him that with insulin and a few changes in what he ate and drank he could live quite a few more years. And that was possible because that old man was as strong as an ox. But only a few months after our conversation, he died. Sinforoso Sándigo, who worked for Don Manrique, saw Don Roque one morning putting a few drops of a dark liquid into his father's *café con leche*. When he asked Don Roque what he was doing, Sinforoso was told that if he valued his life he would keep his mouth shut. I've always believed that bastard was capable of killing anyone, even his own father. Of course, no one ever proved it."

Immediately after Don Manrique's funeral, Don Roque proceeded to claim his share of Las Dos Balas. He kept the most productive half, which also included the hacienda house, arguing that because he was the eldest he had first choice. Several years later, shortly before the Sandinista Insurrection, Julio, because of an ill-advised investment he made in partnership with a *coronel* in Somoza's Guardia Nacional (they had opened an elegant restaurant in Masaya without either of them having the slightest notion about running such a business, and in a time of great political and economic turmoil) found himself on the verge of losing everything. Don Roque helped his brother out, buying his share of Las Dos Balas (at a bargain price, of course) with the exception of ten hectares, which he allowed Julio to keep (he was, after all, his only legitimate brother).

The morning of my visit, in spite of my dread and misgivings, after a few moments sitting next to Don Roque, I did not find him frightening. Instead of the beast everyone had described, what I saw was a withered old man in his early seventies, sitting dejectedly on a rough, hand-carved wooden chair, with his chin on his chest and his body slumped, like a bundle of dirty laundry. In other words, the *hacendado* looked like a man defeated by his own abysmal choices in life, and I assumed that the three years this tall, bony man served in prison had shattered much of his spirit.

During the initial part of my interview with the landowner, he remained reticent, unwilling to fully answer my questions. Undeterred, I continued interrogating him until, after more than an hour, my gentle perseverance started to wear him down. Turning his head to glare at me, Don Roque said in a cavernous voice, "You know something, writer? I don't trust you for shit." I appreciated his forthrightness. Once he had declared his misgiving, I felt as if I had finally placed my feet on firm ground.

Prior to this admission, Don Roque had only spoken in half-sentences and grunts. But after he revealed his absolute mistrust of me, knowing that I had nothing to lose, I gambled, hoping to get him to lower his guard, if only just a bit.

"I don't blame you for not trusting me, Don Roque," I said. "You've been through quite a lot the last few years. And I, for one, believe that none of it is your fault. If anyone is to blame, it's Ixelia. Whatever she became involved in always ended up a mess, and in the case of Adela, a horrible tragedy." The moment I suggested that Ixelia was the cause of all his problems, Don Roque's eyes became teary. He lifted his head and gazed sorrowfully at the ceiba. We sat in silence for a long time, the tension of the moment running through my body like an electric current. I was about to get up to leave, believing that I had failed in that day's quest, when, to my relief, Don Roque began to speak in a voice that creaked like a withering branch of an ancient tree during a hard wind.

"I wanted Ixelia for myself the moment I first set eyes on her. Even though she was only ten years old then, I could already tell that she would someday grow up to be a beautiful woman."

For the first time that morning, Don Roque raised his head to look directly at me while he spoke. In a still raspy voice, he continued. "When Ixelia was eleven, I overheard a man in Don Gumersindo's cantina telling everyone that her mother had put her up for sale. That same night I went to their house and asked Erlinda to give the girl to me. I promised her that I would take good care of Ixelia and would make sure that her daughter had everything she needed. Of course Erlinda said no. Still, I continued visiting the house to try to get that woman to stop selling her daughter and allow her to come live with me. But every time I brought up the subject Erlinda refused to listen. When I got tired of asking her to let Ixelia live with me, I decided to win the girl over myself."

Don Roque, then a man in his mid-sixties, began to court Ixelia. It was an awkward pursuit, the *hacendado*, a man of few words, trying to engage a girl who was barely reaching adolescence in mature conversation. Throughout, Ixelia kept rejecting Don Roque's offers to go live with him, and it hurt the landowner to see how she pouted every time he'd show up at the house. But he persevered, often taking dolls, candy, and clothing as gifts. During his visits Don Roque sat in the living room, conversing with the mother, while Ixelia played with her brothers and sister. On occasion, the girl could be very sweet, particularly when she wanted to ride Don Roque's palomino through the streets of Nandasmo, to which he always consented.

According to Don Roque, after more than a year of this odd, one-sided courtship, just as he was beginning to consider giving up, he again asked Doña Erlinda to allow Ixelia to move in with him. This time, instead of the usual excuses she put forth to turn down his offer, she raised a different concern.

"Don Roque, I can't let Ixelia do that. You already have a woman and three kids to think about."

Sensing that he had an opportunity to win over the merchant from El Oriental, Don Roque answered, "Don't worry about that, Erlinda. I can get rid of them the day you give me Ixelia."

"But, Don Roque, you know that if I didn't send Ixelia out with these men, my children would go hungry. Thanks to her, the kids and I are surviving." Doña Erlinda waited a moment and then leaned toward the *hacendado*. Putting her mouth close to his ear, in a husky whisper, she asked, "Don Roque, what's in it for me if I let Ixelia become your woman?"

For a moment the landowner stopped telling the story. He rose from his seat and moved it so that he could better face me, and then continued with his tale. "I promised her all the plantains, oranges, and tangerines she could sell. But that wasn't enough for that woman. She didn't agree to let me have Ixelia until I promised to make the girl my sole heir."

The next morning, Don Roque had his woman and their three children move into an abandoned shack in the remotest corner of Las Dos Balas, and he ordered several of his workers to clean the house for Ixelia's arrival. That same afternoon, she showed up on foot, carrying a suitcase, and bearing the whip marks her mother had given her the night before.

"Ixelia lived with me for two years. I did what I could to make that girl happy, but Erlinda had ruined her; that child was wild. Still, I made sure Ixelia had everything she ever needed. I did my best to keep her happy." Don Roque glowered at me when he said this, as if daring me to contradict him. I remained quiet, only nodding in agreement as I took notes.

After a long silence, during which the *hacendado* sighed twice as he gazed at the ceiba, he went on with his story. "Believe it or not, after a while Ixelia and I settled into a peaceful life. She seemed to be content. The only problem I had with her was that she was always asking for something. One day it was money, the other it was clothes—and afterwards we would have big arguments because she liked to buy these awfully sluttish outfits, and I will never permit a woman of mine to dress like a whore. Another day she'd want a stereo, and after that she needed to buy cassettes. Like I said, it was always something. Ixelia could never be happy with what she had. In spite of this, she started to settle down, to behave well. And then, just when I thought she had finally come to like it here with me, the *cochona* shows up."

Don Roque had already encountered the chaos that Adela's amorous escapades were capable of creating. It happened when Doña Gabriela, the wife of Don Enrique, the former foreman of Las Dos Balas, allowed the legendary lesbian into her life. Don Enrique, distraught over his spouse's infidelity with a woman, came crying to his boss.

"Don Roque, Gabriela hooked up with the *cochona*, that freak from La Curva. I don't know what I'm going to do. This is so humiliating, Don Roque. I still love my wife, but I don't know if I can ever take her back after what she has done."

Although Don Roque thought that his foreman's predicament was funny, he chose to show restraint and offered a few words of advice.

"Enrique, you should have been firm with your woman. I saw how you pampered her. That was very wrong. If from the very beginning you'd let Gabriela know that you were the man of the house, this wouldn't have happened."

"Don Roque, excuse me for saying so," I interrupted, "but it looks like you are guilty of not following the advice you gave. I mean, with all those gifts, don't you think you were also pampering Ixelia?"

The *hacendado* stared fiercely at me for a moment, but then his gaze softened as he considered his reply. "Those were just gifts," he said at last. "When Ixelia needed to be disciplined, I didn't hesitate. I didn't think twice about punishing her as she deserved. That's what I mean by being the man of the house."

As it turned out, Doña Gabriela's affair with Adela was short-lived, but she never returned to her husband. She told him that Adela had freed her. She then fell in love with a woman from Managua and continues to live with her in the capital to this day. Don Enrique quit his job at Las Dos Balas (a position Don Carlos Somarriba filled) and disappeared into Nicaragua's Triángulo Minero, where he spends most of his waking hours deep under the earth, searching for gold.

Although Don Roque was well aware of how Adela had disrupted the life of his former employee, he didn't object when Don Carlos decided to pay her a bonus to work for them during the coffee harvest. Neither did the *hacendado* become concerned when Ixelia told him that she had spent several evenings at home talking to Adela, just the two of them. He was absolutely sure that his mate only liked men and that she would never be interested in jumping into bed with another woman.

"Honestly, in spite of what I knew," Don Roque said sadly, "I didn't give Ixelia and the *cochona*'s friendship a second thought."

The real problem didn't start, in the *hacendado*'s estimation, until the night he took Ixelia to the Feast of the Immaculate Conception, in Pío XII. "She loved going to parties, dancing, hanging out in bars, anything that got her out of the house." For once he smiled, recalling those pleasant memories. "Ixelia especially loved going to festivities honoring a patron saint. These turned her into a little girl again. We never missed the nearby fairs: San Jerónimo in Masaya, Santa Ana in Niquinohomo, Santiago in Jinotepe, San Sebastián in Diriamba, la Virgen de Montserrat in La Concepción. We went to all of them. That's why, when she asked me to take her that night to the fair right here, in Pío XII, I was happy to do so. Usually, we'd start by going to watch the riding of the bulls. Ixelia enjoyed cheering for the bull whenever it gored a rider or one of the drunks that wandered into the ring. I'm surprised no one ever tried to pick a fight with her. After that, I'd take her dancing. Since I'm too old for that sort of thing, I'd let her dance with other men. I'd just sit at a table and watch as she got lost in the music. She was beautiful when she danced, really. Once she was done dancing, we'd get something to eat. And after that, Ixelia liked to get on as many of the carnival rides as I'd let her."

Don Roque paused for a moment, his eyes darting back and forth, caught in a specific moment of his recollections. I remained still, allowing him to relive the experience. Once his thoughts settled again, he sighed deeply, and continued. "That night, in Pío XII, since we got there late, we skipped the bulls and went straight to a tent that had dancing. Ixelia danced for about half an hour before getting tired. We then went to play cards. Early that night, the decks were in my favor. I won the first three hands. At the beginning of the game Ixelia stood behind me, watching. But, as usual, she got bored. She then told me that she was going to walk around to see what else was happening. When Ixelia kissed me goodbye, she promised that she wouldn't be long."

Shortly after Ixelia left, Don Roque's streak of good luck abandoned him. When the *hacendado* lost the fourth hand in a row, he rose from the table and told the other players that he'd be right back, that he needed to stretch his legs. He walked to the gazebo in the middle of Pío XII's park and climbed the stairs to the top. From there he could see most of the booths of the fair. He scanned the crowd until he spotted Ixelia: she was sitting at a table in a beer booth, drinking and chatting with Adela. Assured that no men were accosting his woman, as many times was the case, the *hacendado* went back to the card game.

Don Roque's return coincided with the resurgence in his fortune, and he won the first hand. But after losing the next three, he went back to the gazebo to check on Ixelia. From the bandstand he glanced over the heads of the crowd. This time it took a while before he spotted her. She was still with Adela. The women were standing in line to get on the Ferris wheel.

Don Roque returned to the card game and won the next two hands. At that point he had made over one hundred *córdobas*. The rest of the evening reminded him of a roller coaster, Ixelia's favorite ride: his luck scaling the splendid heights of victory only to plunge abruptly into a raging, losing descent. Don Roque took out his wallet for the fourth time that night and made a quick calculation. He was now behind one hundred *córdobas*, so he decided to call it quits and return home.

He rose from the table, wished the other players a good night, and left to search for Ixelia. Once again, the *hacendado* climbed the steps of the gazebo to scan the gathering. This time he couldn't locate her. Without becoming alarmed, Don Roque went down the steps and started to stroll among the crowd. He didn't become concerned about the whereabouts of his woman until he had finished circling the town fair a third time without seeing her. The landowner then began to stop every man he knew to ask if he had seen Ixelia. They all answered no. At last, Don Roque spotted Don Carlos Somarriba, foreman of Las Dos Balas. "Carlos, have you seen Ixelia? I can't find her. I'm tired and ready to go home."

The *hacendado* noticed that his foreman seemed uncomfortable, diverting his gaze toward the tent of the man who had become translucent because La Llorona had touched him. Don Carlos then cast his eyes on the ground and, with the point of his left boot, began to kick a few pebbles aside. At last, deciding that his employer deserved to know the truth, the foreman of Las Dos Balas confessed.

"Yes, Don Roque. I saw Ixelia about thirty minutes ago. She was with Adela Rugama. They were both riding on Adela's bicycle, headed in the direction of La Curva." Don Carlos, looking at his feet again, thought carefully about what he was going to say next. He took a deep breath, composed himself, and then continued. "As I was walking, they almost ran over me because they weren't paying attention to the road, and I still can't explain how they could keep their balance. They were very distracted, Don Roque, because . . . well . . . they were too busy kissing."

PART III
Declarations and Confessions

TEN

The Messenger

As soon as Don Roque, Doña Erlinda, and Arquímedes Guadamuz were arrested and taken to the Niquinohomo police station, each of them started to accuse the others of having planned and committed the murder. "I'm innocent," they each proclaimed with nearly convincing righteousness throughout the investigation and, later, during the trial.

Testifying under oath, Don Roque declared that Doña Erlinda had been the mastermind of the crime, and he stated that Arquímedes, the messenger, had pulled the trigger. Doña Erlinda professed knowing nothing about the plan to kill her daughter's former lover. But in her sworn statement to Commissioner Gilberto Wong, Niquinohomo's chief of police, who personally took charge of the investigation, she submitted the theory that Don Roque and Arquímides had conspired to murder Adela Rugama, one out of jealousy and the other because he had been paid to assist. And Arquímedes steadfastly maintained that Doña Erlinda had planned the murder, Don Roque had been the executioner, and that he had been merely an unsuspecting person whose only sin had been to agree to tell Doña Erlinda about the contents of the letters exchanged between Adela Rugama and Ixelia Cruz.

Whenever I tried to piece together the motives of the three who had been accused, tried, and sentenced for the homicide, Arquímedes Guadamuz always came up as the shard of the broken mirror that didn't quite fit: the messenger seemed to have nothing to gain with Adela's death. It's true that he got paid for his services as scribe, letter carrier, reader, and informant, but the sum was so paltry that I couldn't imagine why anyone would risk a long prison sentence for what in the end amounted to less than a thousand *córdobas*—ninety dollars, or so.

Since I only had a brief period in which to conduct my investigation, I was frustrated to learn that as soon as Arquímedes was released from prison, he had gone to Costa Rica, crossing the border illegally in the hope of starting over, far away from the bedlam his life had become. But as I entered the fourth week of my research, the messenger was caught in an immigration sweep of undocumented Nicaraguans in Parque de la Merced in San José, and deported to his homeland. Mariela called me from Gloria Obando's house as soon as she heard the news.

"He's back! The Curl is back!" the surviving sister shouted into the telephone. "He's the only person who might tell us the truth. You've got to talk to him before he leaves again."

The next morning I drove to Pío XII, determined to interview Arquímedes Guadamuz. His house was not difficult to find. It looked just as Mariela had described it: a simple, whitewashed building with green doors located directly across the street from the bus stop at the entrance to the town. I knocked several times, but there was no response. I was about to walk over to a neighbor's house to ask where I might find Arquímedes, when the door opened. A young woman—really, still an adolescent—stepped out. With the palms of both hands she was smoothing down her light-blue dress, trying to get rid of a few wrinkles.

"Good morning," I greeted her. "Is Arquímedes Guadamuz in?"

The girl said nothing. Instead, she glanced inside nervously. From somewhere behind a blood-red curtain that separated the living room from the rest of the house, a cranky voice, thickly coated with the ill humor of a severe hangover, shouted, "What do you want?" I glanced at a small table at the center of the room: two empty bottles of rum and a dirty glass stood as testimony to a solemn bout of drinking. Since it was still rather early in the day, I assumed the event had taken place the night before.

"I'd like to ask Señor Guadamuz a few questions," I said loudly enough for the person inside to hear.

"About what?" the voice answered, now sounding exasperated.

"About Adela Rugama."

There was a long, grave pause. At last, breaking a silence so tense the slightest sound would have seemed like a gigantic explosion, the voice asked, "Who are you?"

"I'm a writer," I answered.

Slowly, a hand covered with coarse dark hairs reached out and pushed the curtain aside. A man in bare feet, wearing a plain white T-shirt, and a dirty pair of jeans stepped into the living room. He advanced haltingly, examining me with great suspicion as he bridged the gap separating us. When he came closer, I saw that the whites of his eyes were a crowded roadmap of spidery red veins.

Arquímedes Guadamuz, a man in his late thirties, was thin and of average height. He had a long, uneven nose that ended in a sharp point. His teeth were small and sharp, rodent-like. Residing high on his left cheekbone was a small birthmark that resembled the profile of a leaping dolphin. Above the messenger's small, black eyes was a single dense row of eyebrow that, even if one didn't know his history, gave him a sinister look. An unruly spiral of thick hair hung over his narrow forehead. Throughout our conversation, he constantly pushed the curl back, but it always returned to dangle in the same place. I then understood why Arquímedes Guadamuz was better known to everyone in the region as the Curl.

Arquímedes probed me with his weary, bloodshot eyes. At that moment, if I read his mind correctly, he was thinking that I was part of a tasteless practical joke. I glanced into the house expectantly, hoping that he would invite me in, but I never got past the doorway.

"No. I don't want to talk about that," he said at last, shaking his head. His reply was so emphatic that his large ears flapped. The Curl turned to leave, and the young girl started to close the door.

"Señor Guadamuz," I said, "you know that you can't be tried again for Adela's murder. Nothing you'd say today can get you into trouble. I'm writing a book about Adela's death. Really, I'm just trying to tell a story, and for that I need to know exactly what took place that Christmas. I've got to know the truth. For example, was it you who set Adela up to be murdered? That's what everyone around here says."

Arquímedes took a sudden step toward me. "I never set anyone up to be killed," he said between clenched teeth, his statement coming out in a spittle-expelling hiss. "Those two promised me that they were only going to scare her. They said that they only wanted to get Adela to leave Ixelia alone. They also said that they were going to convince her to move as far away as possible. *¿Comprende?* That's what they told me. If anyone was set up, it was me."

"Well, then, Arquímedes, there's only one way to get people to stop saying that you helped them murder Adela: by telling me your side of the story. You can start from the beginning. I have lots of time."

The messenger took a couple of steps back and turned. He then started to pace across the living room. His breathing became labored, and the way he kept treading back and forth reminded me of a caged animal. The entire time he kept brushing his curl back, but it would immediately return to droop over his forehead.

When Arquímedes finally stopped pacing, he turned to the girl and growled, "Go back inside." Once she had gone beyond the curtain, Arquímedes sighed, leaned against the doorframe, and, seemingly persuaded by my argument, began to tell me his version of events.

"For a while I had a small business: buying raw coffee beans and then reselling them to Don Victoriano Huerta, who owns a small processing plant near San Marcos. One day, Adela showed up here selling a hundred pounds. She had snuck into Las Dos Balas the night before to steal the beans. I'm not making this up. She told me herself. She said that she wanted to get even with Don Roque because he and Doña Erlinda were doing everything possible to make her life miserable.

"I already knew who Adela was. Who didn't? She was famous around here. Still, when she introduced herself, I pretended not to know a thing about her. Anyway, we started talking, and we were getting along so well that, after I paid her for the coffee. I invited her to stay for a drink. She accepted, and I brought out a bottle of rum. After a few shots I was surprised to find that I liked her . . . as a person, that is, even though she was a pervert."

According to Arquímedes, when he mentioned in casual conversation that he knew Ixelia, Adela became very excited. "You know," she said, "it's not only coffee that I've stolen from Don Roque . . . I took her away as well."

"You've got to be kidding!" the Curl answered, feigning surprise.

"Ixelia and I are separated at the moment," Adela added, and at once she started brushing tears away with the back of her hand. When she stopped, she asked, "Do you ever see her?"

"I told Adela that once in a while I did odd jobs for Doña Erlinda, mainly hauling fruits and vegetables from Las Dos Balas to El Oriental, and that Ixelia would usually hang around to talk while I loaded my pickup," Arquímedes explained. "I also told Adela that later that week Doña Erlinda wanted me to haul a load of plantains."

"In that case," Adela said, leaning toward Arquímedes and placing her hand on his hairy forearm, "would you deliver a message to Ixelia for me?"

"I answered yes, of course," the Curl said. He paused, took a deep breath, and then let the air out slowly, the sour remnants of alcohol still on his breath. "Let me tell you something: I never thought that agreeing to take messages back and forth between those two would get me into so much trouble. And I surely never imagined that poor Adela would end up dead. No, sir. If I had to do it over again, that's one favor I would definitely say no to."

In his declaration to Commissioner Wong, as well as in his testimony in court, the messenger had always referred to the murder victim, without qualms, as the *cochona*. Upon reviewing the court records, in the coldness of print, the Curl's use of the epithet suggested that he strongly disliked her. Not once did he identify Adela by her name. But throughout our meeting, he appeared to be genuinely remorseful about the role he had played in her death.

"Do you know how to read and write?" Adela asked Arquímedes as soon as he agreed to act as messenger. When he replied that he could, she asked him to get a pen and a sheet of paper. Once he had done so, Adela began to dictate a note.

"I don't exactly remember every word," Arquímedes said to me, holding back the spiral of hair as he tried to recall the letter, "but the message went something like this:

My beloved Ixelia:

I miss you terribly. I want us to get back together. I want that more than anything else in the world. We have every right to be happy and live as a couple. I hope you believe that and feel the same way. If so, we can start planning to run away together. We can go somewhere where we'll be left alone, where we can live openly, like any regular married couple. Please say yes. Please say that you need me as much as I need you.

You can trust Arquímedes. He has agreed to be our messenger. Just tell him your answer, and he will make sure that it gets back to me.

With all of my love,
Adela

"Even though they had been apart for several months and Ixelia wasn't really a lesbian herself, she began to cry as soon as I read the note to her. I could tell that she had deep feelings for Adela," Arquímedes said. His voice became hoarse at the recollection. "Right after I was done reading, Ixelia asked me to write down her response. In it, she said that she still cared for Adela, but that it would be too dangerous for them to get back together. The next day, when I delivered Ixelia's reply, Adela was so thrilled to hear that Ixelia still loved her that she gave me a kiss and a big hug. From that day on, I started taking messages back and forth a couple of times a week. Both women always looked forward to receiving the letters; they'd run out of their houses to meet me whenever they'd hear my pickup pull up in front.

"Soon Adela began to plan their escape. She told Ixelia that she almost had enough money saved up for them to take off for Costa Rica, where a friend of hers would help them find work and where they could live in peace. To be honest, I think that Ixelia was very interested in the idea. But then the trouble began.

"When they first started exchanging letters, Ixelia was very cautious. She always made sure that her mother was not around before asking me to read a message. But as time went by she grew careless until, one day, just as I had feared, Doña Erlinda saw us hunched close together over a letter."

"'What were you reading to my daughter?' she asked me afterwards. When I told her, Doña Erlinda responded, 'From now on, I want you to tell me everything those letters say.'

"I protested. I told her that I thought their messages were a private matter. Doña Erlinda didn't answer. She just stared at me with those creepy eyes of hers. I could tell that she was angry, but I didn't want to betray Adela and Ixelia.

"Doña Erlinda then said, 'Curl, we need to break up this relationship. Don't you see that it's unnatural for two women to be together like that? We can't allow it. It's not right. You have to help me put a stop to this perversion.'

"At first I refused, but Doña Erlinda was so used to getting her way that in the end I had no choice but to do as she asked. I knew it would be useless to go against her. So from then on, I kept Doña Erlinda informed about what the letters said." Arquímedes, to avoid meeting my gaze, stared fixedly at an oxcart loaded with firewood that was passing in front of his house, leaving Pío XII.

I had grown impatient. I already knew everything the messenger was telling me. I wanted him to skip ahead. I wanted him to tell me about the message that, to me, mattered most, so I interrupted his tale. "Arquímedes, was it you who wrote and delivered that last letter? The message that lured Adela to her death? You know which one I'm talking about, the one where Ixelia asked Adela to meet her at Las Dos Balas the evening of Christmas. Tell me about that letter."

The Curl paled. With an anguished expression he reached out and held on to the doorpost. He then turned away from me to stare south, toward the center of Pío XII. I remained quiet, waiting for him to confess, to tell me the truth about that fateful day. But Arquímedes clung to his silence like a drowning person hangs on to anything that floats. I sensed that he wouldn't cooperate further, but I tried one last time to persuade him that it was in his best interest to talk, to help me recreate Adela's last moments.

"Listen, Arquímedes, in the case of Don Roque and Doña Erlinda, I'm absolutely certain that both of them are guilty. But you . . . I'm not so sure. The pieces don't fit. Do you understand what I'm saying? I believe that you were used. I believe what you told the police and the court: that you were simply the messenger and that you stepped unknowingly into a plot to kill Adela."

My words seemed to stir Arquímedes. His coal-black eyes widened, and he opened his mouth as if he were about to speak. But he closed it again, almost immediately. He then looked away, continuing to hold fast to his silence. Still, I knew that the messenger wanted to talk. I could see that the burden he was carrying in his soul had become enormous, almost too much to bear, and that it was devouring him from within, like a malignant tumor. But in his gaze there was also an unspoken terror, a fear so overwhelming that it forced him to keep everything he knew about the Christmas of Adela's death locked deep inside him. I waited patiently, hoping that the quietness would place an enormous strain on his resistance until, like the swelling walls of a dam during the torrential rains of a tropical storm, he would burst, releasing the truth and flooding this story with light. But the Curl kept quiet, and he now refused to look at me.

"Arquímedes," I said at last, "if you remain silent about this, you'll be missing your best shot at clearing your name and, possibly, of redeeming yourself. I wish you'd reconsider and tell me what happened that night."

I waited for his response. Sadly, my words had no effect. Under those circumstances, I had only one question left on my list. "I'll leave you alone then, Arquímedes. But before I do, please clarify this for me: why did you help Doña Erlinda and Don Roque? What did you stand to gain by sharing the contents of those letters with them? I realize that Doña Erlinda can be intimidating, and I know that they paid you for the information as well, but I suspect that you were offered something else and that it must have been very valuable to keep you so deeply involved in their plans to keep Adela and Ixelia apart."

The Curl lifted his head and glared at me. Clenching his jaw in anger, he stepped back and, without saying goodbye, shut the door.

The interview had lasted half an hour. Since I had left Granada early, without breakfast, I was both hungry and thirsty. Across the street, next to the bus stop, was a refreshment stand. I walked over and ordered a *quesillo* and a glass of *tiste*. I took a seat at a vacant table and, while the details were still fresh in my mind, began to jot down a few notes about my conversation with Arquímedes. I was so absorbed in this task that I hadn't noticed the person standing next to me until she cleared her throat. It was the girl who had answered the Curl's door.

"May I speak to you for a moment?" she asked, almost in a whisper.

"Of course," I answered. "Please, sit down."

"No," she replied, shaking her head. "I'd better stand. I might have to hide in a hurry if Arquímedes comes out to look for me."

Later that same day, in La Curva, I asked Mariela about her.

"Her name is Soledad. She's the Curl's woman."

"Isn't she a little young to be with him? She can't be more than fifteen," I said.

"She's sixteen, but she has been with him ever since she was eleven. The Curl has a reputation for liking his women on the young side. Everyone around here knows that. A few years ago, when Soledad's mother discovered what was going on, she had the Curl arrested for statutory rape. Soledad became furious when she found out that he was in jail. She told her mother that if she couldn't be with the man she loved she would run away and never return. The mother knew that the girl meant it, so she dropped the charges, and the police let him go."

Back at the refreshment stand, Soledad said, "I was in the back room listening to your conversation. I think you need to know what Doña Erlinda offered Arquímedes if he told her about the messages."

"Go ahead, please," I said. The urgency in my voice betrayed my excitement at this unexpected stroke of good fortune. Composing myself, I leaned forward so as not to miss a word she said.

"Arquímedes, like every stupid man around here, was crazy over Ixelia. I always knew that. And although I hate to say it, he would have left me in an instant if she'd asked him to. He would've acted as if I had never existed. That's how much he wanted her."

Soledad's candor stunned me, and at once I knew that I was in the presence of someone whose honesty was unquestionable.

"Arquímedes thought that if he helped Doña Erlinda break up the relationship, then maybe she would let him have Ixelia, all to himself. I'm certain that's why he got involved in the first place. But when Doña Erlinda began to suspect what Arquímedes really wanted, she told him that she would never allow it, that Ixelia belonged to Don Roque and to no one else."

"If he knew that, why did he still help?"

"Because Doña Erlinda offered Arquímedes something almost as good: Zuleika, Ixelia's younger sister. Zuleika's a lot like Ixelia, in looks and in personality. Only she's not as pretty. But that promise was enough for Arquímedes. Zuleika was going to be his reward."

Soledad paused for a moment as she met my gaze directly. She then placed both hands on the table and leaned forward to stress her point. "Now, I know that Arquímedes is not the most honest or the brightest man around, but I do know that he's not a murderer. I swear that he didn't know that they were going to kill that poor woman."

The Curl's young woman stood straight again, glanced worriedly toward the house, and said, "I've got to go before he sees me talking to you." Without saying farewell, Soledad dashed across the street, carefully opened the door of the house, and snuck back in.

ELEVEN

The Threat

N early a month went by since the Christmas Day of Adela's disappearance before Mariela, in the company of her four children, went to the Niquinohomo police station to file a missing person's report.

"Why did you wait so long?" I asked during our very first interview.

Lying in her hammock, Mariela gazed pensively at the central wood beam that helped support the zinc roof. After a moment, she replied, "I kept on hoping that the Curl's story was true: that Adela, tired of this mess, decided on the spur of the moment to run off to Costa Rica. He came by the house the day after Christmas to give us the news and to return Tulio's bicycle. He said that my sister and Ixelia asked him to say goodbye to us and to return the bike because they were leaving that same evening. According to the Curl, Adela said that she would be getting in touch once they were settled in San José. Although a voice inside of me kept saying that something was terribly wrong, I didn't want to listen. I know it was foolish of me to not follow my instincts, but . . . honestly, I desperately wanted to believe that my little sister was doing well and that she would find a better life."

Shortly after Mariela reported that her sister was missing, the police, under the direction of Commissioner Gilberto Wong, began to question Adela's relatives, friends, and neighbors. From the onset, virtually every person pointed a finger toward Don Roque Ramírez, Doña Erlinda Cruz, and Arquímedes Guadamuz, saying that they were the ones most likely responsible for Adela's disappearance.

The Curl became a suspect because Adela vanished the day after he delivered a message, supposedly from Ixelia, which said, "Meet me under the ceiba next to the old man's house, tomor-

row evening at seven." Gema and her brother, Javier, had read
the letter as Arquímedes was delivering it. They told the police
that the Curl advised Adela to burn the note because if either
Don Roque or Doña Erlinda found out that the women were
thinking about running off to Costa Rica, they would do everything possible to stop them. Adela followed his advice. Thus, the
most damaging evidence against the Curl, the piece that linked
him directly to the plot to murder Adela Rugama, was destroyed.
But the testimony that Gema and Tulio gave in court was so
detailed, so vivid, so convincing, that in spite of Arquímedes's
vehement denials about the letter's existence, the jury concluded
that he was lying.

Doña Erlinda Cruz's name, of course, was immediately
placed on the list because she had often stated, in front of witnesses, that she absolutely hated Adela Rugama. Plus, many
persons eagerly recounted, for the benefit of the police or, for
that matter, anyone who showed the slightest interest, Doña
Erlinda's stunt with the machete and the melon.

But the instant Commissioner Wong set the search for Adela
Rugama into motion, Don Roque Ramírez became the prime
suspect behind her disappearance. For two days, the
Niquinohomo police station was crammed as dozens volunteered
their declarations. As it goes with Nicaraguans, each one believed
that his or her version of events would surpass all others in rele-
vance, importance, and style. Although the testimonies were
astoundingly varied, there was a distinct common denominator:
virtually every witness theorized that the *hacendado*, out of jealousy and because of the humiliation he had to publicly endure,
was the person who most wanted Adela Rugama out of the way,
and permanently.

Two episodes, above all others, helped place Don Roque's
name at the top of the commissioner's list. Mariela's eldest
daughter, Gema, told me of the first one during the second week
of my investigation, after she had served me a cup of lemongrass
tea. A light morning rain fell with a soft, tinny whisper on the
zinc roof as she recalled what had occurred.

"About a month after Ixelia left Don Roque and moved in with my aunt Adela, I dropped by to visit them on my way home from school. They invited me to stay for dinner. I helped out in the kitchen as they prepared a simple meal: *gallo pinto*, tortillas, and cheese. I chopped onions while my aunt fried the rice and beans, and Ixelia made the tortillas.

"Later, we were seated at the table, eating, joking, and having a really good time, when Ixelia suddenly stood up. She put a finger across her lips, and my aunt and I stopped talking. We heard the sound of hoofs. Ixelia ran to the living room and hid behind the front door. From there, through the hinges, she could see whatever was going on in the street without being noticed. And then she saw what we feared most: Don Roque heading toward the house, mounted on his palomino.

"'Shit! Why is that son of a bitch coming here?' Ixelia spat out on her way back to the kitchen. 'Adelita, my love, go hide somewhere. I don't know why that asshole is daring to show his face around here. You have to hide . . . and quick. Let me take care of this. Please, hurry. I'll get rid of him.' Although Ixelia tried to sound confident as she said this, her voice was trembling.

"My aunt nodded and went into the bedroom. Ixelia returned to the table, sat down, and took a deep breath. After that she went on eating dinner, acting as if nothing was going on.

"I felt like running into the bedroom with my aunt Adela, but I was so scared, so terrified, that my body wouldn't listen. Believe me, I tried, but I couldn't get up from the chair. When I heard Don Roque's horse stop in front of the house, I started to shiver. The echo of his boots as he entered the house sounded like violent cracks of lightning to me, and my hands started to shake so much that I had to put my fork down.

"'Good afternoon,' he said, tipping his sombrero as he strolled into the kitchen. Although he had greeted us both, he barely glanced at me; the old man only had eyes for Ixelia. He was staggering a bit as he came toward us, and that's when I realized that he was drunk.

"Ixelia, with her back to the door, didn't even turn to look at him. She just kept eating. The old man walked up to her and, with his right hand, reached out and started patting the top of her head, the way one pats a dog. Ixelia looked at me and rolled her eyes, but she continued acting as if he weren't there. Don Roque then started to play with her hair and, soon after that, like the pervert he really is, he began to press his groin against her back.

"'Ixelia, you're looking so beautiful, so precious. I miss you. You're my woman. What are you doing here with the *cochona*? The truth? You belong with me. You know you're mine. Come back home, please.' While he spoke, the old man continued rubbing himself against Ixelia.

"'Roque, I'm never going back. Never. I don't care what you say or do. I'm staying here, and that's it. It doesn't matter whether you like it or not. Do me a favor, please. Get back on your horse and please, please, please leave me alone.'

"In spite of what Ixelia said, Don Roque kept on insisting that she return with him. He kept on saying how beautiful she was and how much he missed her. The old man then stopped his pressing and began to massage Ixelia's shoulders. But she was unmoved. Over and over she kept asking him to leave. At last, when Don Roque realized that she was not returning with him, he took a couple of steps back and shouted. "'Yes, woman, you're a whore! You've always been a whore, and you'll always be a whore! And now, on top of that, you're a pervert!'

"Right after Don Roque said that, he lunged at Ixelia, grabbing her by the neck. I started to scream and, although I was terrified, I jumped out of my seat to help her. But the old man was so drunk that by the time I reached the other side of the table, she had knocked him to the floor and was sitting on his chest with her hands around his neck, strangling him. At that point, my aunt ran out of the bedroom, put her arms around Ixelia, and began to lift her off of Don Roque.

"'Adela, you have to let me kill this old man! Let me kill him! If we don't do him in first, he's going to end up killing us!' Ixelia was so furious, so determined to wring Don Roque's neck that it was difficult for my aunt, who was much stronger, to pull her off. But once she did, the old man crawled to the nearest wall, propped himself against it, and sat on the floor.

"After Ixelia calmed down, my aunt went to stand before the old man and said, 'Don Roque, this is my house. I expect you to behave respectfully while you're here. I'm going to have to ask you to leave.'

"The old man, looking a little dazed, just rubbed his throat while he squinted at my aunt. I don't think he recognized her at first. Before he spoke, he wiped away a string of spit that was dangling from the corner of his mouth.

"'Ah, the *cochona*,' he said as he cleaned his hand on his shirt. 'You're going to get what's coming to you. You'll see. I'm not going to rest until I see you dead. I'm saving two bullets just for you. Your name's engraved on them. Wait and see; I intend to keep this promise.' After saying that, Don Roque stood up, stumbled out of the house, got on his palomino, and left."

Lizbeth Hogdson, the woman from Pearl Lagoon, was called upon in court to testify about the second incident that helped place Don Roque's name at the top of the list of suspects. When I learned that she had witnessed this occurrence, I stopped by her store to interview her a second time. Unlike my first visit, where we sat comfortably in her living room to discuss her relationship with Adela, on this occasion we talked in the store.

"Oh, yes. I definitely heard the commotion the first time Don Roque threatened Adela," Lizbeth said as she measured a quarter pound of sugar for a client, a girl of about eight. "As soon as I heard the noise I ran over to Adela's house to see what was going on, but by the time I got there Don Roque was leaving. He was still rubbing his throat as he rode off," she added with a smile.

"Because of what happened that day, about two weeks later, when I saw Don Roque headed for Adela's again, I closed the store and hurried across the street. Once more, the old man was drunk. This time he didn't go inside Adela's house. Instead, Don Roque got off his horse and stood in the street, about three yards away from the sidewalk, facing the front door. All the time he swayed back and forth. After a while, he took off his hat and began to scratch his head. I think he was trying to remember why he had come. At last, when the old man appeared to have figured it out, he took a deep breath, and yelled:

"'Ixelia!'

"The old man waited a moment. When he saw that no one responded, he yelled again, this time louder, "'IXELIA!'

"Adela told me afterward that she and Ixelia were inside, discussing what would be the best way to handle Don Roque. But the old man wasn't going to wait for long. When he saw that Ixelia wasn't coming out, he started shouting:

"'Come out of that house now, you shitty whore! You pervert! You're with a *cochona*! Come out of the house now, you pervert!'

"Everyone in the neighborhood ran out of their homes to see what was going on. But that didn't stop Don Roque from making a scene. He continued shouting until Ixelia, angry, came to the doorway and started yelling back:

"'Get out of here, old geezer! Can't you see that I'm never going back to you! Get that through your thick skull! Get out of here and leave me alone! Now!'

"That pissed Don Roque off. He raised both arms with his hands outstretched, like the Egyptian mummy in those old Hollywood movies, and took a couple of steps toward Ixelia. It was then that Adela, who had been watching from the living room, rushed out of the house and stepped between them. As soon as the old man saw Adela, he stopped, put his arms back down, and stood there, glaring at her.

"'Once again the dyke comes to rescue the damsel in distress,' the old man said at last. 'Well, I've still got those two bullets with your name on them.' Don Roque held up two fingers of a wobbly hand as he said this. 'I'll take care of you, *cochona*. That's a promise I'm going to keep.'

"Adela didn't move. She stood solidly between Ixelia and the old man. She didn't look angry or scared. If anything, she seemed to be feeling sorry for Don Roque. I now think she saw a reflection of herself in his obsession with the girl. I mean, we know they both suffered from the same affliction.

"The old man then got back on his palomino, almost falling off as he did so, and he rode away in the direction of Las Dos Balas."

As soon as the woman from Pearl Lagoon had finished the story, I blurted out the question that, at that moment, weighed most heavily on my mind. "Lizbeth, if everyone knew that Don Roque was threatening to kill Adela, why didn't anyone try to stop him?"

"I *did*," the beautiful *mulata* asserted. "I asked Padre Uriel to talk to the old man. I wanted him to stop Don Roque from doing something stupid."

Lizbeth's declaration surprised me. I was unaware that the parish priest of La Curva might have known beforehand that Don Roque had publicly announced his intention to kill Adela.

"Did Padre Uriel talk to him?" I asked.

Lizbeth looked at me, smiling sadly. She then reached behind her to get two Belmont cigarettes for a customer, a young man in his early twenties who was wearing an old, threadbare Cat-in-the-Hat T-shirt—probably part of the U.S. relief shipment sent here after Hurricane Mitch. Before answering my question, the woman from Pearl Lagoon sighed and then said, "Yes. Padre Uriel did talk to the old man. But, obviously, it didn't work."

TWELVE

The Arrangement

When I called Padre Uriel to make an appointment, he didn't ask why I wanted to see him. He merely gave me a date and a time.

Three days later, at nine o'clock in the morning, when I arrived at La Curva, I parked Si Dios Quiere at the rear of the church. Several old men from the town sat on the stone ledge near the walkway leading to the rectory, drinking *café con leche*, eating *rosquillas*, and catching up on the latest round of town gossip.

"*Buenos días,*" I said to the gathering.

"*Buenos días,*" they answered in chorus.

It was a Thursday. That meant that Lizbeth Hodgson had been there earlier for her regularly scheduled twice-a-week confession. At the end of the pathway, I climbed the five steps to the back entrance, took a deep breath, and knocked.

The door opened with startling suddenness. Padre Uriel, as if he had been standing there all along waiting, solemnly examined me. At once, all of my ecclesiastical phobias surfaced: a swift, forceful rush of guilt brought on by several decades of severely neglecting my sacramental duties. The irreconcilable gap between the mental picture I had formed of the priest and the reality of the man also surprised me. I had been expecting a tall, muscular *macho* with a robust build that perfectly complemented Lizbeth Hodgson's voluptuousness. Instead, Padre Uriel was thin and rather short. Some people would go as far as to call the priest frail. The frames of his glasses, of a thick, black plastic, did not flatter him. They did, nevertheless, make the cleric seem erudite, as if he spent most of his time hunched over the open pages of a book. His black, wavy hair was gray along the sides, signaling his age as well past forty.

"Good morning," the priest said in greeting, instantly breaking into a wide, friendly grin. "Come in, please," he added, and with a sweep of his right arm, he ushered me into his office. A crucifix bearing a flesh-colored Jesus, with alarming amounts of painted blood dripping from the wounds, was the sole item adorning the office walls. A missal was the lone book in sight, and it rested on the uppermost right-hand corner of his large mahogany desk. This piece of furniture was the only item that gave warmth to the room's austere, monastic appearance. Padre Uriel walked around the desk to sit in an office chair so old and weathered that the wooden bars supporting the backrest were splintering. With an open palm, the priest motioned for me to take the seat opposite from him.

"From our conversation on the telephone, I gather that you don't live in Nicaragua. Am I right?" he asked.

"Yes, you're right, Padre Uriel. I live in the States. That's where I was born as well, but both of my parents are Nicaraguan."

"That explains your accent," the priest said. "I've found that Latin Americans who live there acquire a listless Spanish, spoken with a dull, bland accent, like Don Francisco, that fellow on *Sábado Gigante*." Padre Uriel then leaned back in his chair, lacing the fingers of both hands behind the back of his head, seemingly proud of his powers of observation. "Well, now," he said, "what can I do for you?"

"I'd like to ask you a few questions about Adela Rugama's death, Padre. I was told that you had spoken to Don Roque Ramírez about the threats he had made, about killing her."

Since I had anticipated that the priest would not want to discuss the subject, I kept my expression as blank as possible while I readied myself for a long, intense debate. My assumption had been correct. The moment I mentioned Adela's name, Padre Uriel's countenance darkened. He turned his chair so that he could stare at the crucifix.

"Who told you this?" he asked after a tense pause. The harshness of his tone made me seek refuge in the hard backrest of my chair.

"Lizbeth Hodgson."

As soon as Padre Uriel heard the name, his shoulders drooped. For a moment, he looked lost. He remained like that, sitting perfectly still until, at last, he let out a long-held breath of air in a thin, drawn-out hiss. Then, as if preparing to pray, he brought his hands together at the height of his chest, his fingers touching at the tips. I waited as patiently as I could for the priest to speak, but after a long pause without him showing any signs of continuing our conversation, I decided to go straight to the point of my visit.

"I was hoping you could share with me what advice you gave Don Roque."

Padre Uriel, again in possession of his wits, asked, "Tell me, what's your interest in that sordid affair?"

"I'm planning to write a book."

"What kind of a book?" the priest asked, turning his chair to face me and then leaning forward to rest his forearms on the mahogany desk.

"An account of the murder."

Padre Uriel looked at me intently, without blinking, as if he were probing my soul to learn the true motive behind my interest in the tragedy. I sat absolutely still, absorbing his glare while trying not to show my growing discomfort. But his cold stare took me to the brink of shattering, and just as I was about to fall on my knees and beg him to hear my confession, the priest spoke, asking, "Why do you wish to glorify this type of behavior?"

As discreetly as possible, I sighed in relief. I was prepared to take full advantage of the wide berth the priest had given me to expand on the nature of the writing craft. He had touched a chord that dwells within every author: one's unwavering passion for the subject.

"Padre Uriel," I said, now filled with the confidence and zeal of an apostle, "Adela Rugama's murder is a chilling story. It's a sobering portrait of human frailty, of what can happen when we allow our weaknesses, our emotional flaws, to take control of our actions. The tale of her death shows how greed, lust, and unrestrained passions can completely cloud our judgment. Just look at everything from your perspective; that is, the perspective of a priest: virtually every single commandment was broken. From that viewpoint, Adela Rugama's murder becomes a remarkable moral tale. This story, then, Padre Uriel, can become quite useful. Perhaps we can prevent something like this from ever happening again."

Padre Uriel listened attentively to my homily. When I had finished, he leaned back in his chair and remained silent, as if contemplating my words. But I was sure that the priest had already made up his mind about whether he was going to confide in me. Now, he simply seemed delighted to keep me waiting. At last, when he calculated that the suspense had reached its zenith, he said, "Perhaps you're right. At worst, I don't think such a book can cause any harm. I don't see how any rational woman would want to emulate her behavior."

"Thank you, Padre Uriel," I said. The relief I felt when he agreed to talk surprised me. After all, his approval of my project meant little to me; I had not come to solicit the Church's imprimatur. All I wanted to hear was his version of what took place during his meeting with the *hacendado*. His opinion, while of interest to me, was secondary. Still, happy to count on his cooperation, I repeated my request. "Would you tell me, then, Padre Uriel, about your conversation with Don Roque?"

The priest nodded and, without delay, stepped back in time to recount his role in the tragedy. "After I was told about the threats Don Roque had been making, I sent a note with the sacristan in which I asked him to come see me. A couple of days later, he dropped by. At that time not much more than a month had passed since the girl left him, so he was still very angry.

"'Good morning, Padre Uriel,' Don Roque said in that low, raspy voice of his. 'What can I do for you?'

"'Don Roque, we need to talk about the threats you've been making.'

"'What threats, Padre?'

"'The ones about killing Adela Rugama.'

"There was a spark of anger in Don Roque's eyes. For a moment I thought that he was going to pound his fist on my desk and accuse me of believing the false, wicked rumors being spread about him. But, instead, Don Roque waited until he was calmer, and then he began to speak.

"'You have to understand several things, Padre. Those women humiliated me, in front of the whole blessed world no less. For someone like me, of such high standing in this community, that's not an easy thing to deal with. You know that, don't you, Padre?'

"Don Roque is a very proud man. I realize that's not a virtue, but he was right: they had dishonored him in everyone's eyes.

"'Also,' the *hacendado* continued, 'those two are involved in an unnatural relationship. You know that better than anyone, Padre Uriel. After all, you've often pointed that out from the pulpit, saying that all *cochonas* are going straight to hell. Isn't that so?'

"But what made things worse for Don Roque," the priest said, interrupting his story for a moment, "is that these women had the audacity to continue to live here, in La Curva, openly and in sin. At least they should've had the decency to move elsewhere, and the further away the better. If they had done this, then, with time, Don Roque's wounds would've healed and the whole incident would've been forgotten.

"'Now, Padre,' Don Roque went on, 'I don't mind admitting to you that the *cochona* has stolen the person I love the most in this life, and I don't intend to let that go unpunished. The *cochona* is going to pay for what she has done.'

"What Don Roque told me that day was true: he was deeply in love with that girl although a bit too obsessively, in my estimation. As you can see, Adela hurt that man deeply, and she shamed him in public as well. That's why, when he came to see me, I was not surprised that all he talked about was getting revenge.

"'Don Roque,' the priest had answered, 'I don't need to remind you that the Church says that we should leave the castigation of sinners to God. If you decide to carry out your revenge, you're bound to spend eternity in hell. I know you're aware of this. After all, you did study with the Salesians, who are fine educators. You do understand what I'm telling you, don't you, Don Roque?'

"He nodded, and his Adam's apple slid up and down the length of his neck as he swallowed his anger and frustration.

"'Don Roque,' the priest had then counseled, 'you need to resign yourself to your loss. Try to move on with your life. I advise you to pray every day. Ask the Lord to reveal His plan for you. Will you do that?'

"Don Roque didn't say anything. He merely stared at me for a long time until, finally, he nodded.

"'One more thing, Don Roque, please stop saying that you're going to kill Adela. Your statements are upsetting a lot of people. It's important that this ordeal be resolved peacefully. Agreed?'

"At the time I thought that Don Roque had taken my advice to heart. I fully expected him to turn away from the path of revenge. As we said farewell that day, he promised to abide by my words."

After finishing the story, Padre Uriel placed both hands on his desk, with the palms facing up. He stared down into them, as if the lines contained a lost thought. After a few moments, he looked at me and said, "Well, as you can see, Don Roque never gave up on his desire to seek vengeance. But this tragedy couldn't have been avoided. I believe it was preordained."

"How can you say that Adela's murder was preordained, Padre?" I found myself protesting in spite of the voice inside that urged me to keep my mouth shut. "What about free will? Don't you believe that Don Roque and the others are responsible for the choices they made, including killing Adela?"

"Of course, I do," the priest answered, nodding emphatically. "But those two women had driven Don Roque out of his mind. By the time I spoke to him, he probably was too far gone, fixated on the idea of getting revenge. But I do believe that when we spoke, Don Roque listened closely to what I had to say; he may have had every intention of following my advice. But I also know that he later became incensed, beyond reason, when the arrangement he had made with the women failed. But ask yourself, how could it not fail? The whole thing was absolutely unnatural."

"What arrangement are you talking about, Padre?"

"The three of them agreeing to live together, of course. Man is only meant to have one wife. The Church is very clear about that, you know," Padre Uriel added, wrapping the top of the mahogany desk with the knuckles of his right hand to underscore his point.

Although the revelation about the agreement stunned me, having come as a complete surprise, I did my best to remain impassive. To mask my shock, I opted to play the devil's advocate. "But, Padre Uriel, in the Bible, in the Old Testament, there are many examples of prominent men, men important to our faith, who had many wives. Look at King David, for one."

"Yes. But then Jesus came to put an end to those hedonistic practices," the priest answered with a triumphant smile. He leaned back in his seat, and his eyes gleamed with satisfaction over the cleverness of his theological riposte.

"I guess you're absolutely right about that, Padre," I said, ready to bring our meeting to a close. I stood up, still upset over the revelation, reached out across the desk, shook Padre Uriel's hand, thanked him for taking the time to meet with me, and hurriedly exited the parish office.

With my hands trembling and my pulse racing, I headed straight for Mariela's house, leaving Si Dios Quiere where I had parked it, behind the church. I needed the time, as well as the exercise, to try to regain my composure. As I walked through the streets of La Curva, my pace faster than usual because of my annoyance, I wondered why Mariela had withheld the arrangement from me.

By the time I turned right on the wide path where the United Fruit Company train used to run, I was much calmer. Still, the feeling that I had been intentionally kept in the dark continued to trouble me.

Upon reaching Mariela's house, I stood at the doorway and called out loud, *"Buenos días"*—the Nicaraguan equivalent of ringing a doorbell.

A few moments later, Javier appeared. "I'm looking for your mother," I said. In my haste to learn why Mariela had not completely confided in me, I had neglected to greet the youngest of her children. Startled by my uncustomary brusqueness, he turned at once and hurried back into the house. Soon his mother came out, wiping her hands on a kitchen towel. Her eyes widened in surprise since I had not called Gloria Obando, as I usually did, so that she could warn Mariela of my visit.

"Good morning. And to what do I owe this surprise?" she said in greeting. "I wasn't expecting you today. Come on in. It's nice to have you here," she said, inviting me into her house. "Would you like some tea?"

"No, thank you, Mariela. I've just come from talking to Padre Uriel. I have to confess that I'm upset with you. From what the priest told me, it seems that you haven't been totally honest with me. I'm very disappointed, and hurt too. You promised to tell me everything, without keeping any secrets."

Mariela looked away, my terseness having caught her off-guard. "What do you mean?" she asked, her voice now unsteady.

"Padre Uriel just informed me that Adela and Ixelia had agreed to live with Don Roque—as a threesome. He suggested that Adela and Don Roque came to some sort of agreement to share Ixelia."

"Oh, that . . . " Mariela said. Her voice trailed off as her gaze fell on the hard-packed dirt floor of her living room.

"Why didn't you tell me about that, Mariela?" I asked. The sharp edge in my voice shocked her, and when she looked up again her eyes were misty. She blinked several times to relieve the sting. Regretting my harshness, I moved toward her and placed my hand on her shoulder. Speaking softly now, I said, "In order for me to be able to reconstruct your sister's life and to find out the truth about her last moments, I need to know everything, Mariela. We had agreed to that. Why, then, did you keep their arrangement from me?"

Brushing away her tears with the fingers of her right hand, she answered, "It's something I'm embarrassed to talk about. I had learned to live with my sister being a lesbian. I can talk about that with honesty because she made loving another woman seem like the most natural thing in the world. But the deal she made with Don Roque was wrong. From the very beginning it was wrong. I told Adela that she was making a big mistake. But, in the end, none of it mattered because the whole thing only lasted a couple of days."

"Yes, Mariela," I said, "but according to Padre Uriel, the moment their deal fell apart, Don Roque's hatred for your sister grew. The failure of the arrangement may have led directly to Adela's death. That makes the incident very important, Mariela."

"I don't know about that," Mariela said, this time far more assured of herself. "Sometimes Padre Uriel likes to exaggerate. Especially when it comes to sex. That man has a lot of hang-ups, you know?"

"Well, then, please, tell me what happened. Allow me to decide if it's important or not." Mariela walked to the doorway that led to the backyard. From there she asked Nubia to bring two cups of lemongrass tea. She then climbed into her hammock and, once we had our tea in hand, reached back into her memory to bring the two women to life again.

"Adela," Ixelia whispered in her lover's ear, "the old man has an offer for us." The women were lying in bed, pleasantly exhausted after making love, their legs and arms entwined as they exchanged slow, lazy kisses.

"What is it?" Adela said as she ran her hand up from Ixelia's stomach to caress her right breast.

"He wants the three of us to live together. That way, he says, you can both have me."

Adela laughed. At any other moment such a proposal would have made her tense, edgy. But every time she was in bed with Ixelia, the world became an astonishing, splendid place, where nothing could go wrong. "He's kidding, right?"

"No, Adela, he's serious. He wants us to move in with him. We should consider it, don't you think? There are some good things about the idea. To begin with, we wouldn't have to worry about money. Roque would pay for everything. And, my love, if the situation works out, my mother and the old man wouldn't be angry any longer. Sometimes those two scare me. You don't know what they're capable of, my love. If you think about it, Adela, we've got nothing to lose. I say we move in with him."

"But Ixelia, you know that the old man will want to have us both in bed with him . . . at the same time, don't you?"

"Of course I do, woman. How could I not know that, my love?"

"So how could you even think about accepting his offer?"

"Adela, you know that I've done worse things with men . . . much, much worse. What's important is that even though he'll be there, with us, I'll only be there for you. I'll always belong to you, Adela, and only you. I say we at least try this. We've got to put an end to this stupid war. As long as we keep on fighting Roque and my mother, they will try to tear us apart or, worse, destroy us. But if we move in with the old man, all our problems will disappear."

"Adela hated the idea," Mariela said. She sighed deeply and then took a sip of her tea. "But my sister went along with it. She was so in love with Ixelia that she would do anything to make that girl happy."

"And what happened, Mariela? How long did the arrangement last?"

"Well, they never really moved in with the old man. Adela and Ixelia first wanted to find out what would happen with the three of them together, in bed. They thought that it was important to see if it would work out before they packed up all their stuff and took it to Las Dos Balas. They spent only part of a night at the old man's house. Adela told me afterward that it was a complete disaster. Don Roque couldn't handle seeing that Ixelia was completely turned on when she was with Adela, but that whenever he'd touch her, she'd pull away. My sister said that he went insane with jealousy. He threatened to kill them both, right on the spot. They got out of his house as fast as they could and ended up walking all the way back to La Curva, in the middle of the night, the two of them wearing nothing but the sheet they had ripped off of the old man's bed."

THIRTEEN

No Harm in Killing a Freak

I n their declarations to Gilberto Wong—the commissioner of the District of Niquinohomo, as well as the officer responsible for investigating the murder—two of the three suspects always referred to Adela Rugama as the *cochona*. In their testimonies, not once did they use her name. In his first statement after the discovery of the body, Arquímedes Guadamuz, alias the Curl, employed the epithet thirty-seven times. Don Roque Ramírez did likewise: on fifty-eight occasions he called Adela "the *cochona*." Only Doña Erlinda Cruz showed restraint. Not once did she use the term "dyke." What's more, she always referred to her daughter's former lover with the affectionate diminutive Adelita. But in her declaration to Commissioner Wong, Ixelia's mother condemned the murder victim's sexual orientation, categorizing it as "the greatest perversion before the eyes of God."

After reading their statements, I was left with the impression that the three conspirators felt that Adela's life had little value solely because she was a lesbian. To confirm this, I needed to speak to Commissioner Wong. As soon as I learned that he had returned from his pilgrimage to China, where he had gone to pay homage to his ancestors, I telephoned the offices of the Niquinohomo police. His assistant scheduled me for an appointment.

Two days later, at mid-morning, I arrived at Niquinohomo's police station. This community of twenty thousand proudly claims the privilege of being the birthplace of Augusto César Sandino, the "General of Free Men." A monument, a cast-iron cutout of the rebel leader's highly recognizable silhouette, stands guard at the city's main entrance. The tribute makes the rebel leader, who successfully fought the U.S. Marines for six years, look like a thin, burnt gingerbread man.

The morning of my appointment the police station was filled with voices, coughing, bodies in motion, and the usual bustle of

128

a chaotic business day as several residents were there filing complaints. Among them: a man who was furious, shouting and gesturing wildly, because his neighbor's Doberman had gotten loose and killed seven of his prizedfighting cocks; a woman with wild white hair and darting, inquisitive eyes who accused a striking teenage girl who lived across the street from her of bewitching her husband, casting spells in the middle of the night, while everyone slept, so she could steal the elderly fellow away; and an Englishman who reported that when he stepped out of his house early that morning to buy a *nacatamal* for breakfast, someone broke in and took his portable computer along with his British passport. He was giving his statement to an officer who spoke perfect English.

I remained in the area, trying to eavesdrop and waiting for the right moment to ask the gentleman why he was living in Niquinohomo, but the officer at the reception desk asked me, in a polite yet firm manner, to wait for the commissioner in his office, and he proceeded at once to escort me into the room. The officer waited until I was seated and then left.

There were few furnishings, and the office smelled of burned incense. In a corner was a file cabinet, and on top of it was a vase with a portrait of San Judas Tadeo, which in a former existence had been a candle. At least three dozen clove-scented incense sticks were inside the empty jar. Next to the file cabinet was a wooden bookshelf. Most of the commissioner's books—in Spanish, English, and French—dealt with religion. A hardbound copy of the Qu'ran rested in an appropriate place, on the right-hand corner of the top shelf. On top of the commissioner's desk was an old metal fan, from the late 1950s, its blades covered in a thick orangey-brown layer of rust. The protective grill bore witness to an era that predated child safety standards: the spaces between the metal rings were so far apart my entire arm could fit through.

Also on the desk were a pewter crucifix, eight inches tall, with a rosary of transparent light-blue beads wrapped around it; a Star of David; a jade statuette of Buddha; a Kachina doll, which, as I later learned, the commissioner had purchased while visiting the

Hopi in Arizona; several Aztec and Mayan stone idols; and a copper dish upon which Ganesha, the Hindu god of wisdom and luck, with a human body and an elephant's head, sat cross-legged. This last piece doubled as an incense holder. Although the sharp, sweet scent of cloves lingered in the room, on that morning there were no ashes on Ganesha's platform.

When the police commissioner stepped into the room, I was holding the Hindu deity in my hands, closely inspecting him. I carefully put Ganesha back. As I had guessed, the commissioner had been the officer taking the Englishman's statement. Gilberto Wong looked much younger than the sixty-two years he would later admit to being. He was thin, rather short, and of dark complexion. His eyes, although showing traces of a mixed racial heritage, still gave compelling testimony to the predominance of his Asian ancestry. The commissioner walked toward me with his right arm outstretched. As we shook hands, he thanked me for waiting and gave me a broad, engaging smile, the kind people usually reserve for old friends.

Because of everything I had heard about the commissioner prior to our first meeting, I had elevated him to mythic proportions.

"Commissioner Wong is a marvelous person," Mariela often said to me. "Without his help, I would have ended up in the psychiatric hospital."

"He's the kindest person I've ever met," said Gloria Obando.

"You know what I admire most about Commissioner Wong?" Don Erasmo Alemán asked me as we sat in his living room, surrounded by our countless reflections. "He's a keen judge of character, which is a unique gift. With the commissioner it's as though he can see right through anyone. Nothing escapes him. But he never sizes you up out of malice; he just does it to get to know a person better."

"Although there's a part of his past that I would normally find disturbing, which I'm not going to discuss with you," said Padre Uriel, "I have to admit that I respect the commissioner because of his professionalism. The people of this region are very fortunate because they have the best police chief in the country."

Indeed, to this day I find Gilberto Wong worthy of the admiration. He's human and makes mistakes like the rest of us, but when he errs it's almost always on the side of generosity. Very few Nicaraguans of Chinese descent remained in the country during La Revolución. After the Sandinistas came to power, the overwhelming majority of Chinese-Nicaraguans, fervent participants in the nation's commercial life, chose the uncertainties of exile over the sacrifices socialism asked of everyone. Of Gilberto's family, which consists of his mother, three sisters, and a brother—his father having passed away seven years before Somoza's fall—only he stayed in Nicaragua. Everyone else moved to Queens, New York, where they still reside. But on the morning of my first visit, I didn't ask the police commissioner a single question about his family's history. Instead, I opened our conversation by commenting on his eclectic collection of religious artifacts.

"Once upon a time," he said, chuckling softly, "I used to be a priest: a Jesuit, in fact. When I was still in the seminary I became interested in other religions, especially those of the Orient. My spiritual advisor warned me about the dangers of 'dabbling in alien belief systems.' But my grandparents taught me to honor all religions, so I never saw them as being at odds with one another. Thus, in spite of my advisor's concerns, I continued with my readings, particularly in the area of Buddhism."

"You and Thomas Merton," I offered.

"Funny you should mention that," Commissioner Wong said, smiling. He glanced at the ceiling with an expression of fondness. I instantly knew that he was visiting a place within his heart where pleasant memories dwell. Once the police chief of Niquinohomo had finished gathering his thoughts, he began to share his recollections. "When I was in the United States, taking graduate courses at Georgetown, I wrote a letter to Thomas. I was surprised, and delighted, to receive a reply. From that point on we started corresponding regularly. After exchanging letters for more than a year, he invited me to visit him at the monastery where he lived, in Kentucky. Of course, I accepted. He was truly a remarkable man. What most impressed me about Thomas was that he didn't fear new ideas or different ways of looking at the world. After my visit, we continued writing to each other—that is, until his death. I saved all of his letters."

We both fell into silence, contemplating the Trappist monk's tragic death while staring at the electric fan. Finally, the commissioner interrupted our thoughts, saying in a slightly trembling voice, "Thomas Merton helped me envision the oneness of life. At the same time, he taught me that reality is multiple. That notion is most useful in police work, you know."

"Commissioner, that brings up my next question, and I apologize beforehand because it's rather personal, but how did you go from being a Jesuit priest to becoming the chief of police of Niquinohomo?"

"You don't need to apologize for that question. I'm used to it by now. People ask me that every time they learn about my previous incarnation," the commissioner said, smiling. The amusement and warmth in his gaze made it difficult for me to believe that someone as gentle as the former Jesuit could survive unscathed in his profession. "When I was a priest," he went on, "I was a fierce advocate of liberation theology. I'm sure you're familiar with it. Those of us who subscribed to this notion wanted the Church to align itself with the poor and their plight. Liberation theology was the occupational hazard for clerics of my generation, and I took its call to heart, as did thousands of others who wanted the resources of the world to be distributed in a more just manner.

"After the Sandinistas came to power, I stopped working at the university, where I had been teaching comparative religion, so that I could minister to the people of San Judas, one of Managua's poorest neighborhoods. The residents there had been particularly hard hit during the struggle to bring Somoza down. By the time the fighting stopped, every house was riddled with bullet holes, or worse. Hundreds, possibly thousands, died in San Judas. We'll never know the exact numbers. Anyway, before long I was spending most of my time mediating disputes between neighbors. It seems that I have an innate talent for that, which was something I didn't realize back then. The commissioner in charge of San Judas heard about my work and started to call on me to help him with the more difficult cases. He'd ask everyone to relate their versions of an event, and then he would turn to me and ask, 'Now tell me, Padre Gilberto, who's lying?' I found the work fascinating, especially when he asked me to help him resolve serious crimes, such as murders.

"I find the investigative part of police work akin to meditating: once you strip away all the distractions, all the shadows, and all the lies, that which remains is what most resembles the truth. Soon, I was hooked and, to be honest with you, being a priest had started to make me feel as if I were always wearing a straightjacket. Besides, I was getting tired of the bitter infighting that was taking place within the Nicaraguan Catholic Church. I therefore requested permission to leave the priesthood. It was granted, and I've been a police officer ever since. In all truthfulness, I see this profession as just another way of pleasing God, as well as serving humanity to the best of my abilities."

"But, Commissioner, in your position you see our darkest deeds, day after day. Don't you find that exhausting? I know that I, for one, would sooner or later give in to despair."

"As a priest I listened to people's failings every day in the confessional. It's true that, on occasion, as a police officer I have to stare malevolence in the face. But my training as a priest helps me see this in the context of the ongoing battle between good and evil. And I absolutely believe that we can't allow ourselves to surrender to evil. In order to live in a loving society, it is essential for us to have faith in the ultimate triumph of good. We need to have that conviction, and I find that most people do. Otherwise, there would be mayhem and terror everywhere and merely walking upon this planet would be sheer hell, don't you think?"

"I couldn't agree with you more, commissioner. I hope you don't mind another personal question, but what's someone with your educational background doing here? I mean, you studied at Georgetown and, to be perfectly candid, Niquinohomo is not a community known for producing great thinkers, even if Sandino was born here."

"Police are no different than priests in the sense that we take a pledge to obey the orders of our superiors. That's how I first arrived, assigned here as commissioner. But it didn't take long for me to learn to love this city and the people who live here. After a couple of years in Niquinohomo, I requested to be stationed here permanently, for the few years that remain until my retirement, and my wish was granted. I now own a home, a simple one, really, in a quiet, wooded area on the outskirts of town. A stream runs through the property and I built a Zen garden near the banks that has turned out very nicely. There, I'm able to step away from the bleakness that sometimes creeps into this job. Every day, as soon as I get home, I step out into the garden, work on it for a little while, and then I sit there to enjoy the sound of the rushing water. This helps me meditate. At the end of each day, I try to clear my mind of everything that gets in the way of tranquility."

Commissioner Wong smiled, brought his hands together to rest on his lap, and said, "But you didn't come here to talk about me, did you? Tell me, how can I help?"

"Yes. I do suppose we'd better get down to business. But I thank you for sharing your story."

"You're welcome," he answered with a slight nod.

"Commissioner, I hope to write a novel based on the murder of Adela Rugama. You handled the investigation yourself. Do you remember that case?"

"I remember it very well. It was most unusual. Fortunately, we don't have many murders around here. The reason I personally took charge of the investigation was because I felt a great deal of sympathy for the surviving sister. That poor woman has gone through quite an ordeal."

"Commissioner, was Adela killed because she was a lesbian?"

"No . . . and yes," the commissioner said. He paused for a moment to reflect on the rest of his answer, closing his eyes as if in prayer. When he opened them again, I noticed that his gaze had become sad. He smiled wanly and continued. "On the one hand, the answer to your question would be yes because, if Adela Rugama had been your typical housewife, she would still be alive.

Gays and lesbians in this country have a difficult time with our narrow-mindedness. Nicaraguans can be bigots, and they will taunt you endlessly if you're different in any way. Thus, it's impossible for homosexuals to live their lives openly without being subject to a great deal of harassment. Our culture is homophobic, and it teaches us that it's perfectly acceptable to act hatefully toward gays and lesbians. Religions tend to endorse these prejudices; at least I know Catholicism does. The thought of homosexuality sickens all of us . . . or so we claim. But I believe that, secretly, we, as individuals, are very curious about what it would be like to love someone of the same sex. If we're honest with ourselves, we have to accept that all humans, at some point of our lives, are intrigued by the idea. Still, outwardly, in Nicaragua, if one wants to be considered a God-fearing member of society, one must condemn homosexuality by ridiculing, and, yes, sometimes harming those who are gay—psychologically and even physically. On the other hand, the answer to your question would be no. You see, Nicaraguans don't go around murdering women just because they're lesbians. What we do instead is try to make their lives as miserable as possible."

"If that's the case, Commissioner, what happened to Adela? Why was she murdered?"

"I think Adela was killed because she fell in love with a young woman who was surrounded by volatile people who were set to detonate at any moment. Sooner or later, because of the circumstances of Ixelia Cruz's life, someone, be it a man or a woman, was bound to die in that explosion. It's unfortunate that it had to be Adela. From everything I've learned she was a person who lived life to the fullest. Had I known her, I think that I would have liked her very much."

"Commissioner, in their statements to you, the killers kept referring to Adela as 'the *cochona*.' In fact, during the official interrogations, only one suspect called her by name. Why do you think they did that?"

"They thought they could use Adela's lesbianism as a shield to protect them from a prison sentence. In their minds, to kill 'a *cochona*' was not a serious offense. When I interrogated them, their general attitude was, 'What's the big deal? She was just a dyke.' They seemed to believe that they had performed a valuable community service and that the rest of us should be grateful to them for what they did."

"Were they surprised, then, when they were convicted?"

"Yes. Definitely. They thought they had an excellent chance of walking out of the courtroom free. After all, in their eyes, there was no harm in killing a freak."

FOURTEEN

The Marriage

"He loved Adela as much as any man could love a woman," Mariela said. She leaned back, closed her eyes, and reached up with her right hand to grasp the cords at the head of the hammock. I recall thinking how that simple gesture seemed to reflect Mariela's wish that her sister had been like most women, for if that had been the case, Adela would still be alive.

"Santiago was such a nice person. He was caring, hardworking, and handsome as well." At that moment a squealing herd of pigs passed in front of the house, their short, squat legs struggling to keep the fast pace set by the boy escorting them. He poked the animals with a sharply pointed stick to keep them from leaving the narrow footpath that runs between the abandoned train station and Mariela's house.

Once the herd had reached a distance such that the noise didn't interrupt our conversation, Mariela continued. "If there was any man who could've given Adela a normal life, it was Santiago Carvajal. For a while, *mi hermana* tried to be like everyone else, but in the end she had to be true to herself. I have to give Adela credit for at least trying. But, if you really want to know the truth, when she first left Santiago I was furious. I thought Adela was making a stupid mistake. I told her that she would never find another man like him: educated and from a good family. I really liked Santiago, and I still feel terrible about everything Adela put him through. He loved my little sister, and he tried to be a good husband."

Mariela shared this with me during our second meeting, but I wasn't able to interview Santiago Carvajal because he had somehow disappeared. It was as if Adela's former husband had walked into the dense green majesty of a rain forest, never to be heard from again. No one in La Curva or in any of the surrounding communities knew where he had gone. I learned that his family had moved far north, to Jalapa, a town close to the Honduran border, to escape the humiliation of their son's blunder. Santiago's parents knew that if they had remained in La Curva their disgrace, as well as the sound of laughter behind their backs, would linger for decades. But Santiago had not joined his family in their new hometown. Several people from La Curva had seen his parents since, always in Jalapa, but they steadfastly refused to disclose their son's whereabouts, saying that his marriage to "the *cochona*" was an abomination, an episode of their lives they'd rather forget.

I tried, in earnest, to find Adela's former husband. I asked everyone who had known Santiago where I might be able to locate him. But after four weeks of seeing people mournfully shake their heads and shrug their shoulders, I gave up on this quest, believing it as hopeless as the search for Las Siete Ciudades de Cíbola or El Dorado.

The unsolved mystery came to an end, however, at a gathering of my father's family.

Relatives from throughout Nicaragua congregated in Managua to celebrate the twenty-fifth wedding anniversary of my aunt Milagros, a nun, to her Divine Husband. Following the mass commemorating the day she took her vows, several of us stood in a cluster, drinking Rojitas, eating *boquitas*, most of them deep fried, and idly chatting. The group included an uncle who's a congressman representing the department of Chontales. When my relatives asked me how the research for my book was coming along, I jokingly mentioned my frustration at having lost a man who could have provided crucial information.

"What's his name? I probably know him. I know everyone," my uncle, the congressman, said.

My first reaction was to laugh out loud, thinking that he was joking: the members of my father's clan being notorious for pulling people's legs. But when I glanced around at the faces in the group, I saw that the rest of my relatives were nodding, waiting for me to state the name. "Very well," I consented. "The man I'm looking for is named Santiago Carvajal."

"I know him," my uncle answered immediately.

Again I laughed out loud, but of everyone in the group, I was the only one who thought that my uncle was kidding.

"Yes, I know Santiago Carvajal. I know him very well, in fact. He lives in my town: Santo Tomás. You said that he was from La Curva? Well, Santiago once told me that he grew up there. He doesn't talk much about his past, you know? I still remember the day he hopped off the bus with everything he owned packed into a single backpack. Can you imagine fitting everything you own into a bag? Santiago's been in Santo Tomás ever since. He's a good man: hardworking and respectful. He has a lovely wife, Miriam, and three daughters, the cutest girls you can imagine."

"What does he do?" I asked, becoming excited at the prospect of having finally found Santiago Carvajal.

"He owns and operates a *barata*. You know what that is, don't you, nephew, or have you been in the United States too long? It's a pickup truck with loudspeakers on the roof. A *barata* drives around a town making announcements like sales, funerals, what movie is showing at the theater, things like that. I hire Santiago every election to help get my name out there among the voters. He covers a lot of ground. Not only does he work in Santo Tomás, but he also drives around the streets of Acoyapa, San Pedro de Lóvago, Villa Sandino, La Gateada, La Libertad . . . all the other little towns in the area. From what I can see, he makes a decent living."

"I'd love to talk to him," I said, "but there's a problem. I suspect that he'll refuse to discuss anything having to do with that period of his life. What he went through, his marriage and the divorce, seems to be something that he and the rest of his family have done their best to erase from their memories."

"I'll have him call you. And don't worry, he'll talk to you. I guarantee it," my uncle added, smiling as he slapped me on the back.

Three days later, just as the congressman had promised, Santiago Carvajal called me. "I'll meet with you out of respect for your uncle," he said, letting me know from the onset that under ordinary circumstances he would have refused to discuss his first marriage. "He has been very good to me and to my family. At the least, I owe it to your uncle to have a short chat with you."

The problem now became that Santiago never left Chontales. That meant that I'd have to travel all the way out there to interview him, to a wild frontier most people in this country avoid. Even under the best road conditions, Santo Tomás is a five-hour drive from Granada, and with this trip taking place during the rainy season, it would take even longer because of the countless potholes that mined the highway, making it look like an asphalt version of the game Twister. Since it would be impossible for Si Dios Quiere to make it to Santo Tomás and back, my only choice was to use Nicaraguan public transportation, which, I can classify, with a clear conscience, as a form of torture, a blatant violation of human rights. In spite of the great affection I feel toward my relatives, and my deep appreciation for Chontales's stark, rugged, majestic landscape, I've always dreaded the journey out there.

I arrived for the interview a day early, knowing from experience that I would need several hours to recover from the jarring ride on buses with minimal leg space whose best years had been devoted to transporting schoolchildren in the United States. My joints throbbed throughout the night as I lay in the guestroom of my uncle's house, my body stubbornly clinging to the memory of the journey.

Early the next morning I accompanied my uncle to his hacienda, where he was to supervise the castration of twenty-two young bulls. When we arrived, they were peacefully chewing their cud, blissfully ignorant of their fate. That afternoon, after a delicious lunch of bull testicle soup, my uncle escorted me to Santiago Carvajal's house. He hurriedly introduced us and then left to attend to his constituents, mostly *campesinos*, who had formed a long line outside of their congressman's house, waiting their turn to plead for boons, both large and small.

Although Santiago was only in his late-thirties, his hair had turned silver-grey, which, in spite of being disconcerting at first, gave him a strikingly distinguished, aristocratic air. Immediately upon meeting him, I had to agree with Mariela's assessment: he was handsome. On Santiago's beckon, his three daughters, between the ages of eight and four, left their television program to greet me with a peck on the cheek. Then they returned to their respective spots on the living room floor, where they instantly became engrossed in a cartoon about a bizarre creature with square pants and a sponge for a torso.

Santiago escorted me through the house to his large backyard. Underneath an orange tree in full bloom were several folding chairs and a round, plastic table. I sat down and at once filled my lungs with the blossoms' tangy scent. Then Miriam, his wife, came out of the house carrying a pitcher and three glasses.

"I just made it," she said with a smile. "Freshly squeezed." Miriam was exactly as my uncle had described her: an attractive woman of light-complexion, who, if dressed in the latest fashions, wouldn't look out of place among Nicaragua's elite. Her large, amber eyes were both intelligent and mischievous. She was at least ten years younger than her husband, and in spite of their age difference, the spouses seemed perfectly suited for each other. After Miriam filled our glasses with lemonade, she placed a chair next to her husband's, sat down, and reached out to take hold of his hand.

I felt awkward, not knowing how to bring up the subject of Santiago's former wife with his current one sitting directly across from me. But Santiago Carvajal was not a man to waste time. Without preambles, he said, "Your uncle said that you wanted to speak to me about Adela."

I nodded and glanced at Miriam. Santiago then said, "Don't worry, Miriam knows all about my first marriage. I own a *barata*, remember? I'm aware of how fast news travels in this country. That's why I confessed all of my mistakes before I asked her to marry me. Better that she hear about them directly from my mouth than from someone else's, don't you think? My divorce has been the most painful experience of my life, and because of the heartbreak, I did a lot of stupid things, making a complete fool of myself. It's a horrendous feeling, you know? That's why I'm in Chontales today. Back then I was trying to run away from my past. I wanted to get as far away as possible from La Curva and find a place where I could bury my shame. And you know what? A person can hide in this part of Nicaragua forever. Think about it, who in their right mind wants to move to Chontales? But from the first moment I arrived here, I fell in love with this place. In fact, I've not set foot outside of the province since, not even to go to Boaco. People have tried to convince me to go to Managua, saying that I should see how much the city has changed over the years. They tell me that they've built a couple of modern shopping malls. But, you know something, I have everything I need right here, in Santo Tomás. Miriam and I have a very good life in this town, as do our girls." Santiago brought Miriam's hand to his lips, kissed it, looked into her eyes, and smiled.

"Santiago, you've renewed my faith in happy endings," I said. "I want you to know that I'm not here to revive old ghosts from an unpleasant past." I then told him about the book.

"As I said over the phone," he said, "normally I wouldn't have spoken to you about this. I'm a private man, and I insist on keeping the details of my life within the walls of this house. One scandal in this lifetime has been enough for me. But I do owe your uncle many, many favors. It's because of my debt to him that I've agreed to this meeting. But I also need to work to support my family and that means I've only got a couple of hours to spare for you."

"I appreciate that, Santiago. I promise to be brief. I'll begin with this question: When was the first time you heard about Adela's death?"

"Well, I had read in the papers that she was missing. Still, all along I had faith that Adela would turn up again, safe. You probably know by now that she knew how to take care of herself. Sadly, things didn't turn out that way. The first time I heard about Adela's death was on the radio. I was in the shower, getting ready for work. I was so stunned by the news that I had to lean against the wall to keep from falling. I have to admit that for several years after the divorce I was resentful toward her, but over time those scars had healed. And since I arrived in Santo Tomás, I started to pray for her happiness and for her to have found whatever she was looking for in life."

"Tell me about your relationship with Adela. How did you two meet?"

"I had just turned seventeen, the age when you think you know everything. I met her at a community dance. Adela was fifteen and had just moved to La Curva from Las Crucitas, where she had always lived until then. She was standing in a corner of the hall with a group of friends, all of them girls. From the moment I first set eyes on her, I knew there was something different about her. She was unlike any girl I'd ever seen. I mean, there was something boyish about her that, to be honest, I found very sexy. And although Adela wasn't beautiful, she certainly was pretty. I gathered up all of my courage and walked over to the group to ask her to dance.

"'Why should I dance with you?' Adela said, defiantly sticking out her chin.

"Because I'm the man you're going to marry." To this day I don't know what made me say that, but I do know that my answer caught Adela completely by surprise. She was speechless, which, let me tell you, was something that seldom happened. Adela always had a quick reply to everything. The other girls started to laugh, and one of them dared her to go dance with her husband. Another pushed Adela toward me, and before we knew it we were in each other's arms, swaying to a slow love song.

"After a couple of dances, we stepped outside and hid behind a *chilamate* tree. We had barely said a word to each other, but there we were, kissing passionately in the dark. From that night on, we'd get together every evening to talk, drink a few beers, and then find somewhere quiet where we could be alone. After only a few days, I was madly in love with her, and I thought she felt the same way about me. Since she was working on a coffee plantation, we decided to wait until the harvest season was over to get married. We needed money to do that, so I also took a job picking coffee. I wanted to become financially independent because my parents, who owned a clothing store in La Curva, were totally opposed to the idea of our marriage.

"'You barely know her, son. She may not be the right woman for you,' my mother would say.

"'*Muchacho*, be careful, please,' my father once said. 'I thought you were going to attend the university in León, to study medicine. You know that's what your mother and I have always dreamed of. And think about this as well. You said that she doesn't know how to read or write. Are you sure you want to spend the rest of your life with someone who's illiterate?'

"'Papá, if marrying someone illiterate was good enough for Rubén Darío, our glorious national poet, then it's good enough for me,' I told him. It's true, you know? Darío's last wife, Francisca Sánchez, a Spaniard, couldn't read or write. But he taught her how. Anyway, my mind was already made up. I was going to marry Adela Rugama and no one, no matter how hard they tried, was going to convince me otherwise.

"By the end of the harvest season we had saved enough money to pay for several months rent on a small, one-room place. We got married in Masatepe, in the courthouse, in a civil ceremony. Adela's family was delighted. From the beginning, they accepted me as one of their own. I liked them, especially her sister, Mariela. Unfortunately, my parents never approved of Adela.

"'There's something that's not quite right about her,' my father would say. 'You'll see, *muchacho*, something terrible is going to come of this. I can feel it.'

"Still, during the first six months of our marriage we were happy, or so I thought. But then, little by little, the way darkness slowly chokes the light out of a beautiful afternoon, Adela grew distant. She wouldn't talk much, she stopped laughing, and our lovemaking became strained, almost always ending in huge fights. I'd often ask her what was wrong, but she'd never give me a straight answer. That would make me angry because I knew that I had done nothing to lose her trust. After a few weeks of this, I turned to Mariela for advice.

"'Santiago, please be patient with her,' Mariela said as she gave me a hug. 'Adela gets into these terrible moods, but they never last long. You'll see. Be patient.'

"I tried being patient, but things only got worse. Soon after my talk with Mariela, Adela started to refuse to sleep in the same bed with me. She slept on the ground instead, on a thin straw mat. I couldn't believe that she preferred sleeping on the hard floor with nothing to cushion her. But what made things worse was that she wouldn't tell me why she was doing that. I kept on asking her what was wrong, but she never gave me a clear, honest answer. Then, one day, during a horrible fight, Adela said something that scared me.

"'You just wouldn't understand, Santiago. All I can tell you is that I'm very unhappy. This marriage isn't working out for me. I think it would be better if we got divorced.'

"But I was still madly in love with Adela. I couldn't stand the idea of losing her. All I wanted was for things to go back to the way they used to be. Following Mariela's advice, I did my best to be patient and understanding, but nothing changed. Adela grew even more distant, and then she became insistent that I give her a divorce.

"I then grew desperate. Shortly after our first wedding anniversary, to try to get Adela's attention, I decided to have an affair. In my mind, once she found out about it, she would want to save our marriage. But just the opposite happened. When Adela learned that I was seeing another woman, she packed her bags and moved back to Las Crucitas to live with her mother. Instead of fixing things, I had given her the perfect excuse to leave. The day after she left, Mariela came by to tell me that her sister wanted a divorce, and as soon as possible.

"Knowing that I had made a stupid mistake, I went to her mother's house to beg Adela to come back. She wasn't there. She knew that I would be coming, so she had left to visit some relatives in Rivas. Her mother, Doña Pastora, had been expecting me, and she said that we needed to talk.

"'Santiago, my boy, I think it would be best if you gave Adela the divorce.'

"'But, *señora*,' I said, 'I love her, with all my heart. I only took up with that woman because I wanted Adela to stop taking me for granted. I promise never to do that again. Please make her come back to me.'

"'I can't, Santiago. Nothing you or I say or do is going to make a difference.'

"Doña Pastora then told me that she and Adela had spent the whole night talking. The poor woman had implored her daughter, over and over, to take me back. She told her to forgive me because I was the best man she was ever going to find. But Adela kept on saying no. Finally, tired of making up excuses for wanting the divorce, Adela confessed the truth.

"'Mami,' she said tearfully, 'I'm a *cochona*. I don't like men. I like women.'

"Doña Pastora's reaction was to slap Adela. She called her daughter a pervert and ordered her to stop liking women. 'You have to go back with Santiago, and that's the last I ever want to hear about you being a *cochona*.'

"'I can't, mami. I tried to love him, but I can't. I don't have a choice. I don't know why, but I've always liked women. I can't change who I am, mami. Even if you slap me for the rest of my life, I will go on being a *cochona*. I have no choice. I've tried to change. I swear it, mami. I've tried. I married Santiago because he really loved me, and I thought that maybe with a good man I could get over my feelings for women. But I can't, mami. You have to accept it. Your daughter's a lesbian.'

"The members of Adela's family are poor, but that didn't stop them from being very close. They got together to discuss the situation. In the end they decided to accept her for what she was and not apologize to anyone. Adela then felt completely free to come out in the open.

"As for me . . . well, after we split up I descended into hell. My parents, who were successful merchants in La Curva, couldn't deal with the thought that I had dishonored them. They kept on telling me that I had ruined their reputation, forever. Not once did they take into consideration how I felt or what I was going through. They were far more concerned about what other people were going to say. That, in fact, became an obsession with them. When the word about what really happened got out, people started to act differently toward them. My parents then closed down the store and refused to leave the house. They wouldn't even open the door when their friends came to visit. The idea of people laughing at them because their son had married a *cochona* absolutely tormented them. A couple of months after Adela and I had split up, they decided to move to Jalapa, where most of my mother's relatives live. They ordered me to go with them, but I refused. I ran away to Managua instead, where I got a job in a print shop.

"But I wasn't doing well. I had started to drink a lot, and the boss fired me after only a few months. I then started to drift from town to town. I'd find a job, start drinking heavily, get fired, and then move on. When I arrived here, in Santo Tomás, the instant I stepped off the bus, I decided that enough was enough; I was not going to run away from myself any longer. For me, this town was the end of the line. I knew that I had to quit drinking or I'd die a broken man. Thankfully, I was able to pull my life back together. I started my business, met Miriam, and after a couple of years dating, we got married. It's now been fourteen years since I last had a drink. Because of that, God has rewarded me with a wonderful family and a great community to live in.

"As for Adela . . . . I never heard from her again. I never tried to find her, and she never looked for me. We were far too young when we got married. Like most kids who rush into a relationship, we made a mistake. I now realize that the way I handled everything was stupid, completely stupid. In spite of the breakup of that marriage, there was no need to put myself through so much misery.

"Yes, the moment I first saw Adela I knew she was different. In large part, that's why I married her. But I was too naïve back then to ever suspect that there were such creatures as lesbians on this planet. Over time, I've come to understand that Adela did us both a big favor by being honest. Just think about it, she could have strung out our marriage for years and years by never admitting to herself who she really was, right? I now know that what she did, to leave me and then come out in the open, took courage. After settling in Santo Tomás, whenever I'd think about Adela, I'd say a brief prayer for her happiness. I had come to accept that, all along, our marriage had been destined to fail precisely because she was a lesbian. But, to be honest, I never dreamed that being one would get her killed."

PART IV

Discoveries, Trials, and Funerals

FIFTEEN

The Discovery

Adela Rugama's body was found nearly two months after the Christmas Day she disappeared. Her remains had callously been dumped into a condemned outhouse on a nearby coffee plantation.

"I looked for my baby sister everywhere," Mariela said. The mere recollection of the exhaustive search seemed to leave her tired and spent. Three-and-a-half years earlier, Mariela's quest to find her sister had come at a great cost. "I was spending so much time looking for Adela that I was forced to quit my job. Because of this, I had to borrow money so I could try to find her. My brothers and I made a list of all of the relatives we could think of, and I went to see every one of them, hoping that they could give me some news about her. I spent a fortune on bus fares. I traveled to Masaya, Jinotepe, Diriomo, El Crucero, Managua, Tipitapa, San Rafael del Norte, Rivas, Matagalpa, Yalagüina, Corinto, and Chinandega to ask about Adela. But no one had heard a word from her."

Believing that perhaps Adela Rugama had been kidnapped, Commissioner Wong ordered his officers to conduct house-to-house searches in La Curva, Nandasmo, and Pío XII, paying particular attention to the homes of the suspects. He also ordered the police to search several nearby haciendas, all without success.

But every human effort, it seems, was destined to fail because, according to Mariela, her sister's body would never have been discovered without divine intervention. "After almost two months without any word from Adela, I was desperate. I barely slept, and I was crying all the time. Sometimes, without warning, my hands would start to shake, and, as hard as I tried, I couldn't get them to stop. My state was such that my daughters, Gema and Nubia, thought that I was going crazy. They were afraid that they were going to have to put me in the psychiatric hospital.

"Finally, one night, when I felt that I was on the verge of losing my sanity, as I was walking home from the bus stop after another long day of searching, I fell to my knees. Without thinking, I started to pray to the Virgin Mary. I was looking toward heaven, begging her for a miracle, when, suddenly, a shooting star streaked across the sky. I watched it closely and saw it come down right behind Don Roque's ceiba. At that instant I knew that Our Lady was sending me a sign. I was sure that if I walked in a straight line, right toward the tree, I would find my sister."

The next morning, before sunrise, Mariela climbed out of bed and started to get dressed. Gema woke up to the sound of her mother shuffling in the dark and asked where she was going.

"I'm going to find my baby sister. I know where she is now," Mariela said as she struggled to get an arm through the sleeve of her blouse. Once she had succeeded with this small task, she shared the mystical experience of the previous night with her eldest daughter.

"Gema ran to my cot and shook me until I was awake," Nubia told me as she fed spoonfuls of Quaker Oats to her three-year-old son, "'Mami has finally gone insane! She says that the Virgin gave her a sign last night, telling her how to find my aunt Adela.'"

"We knew we couldn't stop her," Gema said, continuing the story. "So we told my mother that we were going with her, and we asked her to wait while we filled a couple of bottles with water and packed some food. From what she had said, I knew it was going to be a long, long walk."

The sun had yet to rise fully when the three women left. The girls had trouble keeping up with their mother who walked at a brisk, determined pace in the direction of the ceiba. Although Nubia, who was six months pregnant, begged her mother to slow down, Mariela kept refusing.

"We can't waste time, not today," she'd tell them.

Because of Mariela's insistence that they walk a straight line, the women often had to cross through fences, with two of them holding the wires apart so the third wouldn't get scratched or have her clothes caught on the barbs. On that morning they traveled through cornfields, orchards, watermelon patches, pineapple fields, coffee plantations, *pitahaya* groves, and pastures where the cows stopped their grazing to gaze mournfully at them. Along the way the women passed several little ranches, and the people who lived in the palm-thatched huts stared wordlessly at the three, unaccustomed to seeing strangers strolling through their land.

After walking nearly eight kilometers, the girls had yet to find an indication that would make their mother's vision credible. Less than two kilometers remained before they would reach the ceiba. But Mariela never lost faith that on that journey she'd find Adela.

"The entire time we were walking," Nubia said, "my mother kept repeating, '*Muchachas*, keep your eyes open. The Virgin is taking us straight to Adela, but it will actually be up to us to find your aunt.' I thought she'd finally lost it. Mami went through a lot the entire time my aunt was missing, you know? But that day she proved me wrong." Nubia stopped feeding her son, rose from her seat, and walked around the kitchen table to stand next to her mother. Mariela looked up, smiled, and placed an arm around her.

Shortly before noon, Nubia said that she couldn't go on another step without some rest. Mariela agreed to stop, and they sat under the shade of an *almendro* tree to eat. Because they were so concerned—Mariela about finding her sister and the girls about their mother's mental state—they only nibbled on the *tortillas* and cheese they had packed for lunch. After only a fifteen-minute break, Mariela announced that it was time for them to move on.

Not long after resuming their search, the women helped one another climb through the fence that marked the boundary of the coffee plantation named La Dulzura: The Sweetness. That hacienda belongs to Don Rosendo Arellano, the wealthiest agriculturalist of the region and an influential politician. Mariela's daughters knew that they wouldn't get too far before Don Rosendo's workers would show up to escort them off the land.

But after walking only a short stretch from the property line, Mariela cried out, pointing toward an outhouse that had clearly been out of use for some time, "There she is!"

"Gema and I both looked toward the rundown shack and saw nothing," Nubia said. "'What did you see, mami?' I asked."

"'Your aunt Adela. She was right there, standing in front of the door of the *pon-pón*. As soon as she saw me, she went back inside the outhouse. Didn't you see her?'"

Both daughters shook their heads. They then discreetly glanced at one another, trying not to let their mother see their alarm.

"I should have known it was Adela's ghost," Mariela sighed. She took another sip of her lemongrass tea and continued the story, her expression somber. "At that moment I saw my sister almost as clearly as I'm seeing you, but there was something odd about her face . . . there was absolutely no emotion. She just wore a blank stare, and that wasn't like Adela at all."

Stirred by Mariela's vision, the women headed straight for the outhouse: a dilapidated, weather-beaten, wooden structure that Don Rosendo had ordered condemned three years earlier. The zinc sheet covering the roof was so badly rusted that it had the consistency of ancient parchment, crumbling at the slightest touch. The front door was ajar because of a missing hinge. The women stepped inside and saw that the platform and seat that had once covered the deep hole in the ground had been removed. Instead, a thick, plywood board had been carelessly placed over the opening, inadequately sealing it. Gema, with some help from her mother, lifted the board and propped it against the outhouse wall. Peering into the deep shadows, all they could see was trash. However, rising in an obscene, invisible cloud from the depths was a startling heavy stench: a smell of putrefaction so nauseating that it forced them to step out of the structure, and gulp desperately for fresh air. Of one thing they were now certain: there was something dead down there, decomposing.

Don Lázaro Guevara, foreman of La Dulzura, met me at the Three Dog Night: a cantina located on the outskirts of the city of Masaya (the lighted sign outside the establishment actually read

"Three Dog *Nigth*"). We discussed his memories of that day while he ordered Victorias, and I, Toñas.

"One of the workers came running to tell me that three women were poking around in the abandoned outhouse on the western edge of the hacienda. I hopped into the jeep and rushed over to see what was going on.

"'Hey, get out of there!' I shouted at them from the vehicle. 'You shouldn't be anywhere near that outhouse! It's dangerous! The earth around there can cave in at any moment.'"

"There's something in there that smells horrible. We want to see what's causing it," Mariela shouted back.

"Of course there's a bad smell. It's an outhouse! I don't have to explain what's in there, do I?" Don Lázaro answered.

"But it smells like something dead is in there. We need to see what it is," Mariela insisted.

"It's probably some animal that fell in the hole, a pig more than likely," the foreman said. "Now, please, get away from there."

"And then the woman walked up to the jeep to tell me the story of her missing sister. I instantly knew whom she was talking about. Everyone around here had heard about the disappearance of the *cochona*, but I never would've dreamed that the people who killed her would have the gall to dispose of the body on Don Rosendo's property. He's a man of influence, and to do that would be asking for a lot of trouble. But let me tell you, if I were going to get rid of a corpse, I would've chosen that outhouse as well. No one has been near that place in years, ever since we built a new one about half a kilometer down the path."

According to the foreman of La Dulzura, Mariela then said, "We looked inside but all we could see was trash. We want to go down there to get a better look. How do you suggest we do that?"

Don Lázaro scratched his head. Although he seriously doubted that Adela's body had been dumped in there, he knew that Mariela wouldn't give up until she was otherwise convinced.

"The only thing I could think of, really, was to have her pay one of my workers to go down there to see what was causing the smell. Although the woman was poor, you could tell that by the clothes she and her daughters were wearing, she immediately reached into her pocket and brought out, bunched in the palm of her hand, all the money she had," the foreman said as I signaled for the cantina owner to bring us another round of beers. For fifty *córdobas*—a little over three dollars—one of the plantation workers agreed to go down the hole to discover the cause of the ghastly odor. He wrapped a length of rope around a tree and tied the other end to his waist. Then, after tying a workmate's bandanna around his nose, he descended. Soon he was throwing out vast amounts of trash: plastic bags full of household garbage, bottles, cans, branches, leaves.

"Someone had thrown enough waste in there to fill a container" Don Lázaro said after taking a sip of his Victoria. "It took the worker such a long time to get all that stuff out of there that I had started to believe that the smell came from the rubbish itself. And then, suddenly, in an alarmed voice, the man called out:

"'Get me out of here! Quick! There's a dead body down here!'"

"'What exactly did you see?'" Don Lázaro asked once the man had been hoisted up.

"'A pair of Caterpillar work boots, and they're still attached to the body. The soles are facing up, as if that person dove in there head first.'"

A few days later, when I shared with Mariela what Don Lázaro had told me, she said, "When the man mentioned the Caterpillar work boots, I almost fainted. The girls had to hold me up to keep me from collapsing. But I knew then that my search was over. I had at last found my little sister." And she started to cry quietly as she recalled that awful moment, dabbing her tears with the handkerchief I offered her. "Once I had regained some of my strength, Gema and Nubia led me to a nearby lemon tree where I could sit and rest in the shade. It was strange, but at the time I didn't cry nor did I become hysterical. The only thing I cared about was getting Adela out of there. I kept on telling myself that once I was home, I could cry as much as I wanted. But getting my sister out of that filthy hole became, at that moment, the most important thing in my life."

Earlier, during our conversation at Three Dog Night, as the bartender brought us another round of beers, Don Lázaro had said, "As soon as I heard that there was a body in the outhouse, I climbed back into the jeep. I needed to call the police, and the nearest telephone was at the hacienda house. Then, just as I was about to pull out, the woman came running to ask for a favor: she wanted me to take one of her daughters to pick up a friend who lived in La Curva. She told me that she needed her there."

"I'm not sure why I felt that Gloria Obando had to be at my side," Mariela told me later. "Maybe it's because she had been the person who most supported me during those awful days when I was running around like crazy, looking for my sister. Also, I knew that Gloria had never stopped loving Adela. Anyway, the foreman was helpful; he said that he first needed to call the police, and then he would take Gema along to go get Gloria."

"When I got there," Gloria Obando said as Mariela and I sat in her living room, the two of them remembering that bitter day, "Commissioner Wong had already arrived, along with three of his officers. One of them, a woman, had a camera, and she was taking pictures of everything that had been pulled out of the hole. Once they had gotten the rest of the trash out, the smell became so bad that we all had to cover our noses with handkerchiefs. At last, the worker who was inside the hole tied a rope around the ankles, climbed out, and then, with the help of a policeman, he started to pull the body out. What happened next was horrible— I'll never forget it. They ended up with only the bottom half of Adela's body; it had come apart cleanly, right at the waist.

"Gema started to cry and scream hysterically," Gloria continued. "'Those murderers tortured my aunt before killing her! They cut her in half! What sons of bitches!' Then, very calmly, the Commissioner walked up to the remains, crouched down low, and examined them. After doing that, he walked back, stood next to Gema, put his arm around her shoulder, and gently said, 'I don't think your aunt was tortured. The body simply fell apart because it's so badly decomposed.'"

"The moment Commissioner Wong asked me to identify the body to see if it was my sister, the gurgling in my stomach started . . . and it hasn't stopped since," Mariela told me, staring at her teacup.

"When the commissioner asked Mariela to help with the identification of the body, she turned to me and said, 'Gloria, I can't do this. I know it will be difficult for you as well, but would you please make sure that it's Adela. I just can't do this.' I went to where the police were examining the remains. I really didn't have to look very long to know that the bottom half of that body did indeed belong to Adela. I instantly recognized the Caterpillar work boots, the white socks with light green trim, and the key chain that she always wore attached to the second belt loop of her jeans. But what broke my heart, what made me start sobbing loudly, was when I saw the brown leather belt, the one engraved with dragonflies that I had given her as a birthday gift five years earlier."

Over the telephone, Commissioner Wong shared with me his recollections of that mournful day. "Whoever disposed of the body had placed a large plastic garbage bag over the top half—the head and the torso—and then poured a generous amount of calcium oxide inside. Then, with speaker wire they tied it shut, right below the waist. As a result, the top half of her body decomposed within a few weeks. The flesh on the bone was in such a putrid state that, after we cut open the bag, we had no choice but to take the remains to a nearby water sprout and rinse everything with a hose. Now keep in mind that we don't have a single decent forensic laboratory in this country. If we did, I would've asked my officers to be much more careful. But we were also working in a difficult environment. Who knows what other evidence was left in that outhouse? We did the best we could, really. In any event, when we finished rinsing the skull, we could see, very clearly, a perfectly round bullet hole on the right-hand side of the cranium, slightly above the temple."

When the officers washed off the rest of the upper body, a blue-and-white checkered, long-sleeved shirt emerged—the shirt Adela had been wearing the Christmas she was murdered. Curious about what was causing the bulge in the right breast pocket, a police officer reached inside and pulled out a pack of Belmont cigarettes, still unopened. He then undid the buttons of the shirt, spread apart each flap, and began to rinse off the rest of the decay. Once this was done, there, glittering in the brightness of the noonday sun and wrapping itself like a silver snake around the loose bones of the rib cage, was a necklace. And attached to that, dangling from the sternum and dripping sparkling, crystalline beads of water, was the medallion of San Jorge, Adela's patron saint.

SIXTEEN

The Foundation

By all accounts, Adela Rugama's funeral stands out as one of Niquinohomo's most memorable. Because of Padre Uriel's turbulent relationship with the murder victim and because he believed that if he presided over the service people would perceive it as hypocritical, the parish priest of La Curva strongly urged Mariela to have her sister's remains buried elsewhere. Fortunately, Padre Lorenzo, of Santa Ana, Niquinohomo's main church, had no misgivings about allowing the murder victim to be laid to rest in that city's cemetery.

"He had heard people say that my sister had been a giving person. 'That,' he said, 'is the true meaning of a Christian life,'" Mariela told me, smiling at the recollection.

Almost every *niquinohomeño* came to witness the funeral. Crowds up to three rows deep lined the streets all the way from the church to the cemetery, which is located far from the center, on the city's western edge. But the people of Niquinohomo didn't show up out of respect for Adela or her family. Sheer curiosity, as well as the promise of a spectacle they would talk about for years, was what drew them there. On that day, the citizens of this community closed the doors of their businesses or left their afternoon household chores undone so they could gawk at the hundreds of gays and lesbians who, in a slow, grim procession, filed silently behind Adela's simple pine coffin.

"It was as if they had come from all points of the country to bury their queen," Commissioner Gilberto Wong told me. "And the mourners were angry. They wanted justice. All of Niquinohomo could feel their outrage. If a spectator had made the slightest taunt, I'm sure that my officers would've had to use force to break up a riot. But the *niquinohomeños* behaved, and Adela's funeral was a solemn, dignified affair."

During the latter weeks of my investigations, I had acquired the habit of stopping by the police station in Niquinohomo to chat with Commissioner Wong. If he had time to spare, we'd walk to the refreshment kiosk in Central Park, order a glass of *tiste* each, and sit at a table under the shade of the *guanacaste* tree. Ironically, we rarely spoke about Adela. Most of our conversations were about literature, spirituality, and Nicaraguan history. Still, on occasion, the subject of her murder would surface.

"I didn't realize that gays and lesbians in Nicaragua were so well organized," I commented to the police commissioner. "I understand that they attended Adela's funeral by the busloads and that they came from almost every region of the country. Who coordinated all that?"

"La Fundación Arco Iris—The Rainbow Foundation. Adela's case caught the attention of the gay and lesbian community when she was still alive," Commissioner Wong answered. "That happened when Ixelia's mother had the poor woman arrested in Masaya under charges of committing sodomy, which stems from an archaic law that makes homosexuality illegal in this country. It was then that the foundation intervened on Adela's behalf. I don't know much about the group, but I do know that they played an important role in getting her released. Afterward, when Adela was murdered, she became a symbol. During the trial, the leaders of the foundation appeared in the news every day, condemning violence against homosexuals. They placed a lot of pressure on the judge and jury to find the suspects guilty."

That same afternoon, I called the Rainbow Foundation at the number listed in the phone book. The person who answered identified himself as Dr. Alejandro Ortega, the organization's president. When I told him about my writing project, he became excited, and, at his suggestion, we agreed to meet me for lunch the following day at the T.G.I. Friday's in Managua.

I arrived early and sat on a bench in the front lobby to wait for Alejandro. To entertain myself, I studied every detail of the antiques that were tastefully arranged along the thick wood paneling on the higher reaches of the walls: an accordion; a bass drum; a scooter; a snow sled; a wood carving of the RCA Victor dog, who was listening intently to his master's voice; and a portrait of an obese baby, who in all likelihood had grown old and passed away long ago.

After twenty minutes, a broad-shouldered man, about six feet tall and carrying a thin leather briefcase, walked in. He had a startlingly wide, flat face, which was accentuated by one of the most pronounced jaws I'd ever seen. Without hesitation, absolutely certain about who I was, he walked toward me with his arm outstretched and greeted me with a firm handshake.

"I'm glad to meet you, and let me just say that I'm thrilled that you're writing Adela's story," Alejandro said, startling me by choosing to speak in English. Then, gesturing toward the dining area doors with an open palm, he said, "Well, I don't know about you, but I'm starving. Shall we go have lunch?"

As the hostess escorted us to our table, I noticed that Alejandro Ortega attracted many not-so-discreet stares from T.G.I. Friday's' lunch crowd, composed mostly of well-off Nicaraguans dressed in the latest Miami fashions. And the truth is that he'd turn heads anywhere with his narrow waist, his bright pink shirt, his light brown hair, streaked with glimmering blond highlights, and the stiff way in which he walked, the tips of his shoulders swinging back and forth as if he were a cardboard cutout.

"Good afternoon, and welcome to Friday's," our waitress said as she handed us our menus. She wore a striped referee jersey under a black vest and an oversized, shocking-pink vinyl cap, the color of which nearly matched Alejandro's shirt. The vest was covered with buttons. One of them proclaimed: *BALDNESS NOW HAS A SOLUTION.* I touched the top of my head, patted my thinning hair, and for a moment wondered if, indeed, this was true.

"Gracias, señorita. I don't need the menu. I know what I'm going to order. I'll have the St. Louis Barbecue Ribs, a whole order, and to drink, an Ultimate Hawaiian Volcano." Alejandro looked at me, smiled, and said, "I'm really famished."

I smiled weakly in reply because I suddenly realized that since I had initiated our contact, I should be the one paying for lunch.

The problem was that I had no idea how much money I had brought along. I only knew that several days had passed since I last visited a cash machine, and I wasn't sure I had brought my debit card along. To help ease my fear, I ordered the least expensive items on the menu: a club sandwich and an iced tea. I then quickly calculated what the amount might turn out to be, including tip, and began to wonder what I'd say to Alejandro if he ended up stuck with the bill. Temporarily setting aside my concerns, when our waitress departed, I thanked Alejandro for meeting with me.

"It's the Rainbow Foundation that needs to thank you," he said. Behind him, above the threshold that led into the kitchen and as part of the restaurant's decor, was a functioning traffic light. At that moment, it turned from red to green. "Nicaraguans need to learn to accept us. In this country, those of us who are gay have every right to live freely and in peace. I think that by writing this book you'll be holding up a mirror where people can see themselves for what they really are: homophobic bigots. Hopefully that will educate them, and they'll change. In telling people what happened to Adela, you'll be providing the community with an invaluable service. Now, how can I help?"

"Thanks, Alejandro. Well, it would be helpful for me to know something about the foundation, its history, and how you became involved in it."

"Of course. First of all, I don't want to seem immodest, but the foundation was my idea. Homosexuals in Nicaragua desperately need an organization to defend their rights. To get the foundation started I applied for funding from similar groups in the United States and Europe. Thankfully, several agreed to help. A few still contribute money; not a lot, mind you, but enough to keep our doors open."

"Why would you take on such a task? To me it seems daunting."

"That's easy: I do it because of the awful things I experienced as a homosexual growing up in Nicaragua. It's as simple as that. Having been raised in this part of the world I know how difficult life can be for gays and lesbians in Latin America. But the only way to change things is for us to join together and fight the blatant discrimination that exists here. That's what motivates me."

At that moment, the waitress brought our drinks. "Thanks, my love," Alejandro said to her. With the help of a straw, he took a long sip of the huge, bright red cocktail, keeping his eyes closed the entire time. Gradually, a smile appeared on his expansive face as he relished every second of the experience. Envious of Alejandro's order, I took a halfhearted sip of my iced tea. When I looked up, I saw the traffic light turning green again.

"Alejandro, I hope you don't think I'm prying into your personal life, but would you mind sharing some of your experiences growing up here? I'm trying to understand the difficulties that gays and lesbians face in this country."

"I'll gladly share them because I know they'll be of help. To begin with, I've always known that I'm gay. As far back as I can remember I've preferred men over women—romantically speaking, of course. But in a macho society, such as this one, I was forced to hide my feelings by pretending, in front of my friends, that I wanted to take every woman I set my eyes on to bed. But, in reality, all I wanted was to be close to a few of these friends (and I don't think I have to explain that any further). This schizoid existence was driving me insane. Emotionally, I was bursting at the seams, but if I wanted to survive in this culture, I had to keep my desire for other men locked deep inside of me.

"When I was sixteen," Alejandro continued, "I told one of my schoolmates that I was homosexual. Sadly, he failed to keep my secret. As the word spread, a group of boys who I once thought of as friends began tormenting me. Not only did they taunt me, but sometimes they'd push me around or, worse, beat me up. Then, one night, at a party where drinking had gotten out of hand, several boys grabbed me, held me down, and tried to rape me. Luckily I was able to make a big enough racket to draw the attention of the neighbors, and they had to let me go. But I've never been able to forget the terror of that episode."

The arrival of our orders broke the tension of Alejandro's story, and, instead, it was the enormity of his meal that stunned me. He sliced off a mammoth rib and proceeded to eat it with supreme control. I was amazed at his ability to keep his fingers immaculate, without licking them once in spite of finishing the entire slab. Throughout lunch, my mouth watered, and my club sandwich seemed unbearably dull in comparison. In between ribs, Alejandro continued telling his tale.

"When I graduated from high school, in the late 80s, the Contra War was still going on. By then I was so fed up with this place that I fled for the United States. Once there, I claimed that I had escaped Nicaragua to avoid the Sandinista draft. I was immediately given temporary residence until the war ended. But I never intended to come back. I blamed all of my misery on my country.

"Fortunately, I had attended a bilingual school for most of my life. That meant that I could set my sights on going to college. I chose the University of Idaho because I wanted to be as far away as possible from Latinos. That's how resentful I had become.

"It was difficult for me to adjust to the United States. For several years I believed that all gringos were cold and uncaring. On top of that, I was far from coming to grips with being gay. Luckily, during my second semester I enrolled in a psychology course. I immediately fell in love with the field. Just think about it: in what other area can you be your own subject? Well, perhaps writing, right? Anyway, I became so absorbed with analyzing myself that I never stopped taking classes until, one day, ten years after I had started, I found myself with a doctorate in clinical psychology. And you know what? At the end of my studies, in spite of everything I had learned, I was still having trouble accepting my gayness. But while I was in graduate school, I had a couple of loving, rewarding relationships—with other men, of course.

"And then something unexpected happened: a Panamanian university offered me a teaching position. And, to be honest, I had started to miss living in Latin America, particularly the pace of life here. So I accepted. Professionally, I couldn't have done better for myself. I was now a full-fledged college professor, which was something I never dreamed possible.

"Inside of me, though, the agony continued. I was terrified to come out in the open because I could still recall, very vividly, how cruel people from here can be if you're different, in any way, worse yet if you're gay. In this part of the world, children and adolescents will call you 'fag' to your face, shouting it in the middle of the street for everyone's benefit, just to torment you. Because I was afraid, I ended up going deeper into the closet. Needless to say, I was miserable."

"Is everything all right?" the waitress asked. Glancing behind Alejandro, I saw the traffic light quickly go from yellow to red.

"Yes, my love," Alejandro answered.

"Can I get you anything else?" she asked.

"Of course you can, my angel. I'll have a brownie for dessert."

"And what about you?" the waitress asked me. "Nothing. I'm fine. Thanks," I answered. I started to worry again, hoping I had my debit card with me. And now I was pretty sure that I didn't have enough cash to cover the bill. As the waitress turned to leave, Alejandro resumed his story.

"The farce my life had become came to a head the night I lowered my guard and visited a gay club in El Casco Viejo, the old sector of Panama City. I went dressed as a woman, which, to be candid, is one of the things I often enjoy doing. The club had a great reputation for being discreet, so I thought that I'd be safe. But as I was leaving, on the way back to my car, in spite of the dress, the wig, the high heels, and the makeup, a group of male students who were coming out of a nearby disco stared until one of them recognized me. They surrounded me and threatened that if I didn't give them all A's they were going to tell everyone at the university that I was a cross-dressing faggot. Well, the thought of being outed like that horrified me.

"That night I actually thought about killing myself. I drove to La Boca, parked, and started to walk across the Bridge of the Americas, wondering whether I should jump off. But then, as I stood at the railing, looking out over the Pacific Ocean, the sun started to rise. (Yes, in Panama City the sun comes up over the Pacific; the way the country is laid out is bizarre; it doesn't run up and down like the rest of the continent.) Anyway, at that moment, I had a surprisingly simple yet profound revelation. I realized that everything would be fine if I just was true to myself. Since then, I've been open about my homosexuality, living my life fully as a gay man. And, for the first time ever, I can say that I'm happy."

We remained silent for a while, reflecting on the lessons of Alejandro's story. Finally I asked, "When did you return to Nicaragua?"

"About a year after the bridge incident, which was five years ago. My mother, bless her heart, wasn't feeling well at the time, so I moved back to Nicaragua to keep her company. I've been living with her ever since.

"Shortly after my return, I noticed that the vast majority of gays and lesbians here were having great difficulties coming to terms with their sexual identity. The suicide rate for gays is alarmingly high. Because of this, I opened a private practice that specializes in counseling homosexuals. I'm pleased to say that it's been very successful.

"Another thing I observed was that gays were dispersed. They weren't united and, because of this, they didn't have any means of advocacy. That made gays an easy target for acts of violence, as well as for other forms of anti-gay prejudice. Those challenges are what inspired me to start the Rainbow Foundation.

"In addition to providing counseling, the foundation documents and monitors every case in which our rights are violated. We also ask our members to be forthcoming about their homosexuality. When we do this, our lives gain a greater purpose, and we're able to educate others. The foundation is always urging homosexuals to rebel, to defy every prejudice and religious belief that harms us, until Nicaraguans fully accept us.

"Now, I'm delighted that you're writing this book. Adela's murder was a horrible tragedy. What makes it worse is that Adela never got the justice she deserved. But if you write her story, then maybe her death won't have been in vain. So, let's get to work. What else do you need to know?"

"I appreciate that, Alejandro. Well, to start, tell me about the relationship between Adela and the foundation."

"In Nicaragua, there's a law on the books that defines sodomy as 'any unnatural sexual practice' or as any sexual behavior that can be construed as 'scandalous.' Under those terms, a married heterosexual couple making loud, passionate love in their bedroom, if denounced by a neighbor who is offended by their behavior, can be charged with committing sodomy. It's a completely idiotic law.

"In Adela's case, this is what happened: Ixelia's mother went to see a lawyer to find out if there was anything she could do legally to keep Adela away from her daughter. The lawyer told the mother about this law and that same day she went to Masaya to file sodomy charges, arguing that Adela was making her daughter perform unnatural acts as well as compelling her to behave scandalously in public.

"In order to file the accusation, though, the mother had to drag Ixelia along and force her to testify. She made a threat so terrifying— Ixelia never revealed the particulars—that the poor girl had no choice but to go along with the plan. Then the judge, a retrograde, petty homophobe, issued a warrant for Adela's arrest. Within hours, the poor woman was pacing back and forth in a jail cell."

"How long was she in there?"

"Twenty-three days. Can you believe that? And even then, at the time of her release, that asshole of a judge hadn't set a trial date. If the Rainbow Foundation hadn't intervened, Adela could've been kept locked up for several more weeks.

"In the meantime, the judge and the police chief of Masaya allowed the director of prisons to transfer Adela to the men's facilities. They thought it was the funniest thing. The director went as far as to tell Adela that that's where women like her really belonged. Incredible, isn't it? She spent a week locked up in a cell filled with the worst kind of criminals. It was a terrifying experience for her; she told me so. Fortunately, a group of prisoners placed her under their protection and kept the others from harming her. Still, while Adela was in there, she was teased, threatened, and ridiculed without mercy. But, like I said, she was well protected."

At that moment, the waitress came to see if we needed anything else. At last, Alejandro answered no, and I then asked her to bring me the bill. Alejandro excused himself to go to the restroom, during which time I was relieved to discover that I had brought my debit card along. As soon as Alejandro returned, we resumed our conversation.

"So, how did the foundation first become involved in the case?"

"Because of Mariela. The entire time Adela was in prison, Mariela had been running around from government office to government office, desperately trying to get her sister out. Then, when Adela was transferred to the men's prison, Mariela nearly went out of her mind, thinking that something horrible might happen to her sister. She went to the offices of a local human rights organization to file an official complaint, and it was there that someone told her about the foundation. Then, Mariela came straight to my office. As soon as she finished telling me the story, I started to mobilize our volunteers. One of our activists must have scared someone high up in the judicial system, probably threatening to force him out of the closet, because less than two hours after Mariela's visit, Adela was on her way back to the women's prison."

"And what role did the foundation play in her release?"

"First of all, we can't take all the credit for that. By far, Mariela did most of the hard work. You know, I greatly admire her. That woman is a fighter. She did everything humanly possible to free her sister. Our role after Adela was sent back to the women's facilities was to help Mariela find good legal counsel. We also contributed some money for the attorney's fees, but not as much as I would have liked. Our budget is limited, you know. The sad thing is that Mariela had to sell Adela's most prized possessions to raise the money for her release. These were things that, as I understand it, Adela had bought with a lot of hard work and sacrifice. The poor woman lost her stereo, her television, her bicycle, and most of her furniture. I still get angry when I think of everything Adela was forced to give up just because of that stupid law. But do you want to hear something interesting? In the end, it wasn't the money or the efforts of the attorney that got Adela out . . . it was the girlfriend."

"Ixelia? I thought Ixelia was the one who filed the complaint to begin with."

"Yes, she did file the charges against Adela, but only because her mother threatened her. Ultimately, her love for Adela won out over her fears. Mariela brought Ixelia to my office and asked her to tell me her side of the story. 'Tell the truth this time,' Mariela ordered. What the girlfriend told me was so astonishing that I immediately called the lawyer and asked her to draft a letter and include it with a new motion for Adela's release. I brought a copy of it along with me. I think you'll find it interesting."

Alejandro reached into his briefcase and, very carefully, as if he were handling a document of immeasurable value, pulled out a sheet of paper. The letter was typed on legal paper, notarized, and addressed to the judge who had ordered Adela's imprisonment.

Your Honor:

I do not have the academic background to address you properly. Because of this, I have asked the attorney to write down my story and present it to you in the best language possible. I thank her for this.

As you know, I made a declaration a few weeks ago against Adela Rugama, accusing her of sodomy. I now wish to tell you the truth in the hope that you will drop the charges and set her free. The reason I accused Adela of sodomy was because my mother threatened that if I didn't she would harm both Adela and me, physically. I believe that my mother is capable of horrible things. She has exploited me ever since I was eleven, pairing me with any man who was willing to pay to have sex with me. As you can see, I've been abused most of my life and that's why I live in fear.

Although society condemns lesbians, I have to confess that it has only been with Adela that I have felt fulfilled. She has taken care of all my needs: emotional and economic. But my mother doesn't care if I'm happy or not. She's insistent that I go back to live with Roque Ramírez. I do not want to do this. I don't love him. Therefore, I have refused. And if my mother continues insisting on this, I will take my own life. I only want for my mother and Roque to leave me alone and to allow me to live in peace.

Because I'm frightened about what they might do, I've decided to end my relationship with Adela. This situation has become very dangerous, and I fear what might happen. I still love Adela with all my heart, but I feel that neither of us will be safe as long as we're together.

I thank you for your time, and I request that you release Adela Rugama at once. She's innocent of the crime for which she has been imprisoned.

Respectfully,
Ixelia Cruz

I let out a long, slow stream of breath once I had finished reading the letter. "Quite prophetic, isn't it?" I said to Alejandro as the traffic light behind him turned red.

"It sure is. As soon as the lawyer had taken the girl's statement, we rushed to the judge's office. He read it without saying a word, looking uncomfortable the entire time. But to his credit, he immediately ordered Adela's release. I was with Ixelia and Mariela when Adela walked out of the prison. There were tears, hugs, and kisses all around.

"'Let's go home,' Adela said as we were leaving the prison. Walking next to Ixelia, she reached out and placed an arm around her shoulders. Although Adela looked as if she had been through a terrifying, exhausting ordeal, she was grinning ecstatically, and she couldn't take her eyes off of Ixelia. 'Yes, I'm ready to go home with you, my love.'

"'No, that's not possible,' Ixelia answered. Rather brusquely, she removed Adela's arm and stepped away.

"Adela stopped in her tracks, standing there completely dumbfounded and with her mouth wide open. At last, when she recovered her speech, she asked, 'And why not, woman?'

"'I'm afraid that if I go back to live with you, one of us is going to end up dead. It's over between us, Adela. We can't see each other anymore. Please stay away from me. That's the way it has to be. I can't go on like this anymore.'

"And with that, Ixelia turned and walked away. After twenty-three long days in prison, being reunited with her girlfriend should've been one of the happiest moments in Adela's life. But when I looked into her eyes, I saw that, at that moment, she would've preferred to have died while in jail."

SEVENTEEN

Smokescreens

A s soon as Adela disappeared, the culprits set into motion an elaborate ruse designed to convince everyone that she was still alive. The hoax had undoubtedly been concocted before the murder, and for several weeks it was successful.

"That's the main reason I waited so long." As Mariela said this, she resolutely locked her gaze onto mine, defying me to question the correctness of her decision to wait nearly a month before going to the Niquinohomo police station to report her sister's disappearance. I didn't take her defensiveness personally. I could easily imagine how difficult it must be for Mariela to justify, especially to herself, the reason she postponed filing a missing person's report. "Although deep down I knew that something terrible had happened to my sister, I very much needed to believe the lies those three were spreading; I desperately wanted to believe that she had run off to Costa Rica, like they were saying. Everyone knew that Adela always talked about moving there. She liked to say that it would be easy for her to find work. And during the last months of her life, Adela kept repeating that she wanted a new start, far away from all the crap she had to put up with here."

In this drama of deception and concealment, the murder suspects played their roles to perfection. The messenger, Arquímedes Guadamuz, alias the Curl, visited all of Adela's relatives and friends to ask if they had heard from her. He told them that she had promised to call him as soon as she arrived in Costa Rica but that she hadn't done so yet.

"The Curl came by the house at least three times, while my mother was out, to ask if we knew anything about my aunt," Nubia said as her three-year-old boy slept in her lap. "He said that he needed a telephone number where he could reach her to remind her to wire the money that she owed him."

173

"The Curl became a nuisance. He'd drop by at least three times a week to ask if I had heard from Adela," Lizbeth Hogdson told me as she sold an ounce of Epsom salts to the mother of three young children. The woman intended to cleanse their insides with a purgative. "Every time the Curl came by he'd say that I should let him know at once if I heard anything from Adela because he urgently needed to speak to her. I really don't like to be around that man. Those dark, beady little eyes of his are almost as frightening as Doña Erlinda's. They both give me the creeps. Plus that habit of his drives me crazy; you know how he's always pushing back the spiral of hair that dangles over his forehead. "

Padre Uriel, during a brief conversation we had one afternoon near the footpath that leads to the church's rectory, said, "I had to ask Arquímedes to stop coming by the church. He started showing up several times a week to ask me if I had heard anything from Adela. Now, of all the people Adela could contact, why would she choose me? It's no secret that we didn't really care for one another. The last straw was the morning that Arquímedes burst into the church while I was in the middle of a baptism. There were at least twenty people there, family and friends of the parents. He had the nerve to interrupt the ceremony to ask me if I had heard from Adela. I told him to get lost and never return . . . and he didn't."

Don Roque Ramírez, on the other hand, played a discreet part in the farce, but it worked to perfection. "On Christmas night the *cochona* came by my house to ask me for a loan. I gave her a thousand *córdobas* so that she could get on the Ticabus and head the hell out of here for Costa Rica. I was so sick of that woman that I would've gladly emptied my wallet if it meant that I'd never see her again," the *hacendado* told his fellow card players. And these men, every single one of them, believing that Don Roque had told them the truth, spread the news about Adela's flight into exile.

"What made me believe that Adela was in Costa Rica, and it made Mariela believe the same as well, was a letter I received, supposedly from her," Gloria Obando, midwife of La Curva, told me during another of my visits. "In that message, Adela said that she was doing fine and looking for work. The envelope had a postmark from San José. I still don't know how they managed to do that. But the letter had certainly been mailed in Costa Rica. That raised my hope that Adela was indeed alive and well. But I also had my doubts because, deep in my heart, I knew that she would have never left without saying goodbye to me in person."

At least twice a week after that fateful Christmas, Doña Erlinda Cruz would drop by La Curva, demanding to know Ixelia's whereabouts. She, of course, accused Mariela's sister of running off with her daughter.

"Five times she came by to yell at my mother," Nubia said, reaching out to hold Mariela's hand. "That horrible woman would stand in front of our house, drawing the attention of all the neighbors, and insist that we tell her where my aunt Adela was hiding. She was also running around the town saying that she was going to file kidnapping charges against my aunt. At the time, I thought the whole thing was terrifying. I honestly expected that any day Doña Erlinda would show up with her machete and chop us all into bits. I was so scared of that woman that it never crossed my mind that she was faking everything, that it all was part of a big show."

"That woman was so scandalous. She'd show up during the hours when my store is usually full and demand that I tell her where Adela was hiding," said Lizbeth, the woman from Pearl Lagoon, her gaze turning hard at the memory. "A couple of times she acted so crazy, glaring straight at me with those eerie, demonic eyes of hers, that she frightened all of my customers away. And during every visit she'd yell so loudly that the neighbors would come out of their houses to find out what was going on."

"I know that you're a good friend of the *cochona*! Tell me where she is, or else! I mean it! Return my daughter this instant!" Doña Erlinda would angrily command before the gathering crowd.

"Let me tell you," Lizbeth went on, "that woman could act. She had me convinced that Ixelia had run off with Adela. And, you know, I was happy for them. They deserved a decent, peaceful life together."

In spite of the sterling performances given by the culprits in Adela's death, many claim that it was Ixelia Cruz who deserved the top acting award. Half of the people who are well versed in the case believe that she knew beforehand about the plan to murder her former lover; the other half believes that she was innocent, knowing nothing. Regardless, the murderers' house of cards came tumbling down the day that Don Erasmo Alemán discovered that Ixelia was still in Nicaragua, that she had never left the country.

"I was shopping in Masaya. I go there about once every two months because they have the only supermarket that's worth a damn in this region. But I also like going there because of the open air market. A couple of merchants sell interesting mirrors, and I'm always on the lookout for those things. Anyway, I'm in the cleaning products aisle of the supermarket, looking for Windex, when who should I bump into? Ixelia Cruz.

"'*Muchacha*, where have you been? Everyone's looking for you, especially your mother. She's driving people crazy, demanding that they tell her where you are. And where's Adela? People are saying that you ran off with her to Costa Rica. Is that true?' I asked. To be honest, my comments seemed to take Ixelia completely by surprise. I don't think she was acting, like a lot of people say.

"'Don Erasmo, I have no idea what you're talking about. My mother knows perfectly well where I've been all this time. The morning after Christmas she sent me to Ometepe, where she got me a job on a coffee plantation. She ordered me to stay there until she sent for me. But, Don Erasmo, there's not much to do around there, you know? I soon got bored to death, so I decided to return on my own. I'm just now getting here. I haven't even been to La Curva yet. I was planning on hiding out in Masaya because if my mother finds out that I came back on my own, she'll kill me.'

"You know," Don Erasmo said to me, "I don't understand how a person can get bored in Ometepe. It's one of the most beautiful places in the world: an unspoiled island on Lake Nicaragua. I could spend all day sitting on the beach and staring at the twin volcanoes. It's paradise, really. If I had to do it all over again, I would've moved there when I left Granada, instead of ending up here in La Curva. Anyway, I told Ixelia that her mother was going around accusing all of Adela's relatives and friends of kidnapping her.

"'Why would she be saying that?' Ixelia said, but she seemed to be talking to herself. 'She knows where I've been all this time.'

"'I don't know, young lady,' I answered. 'But what I do know is that everyone is talking about you and Adela, wanting to know where you two have been hiding. All I can say is that once you get home you're going to have a lot of explaining to do.'"

"When Ixelia returned from Ometepe, instead of going to her mother's house in Nandasmo, she came straight to ours," Gema told me, recalling the moment when the family began to grasp the reality of that dreadful situation.

"'Mariela,' Ixelia said, 'please, tell me that you know where Adela is.'

"My mother answered that she didn't know. She told Ixelia that she was hoping that the two of them were in Costa Rica. That's when Ixelia began to cry. She was sobbing so hard that it took a long time before she could speak again. Finally, when she did, she said, 'Mariela, I think something terrible has happened to Adela.'"

Fifty-seven days after that fateful Christmas and twenty-seven days after Ixelia's return, Mariela's worst fears were confirmed. As soon as the police had recovered Adela's body, Commissioner Gilberto Wong ordered the arrests of the three suspects.

"From the moment I began investigating Adela Rugama's disappearance," Commissioner Wong told me, "I was certain that she had been killed. Plus, I was absolutely sure that the only three names on my list of suspects were responsible for her death. Let's face it, these people did not plan the perfect murder . . . no, far from it. The problem was that I couldn't arrest anyone until I had concrete evidence that a murder had been committed. Still, before the body was found, I was able to bring them in for questioning. But throughout the interrogation they stuck to their story, saying that Gloria Obando had a letter that proved that Adela was in Costa Rica.

"From the onset of the investigation," the commissioner continued, "I was absolutely clear about the roles each of them had played in the murder. The woman, Erlinda Cruz, had done most of the planning. The fellow everyone calls the Curl had sprung the trap, delivering the message that lured Adela to her death. And Roque Ramírez was the executioner as well as the person in charge of disposing of the corpse, perhaps with the help of the messenger."

After the suspects were arrested, Commissioner Wong asked that Ixelia Cruz also be brought in for questioning. "She may have not known that they had planned to kill Adela, but I think she knew that something was going to happen to her former girlfriend.

"I was surprised when Ixelia showed up with an attorney. For me that was a clear indication that she knew something and that her mother and Roque Ramírez had ordered her to keep quiet. When I asked her a question, she'd turn to her lawyer, and they'd whisper back and forth. On these occasions, her answers were concise and to the point. But, in a few instances, Ixelia answered my questions spontaneously, not giving her replies much thought. It was then that I gained some insight into her character.

"We'll never know exactly how much Ixelia knew. That question will linger for eternity. But of one thing I'm sure," the chief of police of Niquinohomo continued, "the day Ixelia was brought in for questioning, that young woman did everything possible to distance herself, and her mother, from the crime. Throughout the entire interrogation, she acted as if Adela had never been an important part of her life, disavowing any feelings, past or present, for the victim."

"'Do you know why Adela was murdered?' I asked."

"'No, I don't,' Ixelia replied after consulting with her attorney."

"'Did you suspect that she was going to be murdered?'"

"Ixelia again consulted with her attorney before replying, 'I knew the *cochona*'s life was in danger. Roque hated her, and he told several persons that he was going to kill her. But I never thought that the old man would go through with his threats.'"

"'Were you involved in planning or committing the murder?'

"'No, of course not! I had nothing to do with it!' Ixelia answered without consulting the attorney. She looked at me in horror, as if she couldn't believe that I had dared to ask that question."

"'Was your mother involved in planning or committing the murder?' I asked."

"'No, definitely not. My mother is innocent. I swear that I'm telling you the truth,' she said. She formed a cross with the thumb and index finger of her right hand and kissed it. 'The old man murdered the lesbian, with the Curl's help. But, Commissioner, listen, I hope you won't make a big deal out of this. After all, it's not like someone normal was killed. No, Adela wasn't normal. Everyone knows that she was nothing more than a *cochona*.'"

EIGHTEEN

The Trial

Considering the multitudes that poured into Masatepe to witness the trial, the judge, Leticia Solórzano, performed an outstanding job of maintaining order throughout the five days of legal proceedings. I met Judge Solórzano shortly after starting my investigation: on the day I went to the courthouse to request copies of the trial transcripts. In order to have access to these, I needed her signature.

A clerk took the form into the chamber; when she returned, she said, "Judge Solórzano wishes to speak to you."

Worried that the judge may have decided to refuse my request, I glanced back at the attorney I had hired to help me file the petition. In response to my look of distress, the lawyer, an eager young man who had just recently graduated from law school, shrugged his shoulders and began to wave his hands nervously in the direction of the judge's office, urging me to hurry and comply with her wishes.

The clerk led me into the chamber, invited me to take a seat, and said that Judge Solórzano would be joining me shortly. The magistrate's battered desk had evidently seen many years of service, probably dating back to the days of the Somoza dynasty, before La Revolución. Although I was fearful about having to argue my own case, my concerns were cast aside the moment I noticed the largest collection of crystal animals I had ever set eyes on: a sparkling, translucent display of most of the passengers on Noah's Ark. On a table to the right of the desk, the judge kept elephants, leopards, tigers, jaguars, cows, anteaters, horses, camels, dogs, monkeys, giraffes, parrots, lions, llamas, chickens, condors, emus, crocodiles, cats, eagles, and iguanas, among many others. I had risen from my seat to take a closer look at the menagerie when the judge, Leticia Solórzano, walked in.

"Thank you for taking a moment to chat with me," she said, walking toward me. Her right hand was outstretched, and she offered me a disarmingly friendly smile. Judge Solórzano was an attractive woman in her early sixties. She dressed with discreet elegance, avoiding the ostentatious attire that most upper-middle-class Nicaraguan women succumb to in order to make others aware of their social standing. Leticia Solórzano's openness took me by surprise, and at once I lost any fear that she would deny my request. "I asked you into my office because I'm dying of curiosity to know why anyone would want copies of the transcripts of this case."

When I informed the judge that I intended to write a book about Adela Rugama's murder, her smile broadened. "You know something? . . . I always thought this case would make a good novel. When will the book be out? I'm already eager to read it."

"In about five years, I hope," I answered.

"Why so long? Please, don't take so long," she said, placing her hand on my forearm. A swell of guilt overcame me, and once again the stern inner voice of my conscience reproached me for being a writer who works at a sluggish pace.

"I'm sorry, Judge Solórzano, but I estimate that it'll take about two years to write the book, and then it will be at least another three years before it's in print. That's because my work is published in the United States, and these things take much longer there. It's a dreadfully complicated business. Also, I write in English, so if you don't read that language you'll have to add another couple of years before the translation comes out," I said, apologizing for the delay before I had written a single word.

We spoke only briefly that morning, as the judge had to be back in court within a few minutes. But that short amount of time was enough for me to sense that Leticia Solórzano was a compassionate person who was deeply committed to doing her share to make the world a better place.

Later, when I asked others their opinions of her, I learned that the judge had a sterling reputation. Everyone, without exception, considered Leticia Solórzano to be fair and impartial in the courtroom. In fact, even though she had known both

Doña Erlinda and Don Roque for years, neither the prosecution nor the defense objected to her presiding over the case.

Still, in spite of sitting behind the judicial bench for more than twelve years, Leticia Solórzano had never presided over a case that stirred such interest. Early each morning, for the duration of the trial, the streets of downtown Masatepe would become jammed as vehicles from every possible news venue competed ferociously for the parking spots nearest the courthouse. Radio stations provided their listeners with regular updates. Television news programs sent their star reporters to cover the event. Newspaper journalists and photographers poured into the city, notebooks and cameras in hand, ready to keep their readers informed of the tantalizing circumstances of this case. For the first time in her career, Judge Solórzano had to reserve most of the seating in her courtroom for the press.

The avid interest that the murder trial sparked was certainly extraordinary, but what turned it into an occasion that the *masatepeños* will talk about for generations were the five busloads of gays and lesbians that invaded the town to monitor the proceedings. From the moment the homosexuals first arrived in Masatepe, they took command of the Central Park, across the street from the courthouse, turning it into their base of operations. They'd remain there into the late afternoon, when the judge would declare the case adjourned until the following day. The group would then march back into the waiting buses for the long trip home; and they'd return the next morning in a slow-moving caravan that plowed its way through the city's main street under the gaping stares of the *masatepeños*.

"Since we had received word of their coming, we were all expecting a carnival to sweep into Masatepe. You know, like the feast for our patron saint, only better," said my cousin Maresa. "Everyone, including myself, thought that the gays would bring music, colorful costumes, and great dancing because . . . well . . . that's the way they are. The first day of the trial, the townspeople got all dressed up, as if it were a Sunday. They took their children to the park, even though it was a school day, so the whole family could enjoy the spectacle. But after a short while, everyone was terribly disappointed. The gays and the lesbians looked and acted just like normal people. There was nothing different or outrageous about them. A couple of men did come dressed as women, and a few others were, you know, brassy queens. But, really, most of them were rather boring. We were all hoping they would turn Masatepe into a first-class fiesta, but instead the gathering was quiet, almost mournful, I'd say. The only thing they seemed to care about was the trial."

"It was impossible for everyone who showed up to fit into the courthouse," the judge said to me. At the conclusion of our chat during our first meeting, she invited me to stop by her ranch house the following weekend so we could talk in depth about the case. Her home had a tropical storybook quality, with the exterior painted bright orange with blue and white trim. On her property, in addition to growing coffee and a wide assortment of fruits and vegetables, all for household consumption, Judge Solórzano and her husband raised iguanas. They were trying to help conserve a species that, in Nicaragua, is quickly becoming endangered. At last count they had nearly two hundred.

"I believe that public interest in the judicial system is healthy for a society like ours, especially when Nicaraguans need to learn how the jury system works, since that feature is new to us. That's why I decided to place loudspeakers outside the building, so everyone could follow what was going on."

"I made all the arrangements so that gays and lesbians would be a strong presence at the trial," said Dr. Alejandro Ortega, president of the Rainbow Foundation. "I even hired the buses. I urged all our members to take a few days off from work to go to Masatepe. I told them that the trial represented a vital test case and that we needed to be there in large numbers to guarantee that what happened to Adela would never happen again. We wanted to send a message to all of Nicaragua that violence against homosexuals would no longer be tolerated. To insure this, we needed to be there to monitor the trial. We needed to make sure that justice was served. We wouldn't accept anything less than a long prison sentence for Adela's killers."

In spite of the wide gap between the first-class party *masatepeños* had hoped for and the solemn reality of the gathering, the townsfolk, out of curiosity, continued venturing to the park each day.

"After the initial disappointment, I thought that the *masatepeños* would stop attending," Maresa told me. "But, little cousin, by the end of the first day everyone was completely caught up in the drama of the case. On the second morning the townsfolk got up early, brought their lawn chairs along, and installed themselves in the park, next to the homosexuals, to listen to the trial as if it were a soap opera on the radio."

Beginning the first day, food vendors appeared. They immediately recognized the golden opportunity the gathering represented. While the crowd attentively followed the proceedings, they could eat *raspados, rosquillas, cajetas,* mangos, papayas, pineapples, pizzas, *fritangas,* ice cream, *güirilas,* and *cuajada,* fried chicken, hamburgers, hot dogs, *polvorones, atol, arroz con leche,* and *cositas de horno.* There were also plenty of native drinks, such as *tiste, cacao, chicha de maíz, chicha de coyolito,* and *pitahaya.* Folks could also purchase every brand of soft drink, Rojita being especially popular.

"I prohibited the sale of alcohol, and I asked the police to arrest anyone violating my orders," Leticia Solórzano told me with a smile. She then took a sip of Flor de Caña Centenario—a magnificently aged twelve-year-old rum—served straight on ice. "That's all we needed, a bunch of drunks hanging out at the trial. Well, as long as I was presiding over the case, I wasn't going to allow that to happen."

"With the Central Park full of gays and lesbians and with all the food vendors present, the *masatepeños* kept expecting the whole thing to turn into a party, a celebration. But it never did," said my cousin Maresa. "Maybe it was because the music of the *chicheros* was missing. They can get any crowd going. But during the entire trial, everyone behaved well. Many people talked, of course, but they kept their voices low because the others wanted to hear what was being said in the courtroom."

The circumstantial evidence against the defendants was overwhelming. Witness after witness testified how they thought the suspects, in particular Roque Ramírez and Erlinda Cruz, were directly responsible for Adela Rugama's death. "The prosecutor was superb," said Dr. Alejandro Ortega. "That young woman did a great job building her case. In spite of the lack of physical evidence against the defendants, the way she presented her arguments left no doubt that those three were guilty as hell."

When I started my investigation, I sought out Asunción Cabrera, the prosecuting attorney whom people described as young, attractive, and extremely bright. I was stunned to learn that only three months after the trial, she had drowned during a family outing to the Isletas de Granada on a hot, breezeless afternoon. Asunción Cabrera dove into Lake Nicaragua from one of the three-hundred and sixty-five small islands spewed forth during a prehistoric eruption by the majestic, and now extinct, Volcán Mombacho. Apparently her head struck the sharp edge of one of the ancient volcanic boulders hidden beneath the murky water.

"That made me so sad," Mariela said. "Señorita Cabrera worked hard to make sure that Adela's killers got what they deserved. She wanted all three of them to spend a long time in prison. I liked her, very much. Señorita Cabrera was a caring person, and throughout the whole ordeal she gave me hope that justice would prevail. I'm sure that wherever she is now, Adela's with her."

In the face of a fierce and able prosecutor, who expertly coordinated the presentation of damaging testimony, the defense attorneys, perhaps at the suggestion of their clients, chose an unusual strategy. In an effort to disparage the murder victim, whenever the opportunity presented itself they'd posit, sometimes not so subtly, that to kill a lesbian constitutes a victimless crime. Upon reading the court transcripts, I was stunned to see that the defense attorneys never referred to Adela Rugama by name. Not once. Instead, they always called her *la cochona*. None of the three members of the defense team responded to my repeated requests for an interview. Thus, I can only assume that they had hoped to exploit the homophobia of Nicaraguans to their clients' benefit.

"Boy, did their scheme ever backfire," said Alejandro Ortega, chuckling. According to others I spoke to, the gays and lesbians outside the courthouse immediately caught on to the ploy. To counter the defense strategy, they began to whistle and hiss every time one of the attorneys opened his mouth. This, at once, made him the villain of that segment of the drama.

"Take it from someone who sat in the jury box, little cousin, the sound of that hissing was rather intimidating," my cousin Maresa said, her eyes opening wide at the memory. "In my mind I could easily envision thousands of snakes writhing on the steps of the courthouse, waiting to strike the members of the jury if we sided with the defense."

The citizens of Masatepe joined the gays and lesbians in mocking the tactic. And toward the end of the third day, whenever an attorney from the defense would question the assertions of a prosecution witness, the hissing increased to a feverish pitch until it evolved into boos.

"I have to say that, even though I was supposed to remain impartial as a member of the jury, it was fun to hear the crowd so involved in the trial," said Maresa, smiling. "Everyone outside would cheer and clap whenever they felt that the prosecutor, or a witness, had made a statement that further incriminated the murderers. And on the fourth day of the trial, many *masatepeños* brought pots and pans from their homes, which they would start banging whenever one of the defense attorneys spoke. Incredible, isn't it?"

"I had to put a stop to that," Judge Leticia Solórzano informed me. "I ordered the Commissioner of Masatepe to have his officers confiscate every cooking utensil out there. Afterward, the chief of police complained that he had lost the use of one of his jail cells because it was full to the ceiling. Still, the commissioner joked that he was going to quit the police force to open a kitchen supply store."

"The crowd put a lot of pressure on the judge and on the jury to render a guilty verdict," Alejandro Ortega said as he leaned back in his office chair, a beaming smile on his square, flat face. "Everyone knew that if the suspects had been declared innocent, there would've been one hell of a riot in Masatepe. During those days I was very proud of being the leader of Nicaragua's gay and lesbian community. The members of the foundation behaved magnificently. But, to be honest, even without our participation I think that things would have turned out just fine. That's because as far as everyone was concerned, the case was open and shut."

"I have to admit that for a brief moment I was worried that if we didn't find the defendants guilty, those of us on the jury would've been lynched," said my cousin, Maresa. "But the thought only crossed my mind for an instant. To be fair, the *cochones* and *cochonas* behaved themselves the entire time, even when they got caught up in the excitement of the trial."

By mid-afternoon of the fifth day, shortly after the lunch recess, both the prosecution and the defense rested their cases. Judge Leticia Solórzano then ordered the members of the jury to discuss the merits of what they had heard and render a verdict. After deliberating behind closed doors for only forty-seven minutes, they returned with a decision.

"I want to make it clear that no one on the jury ever mentioned that they feared what the crowd might do if we found the defendants innocent. We arrived at our decision quickly because every one of us was absolutely sure that those three were guilty. It's as simple as that, little cousin," said Maresa. "We performed our duty as citizens, and we handed the judge the correct verdict."

"The jury has found the defendants—Roque Ramírez, Erlinda Cruz, and Arquímedes Guadamuz—guilty as charged in the murder of Adela Rugama," Judge Leticia Solórzano announced.

"The town exploded," said Alejandro Ortega. "I was later told that the roar could be heard in La Curva."

After the crowd had quieted down, Judge Solórzano continued. "I concur with their finding, and I sentence each defendant to thirty-five years in prison. I thank the members of the jury for their service. Case closed, and court adjourned."

"The second roar was heard as far as Monimbó or so a friend told me," added the president of the Rainbow Foundation.

Outside the courthouse, those who had made the trip to Masatepe every morning cheered, embraced, and wept. But the victory celebration didn't last long. The hour was getting late, and after listening closely for five days to every second of the court proceedings, the visitors were exhausted. Plus, they now faced long, tiring bus rides home. The joyful explosion that followed the announcement of the sentence soon became a hushed, sober march as the gays and lesbians, many of whom had traveled very far to see that Adela Rugama's murderers received a severe prison sentence, silently filled the buses and left Masatepe, never to return.

NINETEEN

Death Without a Statement

Roque Ramírez, Erlinda Cruz, and Arquímedes Guadamuz served only a fraction of their thirty-five-year prison sentences. Toward the end of the third year, an attorney representing the convicted murderers filed an appeal for a new trial on the grounds that the prosecution had failed to present a single shred of material evidence that directly linked his clients to the murder.

"It's true," Commissioner Wong told me. "A few letters that the victim and her girlfriend had supposedly exchanged were the only solid evidence we had. But it proved that, in the end, the killers had set Adela up. Other than that, nothing could be traced back to them. The autopsy showed that the wound to the skull was produced by a .22 caliber weapon, but as much as we looked inside the latrine, we never found the bullet. That would have definitely been our strongest piece of evidence. I'm certain we could've proven that it had come from Roque Ramírez's rifle. But, honestly, in terms of physical evidence that could be deemed conclusive, we had absolutely nothing."

"They wanted to file an appeal as soon as the trial ended," Mariela said. "Asunción Cabrera, the prosecutor, told me that. But since I didn't hear anything more about it for nearly three years, I assumed that they were convinced that another trial would end up with the same result: with their sentences upheld. Later I found out that shortly after they had been convicted, they hired an expensive attorney who told them to wait at least three years before doing anything. He said that if they filed right away, the gays and lesbians would be back in the courthouse, making their lives miserable. So the lawyer advised them to wait until everyone had forgotten about the murder because then their chances of going free would be better."

In Nicaragua's quirky judicial system—a hodgepodge of American, European, and Cuban-inspired laws—when an appeal is filed in a murder case, the victim's family has thirty days to submit a petition requesting that the judge keep the prisoners behind bars until the matter is settled. The family's petition is invariably granted. On the other hand, if the victim's relatives fail to act within the month, the prisoners are set free. What's more, if released, those who had been convicted of murder could not be retried. The cost for filing the petition to keep the prisoners in custody is two thousand *córdobas*, or about one hundred and thirty dollars.

"I urged Mariela to file," said Leticia Solórzano, the judge who presided over the trial. "I didn't want those people to go free. I knew they were capable of killing again. I thought about offering Mariela the money myself. But that would've been unethical, and if someone ever found out what I had done, I could've been disbarred. Still, I admit that I was tempted."

"The Rainbow Foundation would gladly have given Mariela the money," said Alejandro Ortega, shaking his head in lament. "It really wasn't all that much. But we didn't know that Adela's murderers had filed an appeal. No one called to inform us. I wish Mariela had come to us. If I'd been aware of what those murderers were up to, I would've rallied the troops to put a stop to it."

"I was broke," said Mariela as she rested in her hammock, staring resignedly at the thick wood beam at the center of the ceiling. "Two thousand *córdobas* is two month's salary for me, and that's when I have a steady job. But you want to know something? It wasn't just about the money. For three years after my little sister's death, I had been feeling terribly tired and depressed. On some days I didn't have the strength to get out of bed. I couldn't have faced another trial. It would've been like reliving Adela's death, and I wasn't well enough to go through that again."

"At the time, whenever Mariela thought about what she should do, she'd become downright miserable," said Gloria Obando. "If Mariela had chosen to file the petition to keep those murderers in prison, she would've needed to take out a loan.

That would have put her in debt for the rest of her life. On the other hand, how could she forget what happened to her sister and let those sons of bitches walk? Throughout all this, Mariela seemed so depressed that I became really worried about her. Those of us close to her felt that she was on the verge of going crazy. We feared that she was going to break down and that we'd have to place her in the psychiatric hospital.

"That's when I came up with the idea of taking her on a pilgrimage to Cuapa, where the Virgin appeared to this man named Bernardo. When we finally made it to the apparition site, I advised her to pray to Our Lady for guidance. I was sure that would work. After all, the Virgin is a woman and a goddess. Who better to ask for help than one of our own?"

"We went all the way to Cuapa," said Mariela, smiling as she recalled the experience. "Let me tell you, traveling to Chontales is exhausting. By the time we got there, we felt as if some thugs had beaten us up. But it was very much worth it. We spent the night in the town, and early the next morning we walked to the apparition site. There's something so peaceful about that place . . . . Anyway, as I sat there, praying the rosary, a beautiful woman's voice, speaking inside of my head and only to me, said to leave all my desire for vengeance and justice in the Lord's hands. And that's exactly what I've done: I've left everything up to God. No one is wiser."

"When the deadline for filing the petition passed, I had no choice but to set those three free," said Judge Solórzano. "It hurt me to sign the forms that allowed them to walk out of prison, but it was my duty."

The release of Adela Rugama's murderers went unnoticed, with the exception of a brief newspaper article in which Esteban Padilla dispassionately detailed the conditions that led to the murderers' freedom. "That was so stupid. How can we allow people like that to walk out of prison? They don't have a conscience; they're capable of anything. But it goes to show that our judicial system still has a long way to go," the reporter said during our meeting at the Mexican restaurant.

"It was so unfair," said Gema, slowly shaking her head as she stared at the dirt floor of her mother's house. "They got away with killing my aunt Adela. I'll never get over that as long as I live."

Because of the part she played in Mariela's decision not to file the petition, Gloria Obando held herself personally responsible for the release of those who killed her former lover. "I don't know if I did the right thing by taking Mariela to Cuapa. If it had been up to me, I would have fought to my dying breath to keep those bastards behind bars. But, honestly, with the passage of time I've come to respect Mariela's decision, especially because she seems at peace with it. Still, when she forgave them for what they did, it made me give up on religion, forever. That part about turning the other cheek is a little too much for me."

"It's too bad we don't have the death penalty in this country," said Lizbeth Hodgson. "I would've loved to have seen those three hanging from a tall tree." Confronted by the memory of the murderers' release, the magnificent *mulata* took out her anger on a *criollo* cigar. The acrid stench of the cheap tobacco made it impossible for me to remain for long in her store.

I did find one person in La Curva who agreed entirely with Mariela's decision to forgive her sister's killers. "She did the right thing," said Padre Uriel. "The Church teaches that it's best to leave matters of justice in God's hands."

But it was Don Erasmo Alemán who, while rocking in his mirrored living room, blurted out what most people in La Curva think but are too cautious to state aloud: "If you have money in this country, like that cursed old man, Roque Ramírez, you can get away with anything, even murder."

Although the notion of the killers going free troubled everyone close to Adela, there was one person who reacted more strongly to the prospect than anyone else: Ixelia Cruz. The moment she learned that the murderers of her former lover might be released, a wave of panic pulled her under, dragging her to the darkest depths of despair, from where she never returned.

While her mother and Don Roque were behind bars, the young woman flourished. For the first time in her life, she was free of exploitation and able to make every decision governing her life. And most people who knew Ixelia thought that she was making the correct ones.

"A couple of years after the murder, I wrote an article about an artist who lives in Nandasmo," Esteban Padilla told me. "This fellow makes incredibly realistic fruits and vegetables out of wood. Anyway, after my interview with him, I decided to stop by Ixelia's house, just to see how she was doing. After talking to her for only a few minutes, I could see that she had placed her life in order. That delighted me. Ixelia seemed happy, and for once she had a boyfriend who treated her well. He was there the morning I dropped by to visit. His name was Oscar Mena. He didn't have much money, but he was in a good trade: making furniture. He had also completed the sixth grade, which for Ixelia was a big deal. During my visit they told me about their plans to get married. I think they would've been happy because they made a nice couple."

"About a year and a half after the murder, the girls ran into Ixelia at the feast for the patron saint in the town of San Marcos," Mariela told me. "They talked to her for a while and saw that Adela's death had affected her quite a bit. The girls told me that Ixelia was no longer the giggly, spoiled brat she used to be when she was with my sister. She had become quieter, much more serious."

"Yes, she had matured a lot from the last time we'd seen her, which was during the trial," Nubia said, adding to her mother's comments. "Ixelia acted like a responsible adult. She was in charge of her two brothers and her sister, who were with her that day. To me it looked like she was doing a good job raising them. I was impressed."

"About eight months after that, I was shopping in Masaya, when I ran into Ixelia and had another chance to speak with her," added Gema. "I had gone there to buy a frame for a photograph I had of my aunt Adela. I wanted to hang it on the bedroom wall. That day, Ixelia's boyfriend, Oscar, was with her. He was nice and kind of cute, too. Ixelia told me that she was happy. And I can honestly say that I was pleased for her. She was doing great without her mother around to mess things up. That was easy to see. She was wearing a nice outfit and no longer went around looking like a whore, which is what her mother wanted: to make it obvious that she was for sale. My aunt Adela would have loved to see Ixelia dressed like that. She was prettier than ever."

According to everyone who knew her, Ixelia had indeed flourished during the three years her mother and Don Roque were in prison. That's why the moment she learned that they might be set free, fearing that her own freedom would be severed at its young, tender roots, she rushed to speak with Mariela.

"She came to see me as soon as she found out about their appeal," Mariela recounted from her hammock. "The poor thing was terrified at the thought of her mother and the old man going free. The entire time we spoke she was shaking."

"You aren't going to let them go, are you?" Ixelia asked. She took an aggressive step toward Mariela, who, for an instant, thought that her sister's former girlfriend was going to strike her.

"Ixelia, I'm tired, sick, and broke. I've already made my decision. I don't want to go through all that again. I'm told there will probably be another trial. I don't think I could survive that. It's time for us to forgive them for what they did. We need to put everything in the past and move on with our own lives."

"What the fuck are you talking about?" Ixelia shouted. "You can't let them go! Stop saying that shit! I know that you believe that you can't handle another trial, but think about me! I couldn't face being around my mother and the old man again. As soon as they get out they're going to start insisting that I return to live with him. You've got to do something to keep them locked up, Mariela. Please, do this for me."

"I'm sorry, Ixelia, but I'm not filing the petition. I've decided to leave everything in the Lord's hands. Try not to worry, Ixelia. Have faith. The Blessed Mother will watch over all of us."

"When the poor thing left she was sobbing," Mariela recalled. "As she walked out the door, she kept on asking, over and over, 'What's going to become of me, Mariela?'"

Within a week of the convicted murderers' release, Ixelia's boyfriend, Oscar Mena, disappeared. On his workbench, Ixelia found a note in which he said that he didn't want to get in the way of what was best for her and that, because of this, it would be better if he moved on.

"Most people believe that Don Roque threatened the poor boy and that's why he left so suddenly," Mariela told me. "He must've been terrified. After all, the old man had killed my little sister and gotten away with it. What was going to stop Don Roque from killing again? One of Oscar's coworkers told everyone that he had gone to El Salvador." Mariela paused for a moment. Then she turned on her side in the hammock so she could look straight at me, and, in a sad, hoarse voice said, "The scary thing is that no one has heard a thing from Oscar since he vanished. Not a single member of his family, who all live in Boaco, knows where he is. He hasn't contacted anyone. That's why people are now beginning to say that the old man probably killed him too."

With the release of Adela's murderers and with Oscar Mena's disappearance, the respectable life that Ixelia Cruz had worked so hard to build for herself and for her siblings was swept away like a village in the path of a hurricane. Exactly two weeks after the prisoners had been set free, and one week after her boyfriend's desertion, Ixelia vanished as well. All that evening and late into the night, her brothers and her sister knocked on the door of every house in Nandasmo, frantically searching for her, without success.

"Early the next morning we received a telephone call from the foreman of El Tostadito, a coffee plantation on the outskirts of Pío XII, saying that two of his workers had found a woman dead among the coffee shrubs," Commissioner Wong told me, recalling the incident as we sat under the shade of a *guanacaste* tree in Niquinohomo's Central Park, drinking *tiste*. "I went with my officers on that investigation. The coffee pickers had placed a sheet over the body. When I uncovered it, I was sad to see that it was Ixelia Cruz. Nearby, just a couple of meters from her body, was an empty canister of rat poison. To this day, what I find most heartbreaking about her death is that, since the poor girl was illiterate, she couldn't leave a note telling us exactly why she killed herself."

PART V

Everything under the Ceiba

TWENTY

What Fate Has Assigned

La Curva, like any small town anywhere in the world, has its share of gossip, jealousies, scandals, and other misfortunes that rob the town of its tranquility, but up until Adela Rugama's murder, nothing had ever so marked the days of its residents. The people of La Curva claim that their neighbor's death diminished their lives, making their existences a shade greyer. Most also agree that they had never experienced an act so appalling, so atrocious, and so easily condemnable.

Violent deaths are not unknown to these simple folk. Not many years before, they had lost children, siblings, parents, and friends to a decade-long armed conflict whose only purpose was, in retrospect, to divide the spoils of war between two greedy, corrupt, and power-hungry factions that dwell at opposite ends of the political spectrum. Still, like most Nicaraguans, the people of La Curva have learned to accept these losses as part of Central America's failed quest for social justice. The planning and execution of Adela Rugama's murder, however, with greed, jealousy, and prejudice at the heart of the vile act, went far beyond everyone's understanding. Her death, they say, was an affront to the entire community, in spite of the victim's lesbianism.

The moment Mariela began to despair over her sister's disappearance, the townsfolk rallied to her side. Even Padre Uriel, who had often expressed his disapproval of Adela, became concerned about Mariela's plight. One Sunday, from the pulpit, the priest asked the congregation to assist in the search.

"I'm calling on each of you to help us find Adela Rugama. As you know, her sister, Mariela, is one of our most devoted parishioners. As Christians, it's our duty to come to her aid during this difficult time."

Through Padre Uriel's plea, every person in La Curva became entangled in the drama. During the two months that Adela was

199

missing, speculation about her disappearance was the town's sole topic of discussion. And today, without hesitation, people can recall exactly where they were and what they were doing when they heard that the body had, at last, been discovered.

Then, for another year, Adela's death continued to alter the small, day-to-day rituals of everyone in La Curva. Family, friends, and neighbors would sit for hours in the park, in their living rooms, in the stands during a baseball game, on the stone ledge behind the church, or in the cantina, discussing every detail of the crime in order to decipher the exact role each of them had played in the affair.

As time passed, however, the pistons of remembrance, which had steadily driven folks to summon up Adela's murder, began to wear out, and, almost imperceptibly, life in the town returned to normal. But for those close to the victim, as well as for those close to the perpetrators, Adela's murder drastically marked the remainder of their days.

The impact of Adela's death on the life of Gloria Obando is the first example that comes to mind. Following the murder of her former lover, La Curva's midwife acquired a peculiar obsession, one with the overtones of a crusade. To this day, Gloria Obando, with staggering fervor, tries to persuade the mother of every girl in whose birth she has assisted to name their daughter after Adela.

"She's become a nuisance," one townswoman, who asked to remain anonymous, told me. "For a while it got to the point where no one wanted to go to Gloria to have their baby because if it turned out to be a girl you had to put up a fight to give the child the name you had already chosen. But, you tell me, where else can we go? There's not a doctor in La Curva and, to be honest, no one is better than Gloria at what she does. We've simply had to accept that that's the way she's dealing with her grief and let it go at that."

Still, in spite of strong resistance to her efforts, Gloria's campaign has succeeded to a large degree: approximately one-third of the girls she has brought forth into this world since the death of her former lover have Adela as their middle name.

The people of La Curva also say that the murder forced Don Erasmo Alemán to give up a treasured ritual he had been known for since the day he arrived in the town. Every evening, for nearly seven decades, beginning at about six and lasting until nine, he'd open the front door, sit in the living room, and gaze at the countless reflections of himself as he rocked in his favorite chair. But shortly after Adela's body was found, he stopped this routine.

Don Erasmo still sits in the living room, beginning at six, but at seven he will move his rocking chair to the sidewalk where he'll remain for the rest of the evening with a glum expression on his face. The townsfolk who spy on him have observed that the man of the mirrors will occasionally lean forward, glance inside his house, and suddenly sit upright, leaning rigidly against the backrest with his eyes wide open, as if he had seen something unsettling.

Although several persons had informed me of the reason Don Erasmo drastically changed a tradition of more than half a century, I decided to pose the question myself. Initially, he, who had been one of the most forthcoming persons during my investigations, wouldn't give me a straight answer. His replies were elusive, and the response he finally settled on was that his doctor told him that the outside evening air was better for the health of his aging lungs. At last, Don Erasmo's reluctance to confide in me gave me no choice but to state the reason people were giving for the demise of his once sacred custom.

"I see that I'm going to have to tell you whether I'd like to or not. But I want you to know that I don't like talking about this. Not in the least. When I told a few friends what was happening, they all said that I was crazy. But what I'm about to tell you is the truth.

"On some evenings, not all of them, mind you, exactly at seven forty-two, Adela will appear in the full-length mirror that's broken in half—the same mirror that upset her that Christmas morning when she came in here to hide from Don Roque. On those evenings, her reflection materializes in the glass, and then, for a couple of hours, she'll step in and out of view. I've asked myself countless times why Adela's ghost always shows up at exactly seven forty-two. My guess is that that's the hour she was murdered. Now, I'm not afraid of her. I say this in all honesty. Adela could never scare me, even as a ghost. But the reason I don't like to sit inside the house any longer is because I become depressed when I see her, and it takes several days for the feeling to go away. You can go ahead now and tell everyone that 'Don Erasmo has gone completely nuts,' but I swear that what I'm telling you is the truth."

Nubia, the younger of Mariela's two daughters at the time of her aunt's death, was pregnant and excitedly making wedding plans. She didn't get married. The father of the child left because the thought of becoming related, especially in death, to such a notorious *cochona* embarrassed him. "I don't want people whispering behind my back as I walk through the streets," he told Nubia when he broke off the engagement. "I'm sorry, but I don't want to be stared at all the time. Wherever I go, people can't take their eyes off of me! And it's all because of your aunt!"

At present, Nubia doesn't have a job. Instead, she stays home all day to take care of the household chores and to look after her three-year-old boy while Mariela lies in the hammock, trying to recover her health, and her sister Gema goes to work, having assumed the responsibility of supporting the family.

Gema graduated from high school the year of the murder, but she was unable to go on to college. Adela had been her benefactor, and without her aunt's financial assistance, a secondary education was as far as she could go. Gema now works in Managua's newest movie theater, behind the snack counter. "It's not too bad, actually" Gema told me. "But sometimes, when I stop to think about it, I become sad because all of my life I dreamed about going to college. My aunt Adela had always promised that she would help pay for my education. But now I'll always be left to wonder what I could've become."

After the trial, Lizbeth Hodgson, the woman from Pearl Lagoon, hung an 8" x 10" photograph of Adela, straddling her mountain bike, in a prominent spot of her store. "This business wouldn't exist without her help," Lizbeth said. "I owe Adela a lot. Because of her, I'm able to support myself and my two daughters. I want everyone who walks through those doors to know that."

But Adela's death had another, more hazardous effect on the beautiful storeowner: so vivid was Gloria Obando's description of the smell of her neighbor's decomposing body that Lizbeth had to start smoking cheap cigars to ward off the deathly stench that haunts her to this day.

Adela's murder also affected Padre Uriel, the parish priest of La Curva. On the first day of the trial, he cast aside his cassock and donned civilian clothing to visit Masatepe incognito. A friend in the archdiocese had called to tell him that gays and lesbians throughout the country had been busily organizing in order to turn up in large numbers. Before going, Padre Uriel told Lizbeth Hodgson that he wanted to see for himself what would happen when the *masatepeños* repudiated the freaks. Instead, the cleric was stunned when, from the first day, the people of that town and the homosexuals developed a strong bond, coming together to form a community that clamored for justice. The experience so changed the priest that he has not openly condemned homosexuality since. Most of the folks in La Curva suggest that his silence stems from guilt, having judged Adela so harshly in life; others say that the incident in Masatepe opened his eyes, allowing him to understand that gays and lesbians are really not that different; and the cynics claim that Padre Uriel has become paranoid, fearing that if he pronounces another sermon condemning homosexuality the throngs will invade the town to set him straight.

Don Roque's gambling cohorts continue to play cards every night. "We were thrilled when the old man was put behind bars because then it became possible for anyone to win. We no longer had to lose just to satisfy a miserable bastard who happened to be rich," said one of the players, who requested anonymity. Don Roque has not rejoined the group since his release.

As soon as the *hacendado* was sentenced to thirty-five years, his brother, Don Julio, moved into the main hacienda house and took possession of Las Dos Balas. He proved to be a far better administrator than his older brother. The hacienda's productivity increased threefold. And Don Julio did something else that shocked everyone in the region: he married his brother's former woman—the one Don Roque had banished to a shack in the remotest corner of Las Dos Balas so that Ixelia could move in with him—and adopted her three children.

One night, during an evening of cards in which Don Julio and the other card players consumed two liters of rum Flor de Caña Seca, with the liquor acting as truth serum, the younger brother blurted out that he hoped his brother would rot in prison. His statement reached Don Roque, who was still incarcerated. Two days prior to the *hacendado*'s release, Don Julio, as well as his family, disappeared without a trace. At once, everyone suspected that the older brother had paid someone to have them eliminated.

Several months later, a smuggler from La Curva, who works with a contraband operation along the Río San Juan, told Mariela that he had spotted Don Julio and his family on a remote ranch along the banks of the river. They live there, engaged in subsistence farming and producing barely enough to survive. Their small patch of land, carved out of the thick rain forests of Nicaragua's southeastern corner, is a three-hour boat ride from the town of San Carlos. It's difficult to imagine anyone wanting to live so far from civilization, but Don Julio has at least succeeded in placing his family safely out of his brother's reach.

Soledad, Arquímedes Guadamuz's girlfriend, was almost fourteen years old when her man was sentenced to thirty-five years. Throughout his imprisonment, she promised the Curl that she'd wait for him, no matter how long it took. When Adela's killers were released after only serving three years, Soledad was the lone person in the entire region to celebrate the event. And then, once again, she waited patiently for another three months as Arquímedes tried to settle in Costa Rica, having promised that he'd send for her as soon as he found work. But before the Curl could secure a steady job, the immigration authorities of that country caught him while playing cards with other Nicas in Parque La Merced, and he was immediately deported. Now sixteen years old, and faithful as ever, Soledad continues at the Curl's side.

Ixelia's siblings, like their older sister, flourished in the absence of their controlling mother. When Ixelia became responsible for their welfare, she insisted that they learn a legitimate trade. By the time Doña Erlinda was released, both boys were competent welders. And Zuleika, their sister, proved to be gifted at sewing. She had even gotten a job worthy of her skills in a shop that makes uniforms, including those of the Nicaraguan police force, in the town of Dolores.

As expected, immediately after her release, Doña Erlinda forced her children to abandon their employment. She wanted them close by and under her total control, working for her. The week after Ixelia committed suicide, the three surviving siblings fled to Pearl Lagoon where, with the help of Lizbeth Hodgson's father, the Anglican minister, they found jobs and live contentedly.

Perhaps it's needless to say that Adela's murder had a profound impact on me as well. During the nine-week investigation, I, along with Si Dios Quiere, became a familiar sight throughout the little towns of the region. After only a short time on the project, the townsfolk were treating me as if I were an old friend, greeting me enthusiastically whenever I'd pull up in the dilapidated car. In my efforts to piece together the events for this account, I interviewed dozens of persons, and as the end of my stint in Nicaragua approached, I became determined to interview dozens more.

So obsessed was I with the subject of Adela's death that I thought of little else, and this included the graduate seminar on Latino and Latina literature that I was teaching at the university. I had even started to resent the course, feeling that it was getting in the way of the only task that mattered.

As the last week of my summer break approached, I called my department's chairperson and told her that I was going to take an unpaid leave of absence so that I could remain in Nicaragua another semester. I informed her that I needed the time to finish my research.

"That's a bad idea," she said. "The dean is a little tired of always hearing you complain that you don't have enough time to write. If I were you, I'd hurry back."

Fortunately, as it turned out, I had already accumulated more than enough information to tell this story accurately.

But there's more.

On some nights I wake up startled, covered in a cold sweat and haunted by a disconcerting recurring dream. In it, San Jorge and Adela are standing side by side under the ceiba next to Don Roque's house. I know it is San Jorge by the flaming sword, but not once has he brought the slain dragon. The two stare at me in silence, smiling the entire time: one like the Mona Lisa and the other like the Cheshire Cat. My therapist assures me that some-day these dreams will fade away, but I'm not entirely convinced.

Three years after Commissioner Gilberto Wong asked Mariela to identify her sister's body, her stomach continues to gurgle: this in spite of drinking four cups every day of lemongrass tea with a drop of a baby boy's first morning urine in it. Also, with Adela's disappearance Mariela started to suffer frequent bouts of insomnia. On those endless nights she distracts herself by counting the hoots of a pair of owls that live in the attic of the former train station. She'll do this until their plaintive calls cede way to the crowing of roosters, which she then begins to count as well.

In addition, Mariela has been unable to hold a steady job because of the dizzy spells that, during the trial, started to affect her balance. Only in a hammock can she find relief from the debilitating lightheadedness that takes hold of her several times a day with unpredictable suddenness. And this, of course, is some-thing most employers do not value: a maid who spends most of the day on her back.

But the bouts of dark, severe depression torment Mariela far worse. During one of our last conversations she confided that there are days when the despair that lays siege to her mind is so unbearable that she is tempted to take her life and join her sister for eternity. Mariela, though, cannot bear the thought of her children having to endure another tragedy. And this notion is what keeps her alive.

Oddly enough, Mariela's sons, Tulio and Javier, the two family members I've written the least about, are the ones who have suffered the most from their aunt's vicious murder. Throughout my investigations, whenever I'd show up to speak with their mother, the boys would look at me wearily, and before long they'd excuse themselves and leave. At first I thought that they were offended by my intrusion into the family's sorrow. And I couldn't blame them. After all, whenever I dropped by, they'd see how hard I'd push their mother to recall even the most insignificant detail of the most painful experience of her life. Because of this, I had assumed that they greatly resented me.

And then, whenever I attempted to interview the young men, particularly during the first few times I visited their home, their answers would be evasive, morose, or both. But with time, as the picture of what took place that tragic Christmas grew clearer, I started to believe that what was keeping them from confiding in me was an overwhelming sense of guilt.

One day I confronted Mariela with this suspicion.

"Those poor boys! They're going to blame themselves for their aunt's death for the rest of their lives," she sighed from the hammock.

Indeed, on the Christmas of Adela's murder, as she and Tulio repaired the Rali mountain bike, the aunt asked him to go with her to meet Ixelia, just in case the whole thing was a trap. She told her oldest nephew that she planned to ask Javier to join them as well.

But that evening, after dinner, the boys went out to shoot pool, promising to be back at six forty-five to accompany Adela on her errand. Unfortunately, they got into a fight and the police detained them both. When they finally returned home, it was already too late: Adela had been gone for over two hours. Never again would they see their beloved aunt.

"The boys are always saying," Mariela told me, shaking her head in sadness, "that if they had made it back on time, their aunt would still be alive. I feel terrible for them. They're too young to carry such a burden. It's as if each of them has a heavy stone tied around his neck. As much as I try to tell them that everything happened the way God intended I fear those boys are going to bear the awful weight of that guilt for the rest of their lives."

TWENTY-ONE

Entryway to Heaven

"**A**dela was neither naïve nor stupid. She knew she might be walking into a trap," Commissioner Gilberto Wong told me as we sat in his office, discussing the murder. He paused meditatively, brought his hands together at the center of his chest, and interlaced his fingers as if he were about to pray. "Keep in mind, though, that she was madly in love, and, as this case proves, love can sometimes be fatal. In spite of the danger, the chance of being reunited with her girlfriend, however remote, won out over Adela's common sense. Love led her straight into the jaguar's lair."

About a week before returning to the States, I visited Commissioner Wong because, outside of the killers, he was the person who could best describe Adela Rugama's last moments. Four incense sticks burned in the Ganesha holder that morning. The scent, "The Seven African Powers," in homage to the most powerful deities of the Santería faith, was woodsy, sweet, and pungent. The metal fan groaned, complaining of old age, and the dull spinning of its rusted blades did little to help circulate the humid, monsoon-season air that filled the room with a dense, balmy heat.

"Adela was lured to her death. No doubt about it. They tricked her into showing up at Las Dos Balas with every intention of killing her," said the police commissioner. After taking another sip of mango tea, he rose from his seat, walked to the filing cabinet, and took out a light-blue folder. Returning to his desk, he placed the file in front of him.

"After Adela's release from prison, although Ixelia had broken off the relationship, the women continued exchanging letters. Arquímedes Guadamuz still acted as their messenger, and, in Ixelia's case, he was the scribe as well. Adela, however, preferred to dictate her replies to Gema. Because of this, the niece

209

knew everything they had said in their messages, and this was of great help to the prosecutor in building her case against the killers.

"According to Gema, Adela's letters were passionate. In every one she'd tell Ixelia how much she loved her, and she kept insisting that they run away together to Costa Rica, where she said that they would find good jobs and finally be allowed to live in peace.

"In her replies, Ixelia always turned down Adela's proposal, saying that it was too dangerous. But in spite of the repeated refusals, her answers were affectionate.

"Since Arquímedes also read the correspondence, the murderers were aware of everything as well, and this made them see Adela as a threat. What must have triggered the murder, I believe, is that during an argument with her mother, Ixelia threatened to run off to Costa Rica. Fearing this, Erlinda Cruz and Roque Ramírez met and decided to eliminate Adela, once and for all."

Commissioner Wong opened the folder and leafed through it until he found what he wanted. Then, he went on with the story. "On Christmas Eve, the messenger delivered a letter to Adela. After Gema had read it to her, he had them destroy it, arguing that if either Roque or Erlinda found out about their plan to run away, they would do everything possible to stop them. Fortunately, since Gema and Javier were both present, they were able to reconstruct it, word for word. In the message, Ixelia states that she has changed her mind and that she's now ready to leave with Adela for Costa Rica." After the commissioner said this, he handed me the letter.

Beloved Adela:

My mother behaved horribly last night. She whipped me, saying that I had to go back to live with the old man. I now realize that you're right and that you and I should be together again. I miss you terribly, and I still love you.

I'm sick of my mother's abuse and of the control she has over my life. I'm especially tired of hearing over and over that I have to move in with the old man. My love, I can't stand this anymore.

I'm now ready to run away with you. I want us to be together. I'm sure that we'll be able to start new lives in Costa Rica and that the Ticos will let us live in peace.

But we have to leave tomorrow, my love. I can't stay here another day. Tomorrow night my mother is going to Masatepe to a party. I'll pretend that I'm tired and stay home. Then, while she's off celebrating Christmas, I'll sneak away.

From there I'll go to the old man's house. As usual, he's going to be out playing cards. I'll break in and steal his money. I know all of his hiding places. That'll make it easier for us to start our new life in Costa Rica.

Meet me under the ceiba next to the old man's house, tomorrow evening at seven. Please say that you'll come.

I love you with all of my heart,
Ixelia

Once I had finished reading the letter, Commissioner Wong said, "Ixelia denied ever writing that message. That's why it became the prosecution's most important piece of evidence. It proved beyond a doubt that Adela was set up." The chief of police of Niquinohomo then pulled another sheet out of the folder, and as he gave it to me, he said, "This is what Adela wrote in response to the false letter, which, again, the niece reconstructed from memory."

Love of my life:

Of course I'll run away with you. Your letter has made me the happiest woman in the world. I've lighted a large candle at the feet of my statue of San Jorge, and I'm praying that you're telling the truth.

You've let me down in the past, Ixelia. I couldn't live with another disappointment, especially one this big. Please be there tomorrow night. I know I shouldn't trust you completely, but I love you so much that I'm willing to take that chance.

Be very careful, my love. Don't tell anyone where you're going. I'll see you tomorrow night under the ceiba.

My darling, please don't let me down. I wouldn't want to go on living if you don't show up. But if you do come, it'll be the best Christmas ever.

I love you, and I promise that we'll live happily ever after in the land of the Ticos,
Adela

Although I knew it all along, to read in Adela's own words the high hopes with which she had embarked on her final journey made the act of her murder seem all the more tragic. For a time I said nothing, and Commissioner Wong respected my need for a moment of reflection.

"Commissioner," I said, at last breaking the silence, "in your opinion, what happened that evening after Adela arrived at Las Dos Balas?"

The chief of police leaned back in his chair and lifted his eyes toward the ceiling. After carefully considering his answer, he lowered his gaze to meet mine, and then, measuring every word, he said, "Keep in mind that what I'm about to tell you is mere conjecture. Now, having said that, what took place seems pretty clear to me. When Adela arrived at Las Dos Balas, they were already waiting for her, probably hiding among the rows of coffee shrubs behind the ceiba. I say 'they' because I believe Arquímedes was with Roque, although he has always denied it. While Adela was searching for Ixelia among the buttresses of the tree, they captured her. This would've been easy because she probably went in between two root walls looking for Ixelia, and this left her without a way to escape."

"Did they kill her there, or did they take her someplace else?"

"I think they killed her there. And they didn't waste much time, either. But since Roque is somewhat of a sadist, I believe that he forced Adela to get on her knees and beg for her life—just for fun. The angle at which the bullet entered the skull supports this theory. The person firing the shot was standing above the victim. Now, the reason they chose to kill her on Christmas Day is that after sunset there are a lot of fireworks. That, of course, would cover up the sound of gunfire.

"After shooting Adela, they had to dispose of the body. Although Roque Ramírez is a strong man, he's getting on in years. I don't think he could've done this by himself. That's the main reason why I believe Arquímedes was with him. Between the two of them, they placed a large plastic trash bag over the victim's torso, filled it with lime, and tied it shut around the waist. They then lifted the body, draped it over a horse, and under the cover of night, took it to the abandoned outhouse. Once there, they dumped the body in headfirst and then filled the rest of the hole with trash, believing that it would never be found. Their plan was simple, really. Nothing very complicated."

A grey, dreary numbness came over me after hearing Commissioner Wong detail Adela's death so clinically, laying out her blanched bones before me, gnawed clean of all flesh. I remained quiet as Niquinohomo's chief of police lighted another four sticks of incense: again, The Seven African Powers. Once done, he gazed at me with compassion, as if I had just heard the news of Adela's death for the first time. Then, gradually, like a man who has just laid down the winning hand in a game of cards, he smiled.

"There is one thing in that scenario that I find uplifting," the commissioner said. "I know it's difficult to believe this, but among all that darkness there's a reassuring beam of light."

"I'm sorry, Commissioner, but I don't see how anyone can say that," I protested, the hatefulness of the crime still weighing heavily on my mind. "Adela was murdered in cold blood. And then, those who killed her were set free after only serving three years. How can you find anything redeeming in that?"

"I say this because Adela died under a ceiba," Commissioner Wong said after taking another sip of tea. He leaned forward and stared at me keenly. "Let me ask you a question: what do you know about this tree?"

"Not much," I admitted. "Only that it's huge and that it grows in the tropics."

"Well, let me then educate you a little about the ceiba." He was ready to expound on what obviously was a topic of great interest to him. "To begin with, several religions throughout the world have held this tree to be sacred. The Mayans, for instance, believed that the ceiba was the link, the artery, so to speak, that connects our world, the world of the living, to the afterlife. And the Yoruban people of western Africa believe that the Orishas, their deities, enjoy taking time out of their labors to rest in the shade of a ceiba. That's why, to this day, followers of Santería leave offerings among the ceiba's roots.

"In Mayan cosmology," the former professor of comparative religion went on, "a colossal ceiba stood at the center of the universe, and the souls of the departed ascended into heaven by climbing up that tree. The most blessed event for a Maya would be to die under a ceiba, for then their souls would be guaranteed straight passage into the celestial homes of their ancestors."

The commissioner smiled. "Now, I don't know about you, but I find it comforting to think that Adela's spirit may have been, at the very moment of her death, whisked straight into paradise."

Commissioner Wong continued, but the tone of his voice changed abruptly, becoming stern, and his expression startled me, for it had lost its customary kindness. "And in the case of Adela's murderers, the mythology of the ceiba teaches us that they won't be able to escape punishment. In both Mayan and Yoruban beliefs, because the ceiba is sacred, those who murder under the canopy of this tree have committed the most appalling offense imaginable: they have usurped the role of the gods. And as a consequence, at the time of their passing, they'll be denied entry into heaven."

TWENTY-TWO

A Fatal Delay

In my last telephone conversation with Gloria Obando, I asked her to relay a message to Tulio and Javier: that they be present during my final meeting with their mother, which would take place three days before my return to the States. The young men held the key to filling one of the gaps that remained in the story. Thus, before leaving Nicaragua, and certainly before embarking on the voyage of writing this chronicle, it was essential for me to know the role they had played on that fateful Christmas.

Javier, the youngest of Mariela's four children, was fourteen years old when his aunt was murdered. By the time I concluded my investigation, he was a handsome, well-mannered young man of seventeen who attended the local high school. Like his sister Gema before him, he was a good student, and every person I spoke to in La Curva regretted that neither Javier nor his sister would be able to attend college. They were responsible young people with great potential, the people would say, lamenting the dim prospects of two futures that once seemed bright.

Adela's other nephew, Tulio, at the time of his aunt's murder, was a short, wiry fifteen-year-old with a penchant for getting into trouble. When we last met he was a tall, athletic eighteen-year-old who was on the verge of making San Fernando's roster: Masaya's semiprofessional baseball team. Although the townsfolk were also proud of him, they were quick to point out that, prior to the tragedy, they were sure that Tulio would most likely be shot, gutted, or clubbed to death in a barroom brawl before reaching his twenty-fifth birthday.

The year of Adela's murder, Tulio had been arrested twice for fighting, and, unlike Gema and Javier, he never performed well at school. He preferred instead to spend his days playing baseball and his evenings at the pool hall, drinking beer while polishing his billiard skills. Tulio was also known as a budding womanizer, and the parents of every teenage girl in the town forbade their daughters from talking to the boy.

"Back then, we all loved Javier . . . and Tulio we all feared," Don Erasmo Alemán, the man of the mirrors, stated flatly during one of my visits. "Thankfully, he changed for the better after Adela died."

After his aunt's murder, Tulio stopped drinking and visiting the pool hall. To honor her memory, as well as to find solace from the senselessness of her death, he devoted himself wholly to baseball, where at the plate he excelled, thanks to a powerful, yet compact, swing; and at third base he stunned opponents and spectators alike with his lightning fast reflexes and strong throwing arm.

Throughout my investigation of their aunt's murder, Tulio and Javier had done their best to avoid me. But on the morning of my last visit both young men were there. What's more, the entire family was present, gathered in the living room to bid me farewell.

In the course of my attempts to unveil Adela's last moments, it became increasingly clear that the young men had played a crucial role that tragic evening, having missed a critical appointment with their aunt. Thus, in order for me to write this account of Adela's murder, I needed to know exactly why they had failed to show up. With the clock moving resolutely toward the hour of my departure, I was prepared to get on my knees to beg for their help.

"Tulio . . . Javier," I started, "as you know, I'm returning to the States in a couple of days, and I have a serious problem: some gaps still remain in the story, two big gaps, in fact. You can help me fill one of them by telling me everything you can remember about the day your aunt Adela was killed, from the moment you woke up until the time you were supposed to meet her."

I had always suspected that Javier would be willing to talk, if only loyalty to his older brother hadn't forced him to remain silent. And on the morning of my final visit, Javier's eyes shifted nervously, darting between his brother and me, which I interpreted as a sure sign that he was eager to rid himself of his burden.

Tulio, on the other hand, sat hunched over, with his elbows on his thighs and his fingers laced together while staring at the hard-packed dirt floor. He didn't look up once as I asked the brothers to share their recollections of Adela's last day. Mariela's sons didn't respond to my plea, and the stillness in the living room became unbearable.

I had started to fear that I'd have to leave the country without hearing the young men's account of what took place that fateful Christmas Day when Mariela's tender, plaintive voice pierced her sons' veil of silence as she said, "*Muchachos*, please, do this for your aunt Adela's sake."

At last, without lifting his gaze from the dirt floor, Tulio nodded.

Letting out a long-held breath, I said, "*Gracias. Muchas gracias.*" Hurriedly, fearing that Tulio might suddenly change his mind, I opened my notepad, grabbed the pen in my shirt pocket, and flexed my wrist in anticipation of taking copious notes. "Tulio," I said, "you spent more time than anyone else with your aunt Adela that day; so, I'd like to begin with you. Starting with the moment you woke up that Christmas, tell me everything you remember, no matter how insignificant it may seem."

With his eyes still fixed on the floor, Tulio commenced his tale. "I remember waking up very excited that morning. For several weeks my mother had been saying that she had bought me a gift I was going to love, so when I got out of bed I was dying to see what it was. But when I stepped out of the bedroom, my aunt Adela was already there, in the same chair you're sitting in now, drinking a cup of *café con leche*." For the first time that morning, as he lifted his head to point in my direction, Tulio's gaze met mine. Then, casting his eyes back onto the dirt floor, he resumed his story.

"I gave my aunt a quick kiss on the cheek and at once started to look around the room for the present. I was about to ask my mother where it was when my aunt handed me her gift. So I sat down, opened it, and as soon as I saw what it was, I stood up and began to dance around the room: a new pair of baseball cleats. My aunt Adela knew that the ones I owned were falling apart, and she also knew how much I loved baseball. She used to say that *béisbol* was God's gift to me: the thing that I did best in this world." I glanced around the room. Every member of the family was smiling, recalling how Adela liked to celebrate the talents of each niece and nephew and how she kept urging them to discover their purpose in life.

"Tulio, your Christmas present is waiting outside," Mariela said then, three-and-a-half years earlier.

The eldest son ran to the backyard. At the sight of the Rali mountain bike, he fell to his knees. Although evidently used, in Tulio's eyes the bicycle was a dazzling, glorious gift. "I was thrilled. My first thought was that I'd be able to fly from town to town, visiting several girls in one night." But his mother had another vision for the bike's use: aware that Tulio had given up on school, she was going to ask him to use the Rali to find work.

"From the instant we first saw the bike, we fell in love with it," Gema said. "And since we knew that Tulio would let us borrow it once in a while, the bicycle was like a gift for all of us."

"I was ready to take the Rali for a spin that very moment," Tulio said, interrupting his sister to resume the story.

But immediately after he mounted the bicycle, his aunt Adela gripped him firmly by the shoulder, preventing him from pedaling away. "You can't ride it like that, Tulio," she said. "That bike is desperately in need of repairs. Let's take it to my house and we'll fix it up. Don't worry, Tulio, we'll have the Rali looking like new before the end of the day."

"Aunt Adela, can't it wait until another day? I can ride it the way it is. It doesn't bother me."

"No, Tulio, it has to be today. I won't have time to fix it later."

"My little sister was very firm when she said that," Mariela interjected, "which shocked me because she never spoke like that to any of the kids. At the time, I wondered why she had to fix the bicycle that same day, but I kept my mouth shut. I now wish I had asked. As I later found out, I was the only one in the house that evening who didn't know that she was planning to run away with Ixelia." Mariela looked sternly at her children. Every one of them glanced away, uneasy under their mother's glare.

As Adela and Tulio walked to her house, Rali in tow, Adela reached out and placed an arm around her nephew's shoulder.

"Listen, Tulio, I'm going to share a big secret with you, but you've got to promise not to tell anyone, especially your mother. Agreed?"

"Yes, I promise."

"Tonight, Ixelia and I are running away."

"What?" Tulio exclaimed, astonished. Still in shock, he asked in one quick burst, "Where are you going?"

"Costa Rica."

"You're planning to come back someday, aren't you?"

"Of course I am, silly boy!" Adela said, mussing her nephew's hair. "We're just going to stay there until Doña Erlinda and Don Roque finally understand that Ixelia and I are meant to be together. That may take a while . . . a few years even . . . , but I do plan on coming back. I'm going to be buried in La Curva, Tulio. I promise you that."

"My aunt was always up to something crazy, but I never thought she'd leave her house behind. She loved that place," Tulio commented. Nodding their heads, the other family members agreed.

"As soon as we got to her place, my aunt went into the bedroom to change," Tulio said, continuing his tale. "But when she came out, she did something strange. She stood in the doorway for the longest time, staring at her medallion of San Jorge, the one that she always wore on a silver chain around her neck. When she finally raised her head again, she looked worried. If I didn't know better, I'd say that my aunt knew that something awful was going to happen to her that day. But she didn't say anything. She simply kissed the medallion and slipped it under the Pura Vida T-shirt she had put on to work. My aunt Adela then repeated that corny joke of hers, the one about San Jorge being her patron saint because he was the protector of good husbands." Tulio chuckled as he said this, but it was an empty gesture, and for a moment, like a passing rain cloud, his recollection cast a shadow over the gathering.

Aunt and nephew then started to restore the Rali mountain bike. Tulio made several trips to Bicitaller El Gordo, four blocks away, on La Curva's main street. Since it was Christmas Day, on each visit he had to knock on the door—the shop also being the portly owner's home—to politely ask for the needed parts.

Most of that day, Adela and Tulio worked in silence. When one of them did speak, it was usually Adela to explain to her nephew what he needed to do to keep the bicycle in good shape. As they waited for the paint to dry, Adela asked Tulio about his plans for the evening.

"After dinner I'm going to play some pool. Then, I'm going to visit Evangelina."

"Ah, the girlfriend," Adela said, smiling conspiratorially.

"Not yet, but I'm working on it."

Suddenly, Adela became serious, her somber expression alarming Tulio. "*Muchacho*, I need to ask you for a favor," she said at last.

"Yes, of course. Anything you want. I mean it."

"Thanks, Tulio." But then Adela just stared at her nephew until he felt a thin sheet of perspiration starting to cover the back of his neck. At last, she broke the silence by saying, "I'm meeting Ixelia tonight, outside of the old man's house. I don't expect anything to happen, but I'd like it very much if you and Javier were also there, just in case. If the old man shows up, when he sees that there are three of us he'll be less likely to try something stupid."

"Certainly. No problem."

"Good. Can you be back at your house by a quarter to seven?"

"I'll be there."

"Please, Tulio, it's important," Adela pleaded. "Don't forget: a quarter to seven. I need you to be on time because we'll need to hitch a ride to the entrance of Las Dos Balas."

"Don't worry. I'll be there."

Tulio gave his aunt a quick kiss on the cheek, touched the Rali to make sure the paint had dried, mounted it, thanked her once again for her work on the bicycle, telling her how proud he was of the way it now looked, and then he started to race home. On arrival, he showed off the bike by coming to a fishtail halt in the backyard. His mother scolded him, upset by the large, thick cloud of dust that floated straight into her home. That afternoon all of Mariela's children took turns riding the mountain bike, with the exception of Nubia, who was four months pregnant and afraid of hurting the baby.

"I had just taken my turn on the Rali when my aunt Adela showed up, freshly showered, and smelling of Mennen aftershave," said Gema. "That's when Nubia and I rushed into the kitchen to get the food ready to serve."

Glancing nervously at his older brother for the first time that morning, Javier spoke. "As soon as my aunt arrived, she quietly asked me to go with her and Tulio that evening."

"Javier, you know how your brother is. I need the two of you there tonight. Tulio says that after we finish eating he's going to play pool and then visit his girlfriend. Please, stay with him and make sure that you're both back on time," Adela said.

"Up to that point it had been the best Christmas Day I'd ever had, mostly because of the bicycle," Tulio said, interrupting his younger brother. "Everyone was in a great mood. Throughout dinner we joked, laughed, and listened to the Shakira CD my aunt had given Nubia. And the food was delicious, especially the turkey."

The gathering suddenly grew quiet, in spite of the pleasant memories of their last supper with Adela, for now the story began to move relentlessly toward the catastrophe that, inescapably, would come.

"We'll be back at a quarter to seven, mami," Tulio said as he and his brother rose from their seats at the dinner table. Although Tulio had said that for his mother's benefit, he had looked at his aunt Adela the entire time to reassure her that he intended to keep his promise.

"Mami, Javier and I are going to take the bike into town," Tulio then announced.

"No, you're not," Mariela countered. "It'll be dark by the time you return home and you boys are not familiar with the roads yet. They're full of holes. Leave the bike here; I don't want either of you getting into an accident, especially on Christmas Day."

"We protested," Javier said, "but mamá can be stubborn. Tulio asked her once more if we could take the bike, telling her that we would be very careful. But she said no, so we started to walk."

"It was close to five o'clock when we arrived at the pool hall," Tulio continued. "Quite a few of our friends were already there, including many of my teammates from La Curva's baseball team. Javier and I went over to their tables. That evening, in the spirit of Christmas, they bought me a few beers. By a quarter past six I was feeling pretty good. That's when I decided to pay Evangelina a quick visit. I was madly in love with that girl at the time. Just as Javier and I were heading out, her brother, Noel, walked in with a few of his friends. When he saw me, he stopped in front of the door, blocking the way. Noel never liked me, not one bit."

"Excuse me," Javier said, stepping between his older brother and Noel, "but we were just leaving."

"And just where do you two think you're going?" Noel asked, glaring down at Tulio. Although today the situation is completely reversed, three-and-a-half years earlier Evangelina's brother was six inches taller and twenty-seven pounds heavier than his adversary.

"It's none of your business," Tulio said, moving his younger brother aside and defiantly stepping forward. He had to crane his neck slightly back to stare at Noel.

"For a while they stood there, toe to toe, and in silence. They reminded me of two boxers who are waiting for the bell to ring so they can start pounding on one another," Javier said.

"It is my business if you think you're going to visit my sister. I've warned you to stay away from her," Noel said as he poked Tulio in the chest with his index finger.

"When he did that, the atmosphere in the pool hall became very tense," Javier recalled. "Everyone stopped playing and started to move toward us. The owner, expecting a fight to break out, sent his son to fetch the police."

"Evangelina is old enough to make that decision for herself. She doesn't need you to watch over her," Tulio said, returning Noel's glare. Bolstered by four bottles of Victoria and the presence of his teammates, the adolescent felt invincible.

"Listen up, asshole," Noel growled between clenched teeth. "You know I think that you're a piece of trash. You have no future, except maybe for drinking, billiards, and baseball. You're going to eat shit for the rest of your life because you're not going to amount to anything. But do you want to know the real reason I want you to stay away from Evangelina? Because of your aunt: the *cochona*. I'm not going to allow anyone related to that freak to come near my sister."

"What happened next was amazing," said Javier, looking toward his brother in awe. "Tulio grabbed a pool cue and smashed it across Noel's face. That jerk didn't even know what hit him. I've never seen anyone move that fast! All at once, blood started to spurt out of that punk's nose. Immediately, a fight broke out between Noel's friends and Tulio's teammates. We were getting the best of them when two policemen burst in and broke it up. But then, instead of arresting Noel, who was the one who had started everything, they took Tulio and me to the station.

"On the way there we told the policemen that we were just defending ourselves. But my brother had been in the same kind of trouble before, so they didn't believe us. At the station I kept checking my watch. When it was twenty to six, I asked them to let us go because we had an appointment we couldn't miss. Again, they didn't believe me. That's when Tulio got angry and began to yell at them."

"You've got to let us go! Idiots! My aunt's waiting for us. It might be a matter of life or death!"

"'Nothing ever happens in La Curva that's a matter of life or death,' the policemen scoffed as they locked us in a cell," Javier said. And although three-and-a-half years had passed since that fateful evening, the frustration of that moment returned to his expression.

I glanced at Tulio. Again he sat hunched over, but this time he held his face in his hands, and his shoulders shook as he cried. It was Javier who concluded their tale.

"We'll always feel terrible for having failed my aunt Adela. When the police finally let us go, which was about a quarter past nine, we ran straight home, hoping that she had decided to wait for us. But she had already left. We tried to go after her, but my mother didn't let us. Tulio and I failed to keep our promise that night. As long as we live, we'll never be able to forgive ourselves. If only we had stayed out of trouble, my aunt would still be alive. Because of us, no one in this family will ever think of Christmas as a happy day again."

The gathering fell silent as Mariela and her children thought about how the slightest difference, the most insignificant twist, could mean that everything they had experienced since that day had been nothing more than a nightmare and that they would all wake up to find that Adela was still alive. At last, Mariela, breaking the heartrending silence, went on with the story.

"While the boys were at the police station, I was here with my little sister and with no idea of what was going on. My children made a terrible mistake when they promised Adela that they wouldn't tell me what she was planning. If I'd known, then at least I would've tried to keep her here until the boys came."

Mariela looked at each of her children gravely, but soon her expression softened, and she offered them a loving, gentle smile. "I've told them many times that they can't blame themselves for what happened. God wanted Adela up there in heaven with Him. And there was nothing we could do about that. I don't know *why* He wants Adela around. Right now she's probably giving San Jorge a hard time. I just pray that Ixelia was able to join her. They deserve to be happy."

The Christmas of Adela's death, as the boys paced anxiously in their small jail cell, their mother and aunt sat in the living room, chatting. "My sister was very nervous that night. She couldn't stop her knee from bouncing. I did most of the talking, even though I could tell that she wasn't really paying attention. I then noticed that she kept looking from clock to clock to clock."

I glanced around at the four clocks in Mariela's living room. Each of them marked a different time, with a divergence of twenty-three minutes between the fastest and the slowest.

"How do you ever know the time in this house?" Adela asked.

"What does it matter?" said the older sister.

"It matters," Adela replied. "Tonight, it matters."

"What's wrong? Why are you so nervous?"

"It's nothing, really. Don't worry about it, Mariela," Adela answered. Then, after a brief pause, she asked, "Where are the boys? They're supposed to go on an errand with me."

"I don't know. They said that they'd be back before seven, didn't they? They're probably on their way. What errand are you going on at this hour? And on Christmas, of all evenings?"

"It's nothing important, sis. Just a little business, that's all. But I wanted the boys to keep me company."

Adela's knee then started to bounce furiously, and she checked each clock one last time.

"I'm late, Mariela. I can't wait for the boys any longer. Can I borrow Tulio's bicycle? I'll only be gone about an hour."

"Adela, does this errand have anything to do with Ixelia?"

"Don't be foolish, Mariela. You know that's over with." Adela stood up, walked to the hammock, reached out with the open palm of her right hand, patted her sister on the cheek, and then kissed her tenderly on the forehead. "Listen, I've got to go."

"Adela, wait a while longer for the boys. I'd feel much better if they were with you."

"I'm already late, Mariela. I've got to go. Don't worry. Everything will be fine."

Ignoring Mariela's concerns, Adela stepped out of the house, mounted the refurbished Rali mountain bike, smiled at her older sister, waved farewell, and took off down the wide dirt path where the United Fruit Company train used to run, in the direction of the town of Pío XII.

"That was the last time I saw my little sister alive," Mariela said. "I knew something terrible had happened to her when the fastest clock said that it was nine and she hadn't returned. When the boys finally made it back, I could see, without them saying a word, that they were very worried about their aunt Adela. They told me that they were going to go after her, but I asked them to wait until midnight, and if she hadn't returned by then we would decide what to do next. After that I went to bed because the next morning I had to catch the first bus for Managua. But I couldn't get to sleep.

"I was tossing around in bed, worrying about my sister when, at about half-past-ten, something strange happened: I heard Adela's parrot trill. The sound passed quickly in front of the house, as if she had ridden by at top speed on the bicycle, on her way home. I thanked God that she was safe, got up to tell the boys that their aunt was all right, went back to bed, and finally fell asleep. Of course, none of that was true," Mariela said sadly. Then, with a faint smile, she concluded, "I know it seems difficult to believe, but today I think that the trilling was Adela's spirit, letting me know that she had made it to the other side and that she was fine."

TWENTY-THREE

Her Last Moments

Adela Rugama rode east on the wide dirt path where the United Fruit Company train used to run. She concentrated on taking long, deep breaths to lessen the pounding of her heart. But Adela's attempts to stay calm failed that evening because being reunited with Ixelia Cruz, and once again embracing the love of her life, was the only thing that mattered in this universe.

Fighting the surplus adrenaline that coursed through her veins, Adela pedaled with restraint. She wanted to arrive at the reconciliation with her skin still exhaling the sweet, spicy scent of Mennen aftershave and not dripping with sweat. Following the abandoned railway path, she rode two-and-a-half kilometers until she came to the highway. At the juncture she turned right and pedaled another four kilometers until reaching the entrance to Las Dos Balas.

As Adela wove her way along the unpaved, rain-gutted road that leads to the hacienda house, she felt relieved that night had fallen. The darkness, she thought, would offer all the protection she needed. Shortly before reaching the house where the road widened, she veered right and headed straight for the ceiba. With the Rali mountain bike still in motion, Adela rose from the seat and stood on the left pedal. Dismounting when she reached the tree, she trotted a few paces to hide the bicycle behind the first row of coffee shrubs. Adela then hurried toward the ceiba, her eyes anxiously searching for any sign of Ixelia in the shadows, who should be there waiting among the massive root walls.

That was as far as my imagination could accompany Adela on her last journey. To fill the remaining gap, the dark void of her actual death, I only had the scenario that Commissioner Wong described to me. But I found his depiction of Adela's final moments too hazy, too vague for me to write a truthful conclusion. To not tell exactly what had taken place at the very end seemed, at least to me, to mock the tragedy. I believed that Adela's sacrifice deserved a full, complete account.

I was also bound by my pledge to Mariela to uncover the truth of her sister's final moments, however horrible those may have been. That left me, then, with only one option: to meet a second time with the one person I was absolutely sure had been there—Don Roque Ramírez.

In our previous meeting, the *hacendado* had spoken about his relationship with Ixelia and about his firm belief that Adela had ruined it. But he refused to discuss anything further. When I asked Don Roque to go on with his story, he rose from his seat, stared menacingly at me, and ordered me to leave.

Still, although I'd break out in chills at the mere thought of meeting again with the *hacendado*, I was prepared to pay him another visit to see if I could get him to talk about the murder.

During my last meeting with Commissioner Gilberto Wong, because I was too scared to question Don Roque by myself, I asked him to accompany me.

"You don't want me there," the commissioner said as he poured me a cup of mango tea. "If I show up, Don Roque will definitely not talk. If you want him to tell you what happened, you'll have to go on your own. But I wouldn't worry too much about that. I'm sure you'll be just fine. I will, though, offer you this piece of advice: if he refuses to talk, don't push the issue; just let it go. If you insist, he'll feel cornered. In that case he'll become dangerous. And you don't want to die just for the sake of completing your story, do you?"

Commissioner Wong also advised me to alert as many people as possible about where I was going and at what hour. Because of this, on the morning of my visit, as I drove through the towns on my way to Las Dos Balas, I stopped to chat with many of the persons I had met throughout the investigation, mentioning casually that I was going to speak with Don Roque.

At precisely ten o'clock I turned off the paved highway onto the rain-gutted dirt path that leads to Las Dos Balas. About half a kilometer before reaching the hacienda house, I drove up to a group of workers who were cutting an enormous bough, the size of a fully grown tree in most parts of the United States, into manageable pieces. The colossal limb had broken off a *guachipilín* tree during a recent, particularly fierce tropical storm. For several days it had blocked the main entrance to Don Roque's property. Don Carlos Somarriba, foreman of Las Dos Balas, was there, supervising the operation. When I stopped the car, he strolled over to the driver's side window to greet me.

"Don Carlos, I'm glad I had this chance to see you before returning home. I want to thank you for all of your help."

"You're welcome," he said, taking off his Pittsburgh Pirates baseball cap to scratch the top of his head. "So you're heading back."

"Yes. In two days."

"You know, I have a brother who lives in the States, in Los Angeles. He's always inviting me to visit."

"You should go, Don Carlos. You'd like California."

"No, thank you," he said, chuckling. "The furthest I've ever been from home is Managua. And I want to keep it that way."

"But it's a big world, Don Carlos. You should get out and see more of it."

He glanced at me, a puzzled expression on his face. Then, after putting his cap back on, he said, "I see much more than I want to see right here."

"I understand," I said, knowing that I'd miss the wise foreman, as I'd miss most of his humble, kindhearted compatriots. "Do you know if Don Roque is home?" I asked.

"Yes, he is. But be careful. He was furious after your last visit. It took him about a week to calm down."

"*Muchas gracias*, Don Carlos. I promise to be careful," I said, his warning increasing my apprehension. We shook hands, said goodbye, and I continued on my way. Where the road widens, shortly before reaching the house, I veered to the right, parked Si Dios Quiere in the shade of the ceiba, and got out. I walked to the building, climbed the porch steps, took a deep breath to try to summon all of my courage, went to the door, and knocked.

A cavernous silence greeted my call, escalating my dread further. I was strongly tempted to race back to the car, hop in, start the engine, and push the old Subaru to its limits. But I knew that if I succumbed to fear, I'd be replaying that act of cowardice in my head for the rest of my days.

Marshalling the scant valor still remaining in my heart, I told myself that I owed it to Mariela, as well as to this chronicle, to try one last time to persuade Don Roque to talk about Adela's death. After taking another deep breath, I knocked again. This time the door opened slowly, and Don Roque peered out of the crack.

"Well, well . . . how marvelous . . . the writer has come to visit again," the *hacendado* said in a low, scornful, sarcastic growl. "What do you want this time?"

"Good morning, Don Roque," I said as I unsuccessfully tried to contain a violent, cold shudder that suddenly ran through me. "I'd like to ask you a few questions."

The landowner didn't say a word. Instead, he glared at me without blinking, his mouth partly open in disbelief. "I've already told you everything," he responded at last. He then stepped back into his house for a few seconds and returned holding a rifle in his right hand. For a moment my throat tightened, making it difficult to breathe or swallow. The only thing missing was the trite cliché of seeing my life flash before my eyes.

"You'd better leave now, writer. This minute," he said in a grim dismissal, worse than if I had shown up to peddle religion. "I've got to take care of a stray cat and her litter. If you're still here when I return, I just might have to take care of you as well."

"As you wish, Don Roque."

Every nerve in my body stood on end as I walked away, imagining that the *hacendado* had changed his mind, taken careful aim, and was getting ready to fire a round into my back. But I was determined not to show him my terror, and so bracing myself for the swift, excruciating impact, I moved slowly toward the car, not looking back once. When I reached Si Dios Quiere, I got in unhurriedly. For once, the old car answered my prayers, starting on the first try. With my heart pounding as if it wanted to break out of my chest and run off ahead of me, I drove away, gripping the steering wheel tightly to keep my hands from shaking.

When I passed the workmen, I didn't stop to chat with the foreman; I merely waved farewell and went on. As I progressed slowly toward the highway, Si Dios Quiere moaning in discomfort as the thirty-year-old Subaru negotiated the sometimes brutal, uneven road, the terror of only a few minutes before gave way to the oppressing weight of defeat. Not only had I failed in my promise to Mariela, but I also started to fear that without knowing precisely how Adela's life had ended, this chronicle would be doomed.

I was being assailed by these gloomy thoughts when a man flagged me down at the juncture where the unpaved road and the highway meet—it was Arquímedes Guadamuz. For a moment I thought I was beholding a mirage. The Curl, more than anyone else, had steered clear of me, scurrying away like a terrified cat every time he saw me interviewing someone in Pío XII. For an instant, the thought flashed through my mind that I might be stepping into a trap, another deadly plan devised by Don Roque and his accomplices to eliminate someone troublesome. But finding courage in the thought that that would be the height of stupidity, I stopped the car.

"Hello, Arquímedes. What a surprise to see you around here," I greeted him, trying to conceal my astonishment behind a casual veneer.

"I'm glad I found you," he said fretfully. "I need to talk to you before you leave." The translucency of his frightened gaze startled me. I felt that I could look straight into his soul and see his torment: a dark, hellish lump, a malignant growth that was feeding on his body as well, leaving him pale and gaunt.

"How did you know where to find me?" I asked.

"Everyone knew that you had come to talk to Don Roque."

I silently thanked Commissioner Wong and then said, "Well, Arquímedes, Don Roque just ran me off of his property, so I've got the rest of the day free. Get in the car, I'll buy you lunch."

Twenty-five minutes later, we were pulling into the town of San Marcos. When I had first started the investigation, Don Carlos Somarriba, knowing that I taught at a university, told me about a quirky group of English-speaking college professors, men and women who lived and worked in Nicaragua. They had come from the United States, Canada, and England and liked to hang out at a restaurant called Lario's. There, over pitchers of beer, they'd have loud, passionate discussions about philosophy, religion, and literature (or so Don Carlos imagined).

That same day I stopped by, eager to learn what such an illustrious group of expatriates was doing in this country. I was disappointed to find out that they had moved on, most of them having returned to their respective countries. It seems they had been run out of the Catholic institution where they taught by a modern-day version of the Spanish Inquisition. Still, in spite of the let-down, I grew to appreciate the restaurant's atmosphere. It was a great place to unwind with a couple of Toñas—as well as with the owner's preference for classic rock—after a long day of interviews. Over the course of that summer, I visited Lario's a lot.

Although Arquímedes and I arrived well before the lunch hour, several *sanmarqueños* were already seated at the bar, drinking beer and watching a soccer match between Manchester United and Real Madrid (the men cheering loudly for the Spanish club).

I requested a table in the covered section of the patio, where I knew we could talk without many distractions. Arquímedes said that he was too nervous to eat, and he asked only for a Toña. I decided to join the Curl, in spite of the relatively early hour, thinking this would help me gain his trust. Once the waiter brought us our beers, the conversation began.

"Arquímedes, please don't get me wrong," I said, "I'm delighted that you're now willing to talk, but I'm also very curious . . . what made you change your mind?"

He reached for the spiral of hair that dangled over his forehead, pushed it back, and held it there. Smiling pitiably, his teeth looking more rodent-like than ever, he gathered his thoughts until, at last, he said, "My woman, Soledad. She said I needed to talk to someone." He then let go of the thick, black curl; instantly, it fell back into place. "If anything good has come out of this mess, it's that I now understand that Soledad is the best thing that's ever happened to me. But only last week, she said that my memories of that night were making it impossible for her to continue living with me. She told me that if I didn't get rid of whatever was haunting me, she would go back to live with her mother. She said that if I wanted her to stay, I had to go see Padre Uriel for confession.

"Because I'm afraid of losing her, a few days ago I went to see the priest and told him everything. But then, once we were done, he took me aside, away from the confessional, and told me that even though he had given me absolution, he didn't believe that would be enough to save my soul. Padre Uriel said that if I really wanted to purge myself, I needed to come clean to the whole world about what happened that night. He then suggested I talk to you and tell you exactly what I told him.

"At first I thought the priest was playing a bad joke on me. But the nightmares haven't gone away, even after the confession. The past couple of nights, I've been tossing around in bed, wide awake and still frightened to go to sleep. I now think that maybe Padre Uriel is right; maybe the only way to get rid of my guilt is to tell you what happened. That's why I'm here. I don't know what the old man will do when he finds out that I've spoken to you, but to be honest, I don't care anymore. I just want to be able to sleep again."

I silently thanked Padre Uriel and the Patron Saint of Chroniclers, whoever that may be, for my good fortune and for the timing of Arquímedes's quest for redemption. Then, thanking the messenger himself, I opened my notepad, took the pen out of my shirt pocket, brought out my tape recorder, and pressed the record button.

"Let me start by saying that I'm innocent," Arquímedes began without prompting. "I honestly didn't know that Erlinda and the old man were planning to kill Adela. They told me that they only wanted to scare her."

"We're going to give her a good scare until she pees in her panties and leaves us alone forever," Doña Erlinda said, her golden eyes gleaming as she relished the thought.

"Yes. One big scare should be enough to keep the *cochona* away, forever," Don Roque said, nodding emphatically in agreement, and the dry, sagging skin under his neck wobbled.

At a quarter to seven, on the evening of Christmas, with rounds of fireworks going off at unpredictable intervals, Don Roque and Arquímedes were hiding between the third and fourth rows of coffee shrubs, directly behind the ceiba and on the far side of the hacienda house.

"Maybe the *cochona*'s not coming, Don Roque," the messenger said after checking his watch and seeing that it was already seven-fifteen. "Maybe she's figured out this is a trap."

"She'll be here," Don Roque said in the low, rumbling voice that, throughout the years, had always unsettled Arquímedes. "The *cochona* is too much in love with that little bitch to pass up a chance like this."

At seven-twenty-three, Adela appeared riding a mountain bike. The men, crouching low and now fully alert, saw her rise from the seat and stand on the left pedal, the bicycle still in motion. They crouched even lower after she dismounted and rushed in their direction to hide the Rali behind the first row of coffee shrubs, a mere twenty feet away from them. They then saw her dash toward the ceiba's massive roots, still on the far side of the hacienda house, and take cover between the lofty buttress walls. After a few moments in hiding, she peered over the root's edge, looking toward the house. Once she thought it safe, she trilled like a parrot.

As I ordered the third round of Toñas, knowing that it was helping to keep Arquímedes's confession flowing, he said, "Adela was so eager to see Ixelia that she didn't even notice when we snuck up on her. She screamed for help when we grabbed her, but the moment Don Roque pointed the rifle in her face, she shut up. She then went peacefully as the old man led her about thirty steps away from the tree."

"Stop right there," Don Roque said calmly. "Now, get on your knees, *cochona*." When Adela had placed her knees on the moist, cool earth beneath the ceiba's canopy, Arquímedes pointed the bright beam of the *hacendado*'s flashlight in her face, making her squint.

"What are you going to do, Don Roque?" Adela said, her voice now quaking in fear. "Are you going to kill me?"

"What do you think? You've given us a lot of trouble, *cochona*. And you don't stop, do you? The time has come for us to be rid of you . . . and this time it'll be forever."

"Listen, Don Roque," Adela started, and although she struggled valiantly to remain calm, her voice cracked. "I've learned my lesson. I promise to leave Ixelia alone. I'll never bother you or Erlinda again."

"I don't think you're capable of learning anything, *cochona*. You can't help yourself. You just can't keep away from Ixelia, can you?"

"Please, Don Roque, if you let me go I promise never to talk to her again. I give you my word. I swear." She formed a cross with the thumb and index finger of her right hand and kissed it.

"It's too late for that, *cochona*. I wouldn't believe you anyway, even if you swore it over your mother's grave."

With her promises failing to convince the *hacendado*, Adela then said, "Don Roque, my family knows that I'm here. If I don't return soon, they're going to come looking for me."

"Let them come. We're not going to be here long, anyway," Don Roque replied dryly. "By midday tomorrow everyone will be talking about how you and Ixelia ran off to Costa Rica. And first thing in the morning, the Curl is going to return the bicycle and tell your sister that you and Ixelia were in such a hurry to leave that you didn't have time to say goodbye. It'll be a while before anyone figures out that you're never coming back, and by then it'll be too late: no one's ever going to find your body."

As Real Madrid scored a goal to take the lead, the loud cheers of the men watching the match interrupted the messenger's story. He took a long pull of his Toña, and then, with difficulty because of the shaking of his hands, he lit a cigarette, inhaling deeply. After letting out a slow, steady stream of grey smoke, he continued. "At that point Adela seemed to realize that that Christmas was going to be her last one."

"Don Roque, please don't," she said, her voice faltering. "Please, Don Roque, for the love of God, don't kill me."

"Oh, how I like this, Curl. I mean it, I really like it. Don't you just love to hear the *cochona* beg for her life? This is much better than I had hoped."

"Please, Don Roque," Adela repeated, now sobbing openly. "For the love of God, don't kill me."

"If you really do believe in God, *cochona*, now's a good time to say a prayer."

Stepping to Adela's right, Don Roque, very slowly, as if he were savoring every second, lifted the barrel of his rifle and aimed it slightly above her right temple. Curious, the messenger pointed the flashlight toward Adela's crotch. He saw that, indeed, she had peed in her pants.

"I think that's good enough, Don Roque. I believe the *cochona* has learned her lesson. She won't be bothering anyone anymore."

"Stay out of this, Curl. This is now between the *cochona* and me.

"But, Don Roque, you said that we were only going to scare her."

Lowering his rifle, the *hacendado* turned toward the Curl, and the messenger, seeing the fury in his eyes, took a step back.

"I swear that I've never been so scared in my life," Arquímedes said. He tried to light another cigarette, but his hands were shaking so violently that I took the matches from him, struck one, and then followed the bouncing tip of his cigarette until it was lit.

"Stay out of this, Curl, or I'll get rid of you too," Don Roque hissed. "And remember to keep your mouth shut about this. If you ever talk, to anyone, I swear that you'll be joining the *cochona*. Besides, you're up to your neck in this now, you know. No one will ever believe that you had nothing to do with it. So, just shut the fuck up and stand back." Don Roque turned to face Adela again.

The men at the bar groaned and cursed bitterly at Real Madrid's defense for allowing Manchester United to even the score. As we waited for their displeasure to subside, Arquímedes wiped away the tears with a paper napkin. Then, in a faltering voice, he continued. "Now here's the part that keeps me awake at night. While Adela is on her knees, sobbing, the old man is waiting patiently for another round of fireworks so he can pull the trigger. Suddenly, Adela lifts her head and looks toward the ceiba. At once she stops crying and the expression on her face changes completely. Instead of being terrified, her eyes and mouth are now wide open, as if she's seeing something absolutely miraculous.

"I can't believe it! You're here!" she exclaimed.

"And then, and I swear this is the truth, I feel that someone's there. I flash the light in the direction she's looking, but I don't see anyone. But Adela definitely sees someone because she breaks into a huge grin."

"'You're here!' she cried out again. Then, with her left hand, Adela reached inside her checkered shirt, grabbed the medallion she always wore on a silver chain around her neck, and clutched it tightly in her fist.

"Throughout all of this," Arquímedes said, continuing the story, "the old man doesn't even blink. He probably thought that Adela was trying to trick him into looking away so she could make a run for it. But I . . . I can feel that someone, or something, is there. And at that very moment, a dark cloud descended over me, making me feel wretched, and it hasn't lifted since. It was then that I knew that if Don Roque pulled the trigger, we'd both be damned for eternity."

As the men who had been watching the match left, terribly disappointed that it had ended in a tie, the owner of the restaurant turned off the television and started to play Pink Floyd's *Dark Side of the Moon* on the stereo. In the meantime, I passed another napkin to Arquímedes so he could dry his tears.

"Whatever Adela saw, it must have been glorious because it showed on her face," the Curl went on. "And then she seemed to be paying close attention to something the presence was telling her."

"Yes, yes," Adela at last answered, nodding earnestly. "I'm ready."

"She had stopped sobbing and now appeared to have accepted that she was going to die. She made the sign of the cross, laced her fingers together over her chest while still holding the medallion, and bowed her head, as if in prayer."

Just then, at seven forty-two, another round of fireworks went off in Pío XII. Don Roque lifted his rifle, aimed it carefully at a point just above Adela's right temple, and pulled the trigger. She collapsed onto her back, her legs folded under her.

Indifferently, as if he were inspecting the slaughter of one of his farm animals, the *hacendado* walked to the other side of the body and pushed it with his foot. Nodding in satisfaction, he said, "She's dead all right. The *cochona* won't be bothering anyone any more."

"At that point, I'm terrified," Arquímedes said. As he lifted the thick curl of black hair off of his forehead, I saw that his tears were flowing freely. "But I still don't know what scared me more: the thought that Don Roque might kill me too or the thought of burning in hell because I had helped him murder Adela."

Don Roque smiled contentedly and glanced up at Arquímedes Guadamuz. In the tone of voice one reserves for telling jokes, the *hacendado* said, "You know, Curl, I always told the *cochona* that I had two bullets with her name engraved on them. I may as well keep that promise."

And on that dark, bitter Christmas night, as yet another round of fireworks shattered the still, tropical sky with bright, thunderous explosions, Don Roque Ramírez, holding his rifle in only one hand, aimed it toward Adela Rugama's chest, pulled the trigger, and shot her once again—this time, straight through the heart.

POSTSCRIPT

On Christmas night of 1999, Aura Rosa Pavón—a humble coffee picker and jack-of-all-trades—was murdered under circumstances close to those described in this novel: a labyrinthine entanglement of jealousy, lust, and greed. Her body was found at the bottom of a condemned outhouse two months later, where the killers had dumped it. It was Aura Rosa's sister, María Auxiliadora Pavón, who, acting on a vision, led the authorities to this heartless resting place.

At the time I was living in Nicaragua; I followed the case in the newspapers with great interest. Needless to say, I was deeply saddened by the thought that Aura Rosa had to pay the ultimate price for loving Carla Vanesa Muñoz, a young woman who since childhood had been the victim of sexual exploitation. In addition, I felt that the murder perfectly illustrated the homophobia that is rampant not only in Nicaragua, but in all of Latin America. To cite one relevant example: Aura Rosa Pavón had spent two months in prison, charged with committing sodomy—including one week, as a penitentiary joke, in a men's facility. In the novel I shortened the time of Adela Rugama's confinement by more than half. I believe that to have done otherwise—in other words, to write the truth—would have dangerously tested the readers' faith in the narrative.

Also, in conditions similar to those related in the novel, three suspects were brought to trial. La Comisión Pro Derechos Humanos de Lesbianas y Homosexuales placed considerable pressure on Nicaragua's judicial system to find these individuals guilty. Perhaps as a result, the accused were sentenced to thirty-five years in prison, each. Nevertheless, through various quirks in Nicaragua's laws, those convicted of murdering Aura Rosa Pavón only served three years of their sentence, and under the law they cannot be retried for the crime. Carla Vanesa Muñoz committed suicide two weeks after their release.

I am deeply indebted to María Auxiliadora Pavón, Aura Rosa's older sister, who, during one exquisitely lucid day-long conversation, gave me the foundation of this novel. She is a remarkably courageous and generous person who has chosen to forgive her sister's killers rather than to seek vengeance. Without her cooperation, *Meet Me under the Ceiba* would not exist. Unlike the fictional "chronicler" of this tale, my "investigation" was limited to a few trips to La Curva, an exploration of the surrounding communities, a chance visit with the judge who presided over the case, and the scrutiny of court records and newspaper articles.

In writing this novel, although I took countless creative liberties, I did my utmost to preserve the spirit of Aura Rosa Pavón's life story.

Those are the facts.

The rest, I guess, is fiction.

Infinitas gracias to those who have blessed me with their support.

Rhonda Patzia

Nina Forsythe

Helen Kiser

Benjamin Murphy

David and Mindy Hunt

Lois and Edwin Rojas

Joseph Dziver and Ingrid Chavarría

Silvio Villavicencio

Bill and Jackie Madonna

Isabel Montoya and the rest of the Montoya-Villegas clan

The Vasco Núñez de Balboa Academy

The Kids: Mónica Martínez, Eloy Benedetti, Carla Pinilla, Vivian Fong, Alicia de León, Ricardo Agurcia, Tomás García, and Leila Nilipour

The Gang at Lario's

María Auxiliadora, Mireya, and Sandy Sirias

(for welcoming back the prodigal son and brother without questions)

Magee (with all my love)

María Auxiliadora Pavón

La Virgen de Cuapa

About
The Chicano/Latino Literary Prize

THE CHICANO/LATINO LITERARY PRIZE was first awarded by the Department of Spanish and Portuguese at the University of California, Irvine during the 1974-1975 academic year. In the quarter-century that has followed, this annual competition has clearly demonstrated the wealth and vibrancy of Hispanic creative writing to be found in the United States. Among the prize winners have been—to name a few among many—such accomplished authors as Lucha Corpi, Graciela Limón, Cherríe L. Moraga, Carlos Morton, Gary Soto, and Helena María Viramontes. Specific literary forms are singled out for attention each year on a rotating basis, including the novel, the short-story collection, drama, and poetry; and first-, second-, and third-place prizes are awarded. For more information on the Chicano/Latino Literary Prize, please contact:

> Contest Coordinator
> Chicano/Latino Literary Contest
> Department of Spanish and Portugese
> University of California, Irvine
> Irvine, California 92697